LEMONADE SPRINGS

Libby young, naive, born into a protective family in Lemonade Springs, Montana, marries Harry, university student and gambler, in San Francisco. Before long Libby becomes uneasy about Harry's secrecy, his preference for gambling to studying. And then their daughter Charlie is born.

Harry takes them off to London. There, Libby and Harry plunge into a dazzling night-life, living on a cloud of glitter, gaming rooms and expensive restaurants. Gradually the dazzle begins to dim as Harry's gambling takes over their lives. How can Libby turn night into day and still make a home for their young daughter?

Charlie plays happily with her father's discarded poker hands; Harry laughs, Libby feels her heart will break. She loves Harry, but she knows that the price she is paying for her marriage is too high, that she must fight for her daughter's future, and her own. But how?

LEMONADE SPRINGS is the story of two people tearing each other apart in the name of love. Denise Anne Jefferies has created in Libby a character who stays on the mind – sensitive and gentle and ultimately strong.

LEMONADE SPRINGS

Denise Anne Jefferies

COLLINS
8 Grafton Street, London W1
1984

William Collins Sons & Co Ltd
London · Glasgow · Sydney · Auckland
Toronto · Johannesburg

BRITISH LIBRARY CATALOGUING IN PUBLICATION DATA

Jefferies, Denise
Lemonade springs.
I. Title
823'.914[F]   PS3560.E/

ISBN 0 00 222740 1

First published 1984
© Denise Anne Jefferies 1984

Photoset in Plantin

Made and printed in Great Britain by
William Collins Sons & Co Ltd, Glasgow

For Rebekah, with all my love
and thanks for her unflagging moral
and very practical support

Oh there's lemonade springs,
And the bluebird sings,
In the big rock candy mountain. . . .

TRADITIONAL

1

I first met Benjamin Harold Franklin when we were freshmen at the same university in the cornbelt of the American midwest. His name, he told me later and bitterly, had been his father's little joke.

We were introduced by a girlfriend of mine who'd gone out with him once or twice, and who thought him far too shy and serious for her.

'He's a grind,' she said, 'to put it bluntly. Studies as if his life depends on it.'

'Maybe it does,' I said, defending Harry even before I met him. 'Is he good looking?'

She shrugged. 'I guess so,' she conceded, 'and he *can* dance. He's okay when he isn't lecturing on the peaceful uses of atomic energy or the theory of sets. Not my type, though. . . .'

And she went on to tell me about the guy she'd met at a freshman mixer who was dynamite, and a few days after that she engineered my meeting Harry by suggesting I meet her outside the chemistry laboratory where she spent the last hour of her Wednesday afternoons.

Harry was her lab. partner, and he was there too, though most of the other students had left. He smiled at me and said hello, and then handed me a sulphur crystal he'd just made, blue and beautiful in the austerity of the tall-windowed, malodorous room full of mysterious apparatus.

'Ever worry about blowing yourself up in here?' I asked him. As a student in the College of Arts and Sciences, and a virtual stranger to chemistry laboratories, this was a semi-serious question.

'All the time,' he answered, grinning. We just stood there talking generalities until my girlfriend made her hasty exit, and when Harry and I were alone he asked me if I had time for a cup of coffee and I said yes, I'd love one.

Harry planned to major in chemistry and mathematics, I in history or English. We intended, each in our way, to change the world.

Almost all the students I knew talked of doing that, sincerely and earnestly, as students do in every generation, their optimism and idealism not yet tarnished by the exigencies of hard knocks and harsh realities.

Such talk was a badge of our status as serious students and fledgling citizens of the world, many of us away from home for the first time, fresh from the regimentation and externally imposed disciplines of family life and high school, privileged with heady if limited freedom and plenty of time to think.

We became students in the late '70s, a full decade after the period of intense student visibility which began in the summer of 1967 in the Haight-Ashbury area of San Francisco.

There young people had danced joyously in the streets, celebrating the dawning of the Age of Aquarius by throwing flowers into the ranks of alarmed police who closed in on them and fought to stop their open marijuana smoking, to curb their barefooted, free-floating frenzied exuberance.

The mood had spread across the bay to the University of California at Berkeley, darkening ominously in transit; it became a political issue between a strangely restless, activist student population and the firmly entrenched authorities of town and campus – over things like whether or not a vacant patch of ground owned by the city could be used as a 'people's' park which, according to the formal demands presented by the militant students, was to be a sort of adventure playground for big kids – to be pervaded by the pungent unimpeded and unprosecuted fragrance of cannabis.

10

When City Hall remained intransigent, the angry students marched in the streets in support of their demands concerning the vacant lot and many other issues; and they were confronted by frightened angry townspeople and angrier police, and they were tear-gassed and clubbed and even shot at for their trouble.

People's Park remained the property of the city of Berkeley, and was protected by an electrified fence; student unrest began to escalate, people began to take furious sides. Polarisation was the word on everybody's lips: cops versus kids.

And that spread eastward across America's college campuses in an increasingly turbulent flood of riotous confrontation until it peaked in horror in Ohio with the accidental shooting and killing of four non-political, non-activist students at Kent State University.

That incident effectively marked an abrupt and terrible end to wholesale campus violence across the country: the Age of Aquarius ended there, teetering on the brink of the Age of Apocalypse.

By the time Harry and I met in his chemistry laboratory in our freshman year at college, American campuses had been fully restored as repositories of an ideal of dreaming spires and ivory towers, and were as peaceful as if they had never been otherwise.

The era of active student protest was a footnote to modern history, widely attributed to a larger national restlessness over the debacle of the Vietnam war; the riotous cacophony of open confrontation in the streets had faded almost without echo. It may as well have happened in outer space, or in another century, or not at all.

The town in which our campus stood was quiet and prosperous and pretty, a market centre set in the heart of the enormous granary that is middle America.

Immaculately painted clapboard houses sat well back in manicured picket-fenced lawns along its tree-lined residen-

11

tial streets. It was a place where it seemed quite likely that housewives left their doors unlocked when they visited one another for coffee in the mornings.

Or when they went out to shop in the thriving business district nestled around the Courthouse square – a district where students were treated kindly and their custom encouraged when they came, where we felt welcome to browse in one of the two boutiques that had been established with us in mind, or to stop for ice-cream sodas at the lovingly restored turn-of-the-century drugstore that boasted its original framed mirrors and dark mahogany woodwork and marble counters.

Above the town, on a long sloping hill to the north, our campus and its immediate environs was almost a town in itself.

The warm red brick buildings were arranged in a loose protective cluster as though to shelter us while we studied arts and sciences or engineering or agriculture, as though to draw us into a love for the act of learning itself.

Just beyond it, still on university hill, there were three superbly stocked bookstores, a couple of beer bars with dance floors, a cinema that specialized in showing *avant garde* films and serving honest-to-God filtered coffee in the lobby instead of the coke and popcorn of our childhoods, an unashamedly up-to-the-minute boutique that catered almost exclusively for rich student clotheshorses, a drugstore, a bank, and a small post office.

But in spite of the inevitable separation of town and gown, the locals were proud of their university, proud of us, genial and sanguine when our two communities meshed and were reported in the local newspaper when we came together at the Kiwanis or Rotary Club, or the Chamber of Commerce.

We students were cocooned on our campus, there to be educated. We were seldom raucous, any of us, except for the occasional ruckus that arose from animal high spirits

12

after a disastrous football game, or one too many beers among the jocks in an off-campus watering hole on a Saturday night.

Some of the older and more restless students among us, and one or two of the younger professors, had been heard to refer to our campus as a hotbed of apathy.

I suppose it was; still, we talked of changing the world, and our changes would be wide-ranging and brave.

They would be political, economic, social, scientific. Some would ban nuclear weapons, or the vivisection of animals, or capitalism, or they would permit abortion on demand. Almost all of us would abolish poverty and ignorance if we could, and racial and sexual inequality, and war on any scale.

The means to these ends would be revolutionary and swift, or systematic and orderly, depending upon the temperament of the speaker, and his or her mood at the time.

No matter what we might burn to change, however, no matter how we proposed to change it, the prevailing mood of the time in which we lived prevented even the most dedicated firebrands among us from taking to the streets. We had read or been told – some of us could even vaguely remember from childhood – what taking to the streets had really been like, and all that it had failed to bring about. No one was willing to defy the lessons of such recent history.

Our actual active rebellions were personal.

We puffed self-consciously at our first cigarettes, and cautiously sipped our first beer or bad wine, accepted furtive drags of pungent joints whenever they were passed around at parties – parties given by older students who were lucky enough or rich enough to have off-campus apartments, who were sophisticated enough to be 'holding' grass or hash, even in the middle of Iowa.

I lived on campus because, at seventeen, I was among the youngest batch of freshmen and could not do otherwise

13

without violating the letter and spirit of the campus rules concerning *in loco parentis*. My parents' home was a couple of thousand miles away in Lemonade Springs, Montana; I could hardly commute.

My father objected to my studying so far away. I was the baby of the family, and the only girl. I was the apple of his eye.

'How come you want to go to college with a bunch of farmers' kids?' he said, when I broached the subject of applying there. 'There's nothing in Iowa but flat land and cornfields and muddy tractors. You'd miss your mountains, mark my words.'

'Well,' I said uncomfortably. 'It's a good university, and they've got students from all over the country. I can come home in the summer, and at Christmas. . . .'

'Hell, there's universities just as good or better right here in Montana, honey. Just as many kids from out of state just itching to come to God's country. If you went to school in Helena you could come home weekends.'

I looked at my mother, signalling for rescue with my eyes.

She smiled at me, then at dad. 'Libby's never been away from home much, John. It'd give her a real taste of independence to go east. And look here in the catalogue, they've got dormitories on the campus. They look real comfortable.'

They did, and they were. Two girls to a room, two beds, two desks, two bookshelves, two lamps, one big window overlooking the campus and the town below it. And, critically important, an internal telephone in every room, just by the door, on which the dormitory switchboard attendants could buzz us when we received calls from boys who wanted us to go out with them on Saturday night.

'Um,' my father said.

'They have curfews too, John,' my mother added, winking at me, running her index finger along the fine print beside the pictures, 'and rules. No boys in the girls' rooms, no girls in the boys', and a couple of acres, looks like, in between the buildings where they live.'

She may have said something else to him, I don't know. But in the end he capitulated. I applied and was accepted, and was assigned a room in one of the women's dormitories that was exactly like the picture in the catalogue, right down to the nubbly-textured brown and beige curtains at the window.

Harry lived on campus too; he told me he was able to earn his room and board by working in the Student Union snack bar as a busboy.

When I asked him where he came from he said, 'Oh, here and there. No special place, really. I moved around a lot as a kid.'

I didn't pry; he was visibly uncomfortable with the question, he didn't want to talk about it.

On our first real date – going out for coffee did not count as a 'real' date because it hadn't been planned beforehand – we scrunched our way through autumn leaves along the campus paths until we came to the graceful arched bridge that spanned the artificial lake. We paused there, and Harry threw a penny into the water because it was the custom.

He told me, looking down into the lake, that his parents were dead, and I fell in love with him.

After that he took me for a glass of beer which I was legally too young to order, and then he walked me back to my dormitory. He said, 'May I kiss you?'

I think I blushed. I'm sure I did. I'd been kissed before, more or less clumsily or even perfunctorily at the ends of dates, but I'd never really thought about it. It was the custom.

I had acquired a fair knowledge of the theory of sexual attraction. My mother made sure I understood the basics, and I had built on that by reading and by talking and listening to my girlfriends.

By the time I went off to university I was acquainted with

15

the guilty passion of Madame Bovary and the deliciously contraband abandon of Lady Chatterley, as well as the thoughts of a few distinguished heavies like Havelock Ellis and Bertrand Russell, thrown in for ballast.

More recently I had been to a party with my dorm roommate where two optimistic graduate students, who seemed wonderfully worldly and sophisticated to us, explained with slightly drunken intensity that it was an existential folly to hang on to our virginity.

'What the hell did that mean?' she asked me later, slightly awed.

'That they were trying to get us to go to bed with them,' I said.

We giggled about that and went to sleep.

So I knew about desire in much the way I knew about geometry: in theory. It was something remote, abstract, not part of my real life.

Until that night with Harry.

His face seemed grave and tender, and his eyes reflected points of the soft light that poured like sudden honey from the dormitory windows.

He was luminous and very beautiful, tall in his jeans and checkered cotton shirt, and somehow – vulnerable.

My mouth felt dry, and my bones seemed to be melting, and I could hear my heart beating in staccato rhythms, and I was aware of the heat of my blood.

He had said, 'May I kiss you?' Just that: undemanding, very gentle.

I wanted him to kiss me. I wanted to reach up and touch his fair tousled hair, and for him to go on kissing me forever.

A universe had exploded within me without warning, and I remember thinking: why? why him? He was a good-looking guy, yes, with nice eyes and a full mouth and dimples when he smiled. Tall, clean-looking, young. But I could have said that about most of the boys I'd gone out with before.

So why him? And I remember realizing there wasn't a

reason, and that it didn't matter. It was so. But it was so new, so unexplored, so overwhelming it frightened me.

I said, 'No. But – someday I'll steam up your glasses, it's a promise.'

I smiled, and he smiled too.

And then he asked me which window of the dormitory was mine, and I took his hand and led him around to the side of the building and pointed up, to show him.

When I got back to my room that night he was standing on the lawn beneath it, two storeys down.

I threw him a slim volume of sonnets, and he picked it up and kissed it, and then he blew me a kiss before he walked away.

That's how it began with Harry.

He didn't ask me again if he could kiss me, and he didn't kiss me, though I saw him every day and my own emotions were so near the boiling point I seriously considered kissing him first – before I took all my clothes off and pulled him down onto the dry grass of the quadrangle of the main library building. Something – shyness, pride, convention – held me back.

Instead we walked, kicking dead leaves, sometimes holding hands and sometimes not, talking for hours.

He didn't have much money, I knew that, but still he insisted on taking me out, and I insisted that all I really wanted was a bowl of soup or a limeade or a glass of beer.

He always laughed at that, and told me I was a cheap date and that it was just as well, and somehow he made the soup or the drink seem like a banquet.

Three weeks to the day after our first date, a Thursday, Harry disappeared.

He knew my schedule, and I expected to see him after my last lecture of the day, at three o'clock.

He wasn't where he usually was, outside on the wide

17

steps of the humanities building, so I loitered there as long as I could bear the curious stares of the passersby, waiting.

At six, I went looking for him. And somebody – one of the guys he worked with in the snack bar – finally took pity on me and told me Harry had dropped out of school.

'He's left the campus?' I asked.

'Yup.'

'Did he say . . . where he was going?'

'Nope.'

'Well, is he – is he coming back?'

The guy shrugged. 'Doubt it. Said he was fed up.'

I was bereft, turned to stone.

For days I didn't leave the dormitory. I slopped around in my bathrobe reading love poetry and drinking the rum my roommate had sneaked into our room in empty shampoo bottles, wailing and hiccuping and grieving.

My roommate grew increasingly impatient, and finally she hauled me bodily out of my rum-stained robe and into a clean skirt and blouse, via a hot shower.

'You're a mess, Libby, do you appreciate that? You smell like a bum straight off the Bowery.' She was from New York City.

'So? So what! Oh God, you wouldn't even begin to know what this pain is like!'

She grunted, searching for my shoes, unmoved.

'I know enough. Like for instance, "Heaven be thanked, we live in such an age, when no man dies for love, but on the stage." John Dryden, 1678,' she added absently, emerging from under my bed with my pantyhose.

'Christ! Freshman English!'

'Come off it, Lib. The guy never even kissed you, you told me that. So from where do you get this tragedy queen act? Come on, shake a leg.'

I shook a leg, but my heart wasn't in it.

I spent the rest of the semester floundering my way

through a prolonged and postponed adolescent crisis, only just keeping my head above the academic waters while feeding coins to the juke box and pinball machines in the Student Union.

When I went home that Christmas, my mother noticed my lethargy and expressed cautious tactful alarm that I seemed to be losing interest in school.

'Mononucleosis,' I mumbled. 'Everybody gets it.'

Naturally enough, long before I reached my senior and final year at university, the brief episode with Harry Franklin had faded well into perspective.

I hadn't met anyone since who came close to touching the wellsprings of powerful emotion Harry had tapped. But at least I knew the wellsprings were there, and that they would undoubtedly flow again when the time came.

Meanwhile increasing maturity and confidence, and a genuine interest in my course work – for by then I had more or less decided to make a career in public relations – had consigned any conscious thoughts of Harry into some remote storage room in my mind, rarely if ever entered.

I knew it was highly unlikely I would ever see him again. But the knowledge was no longer actively painful.

And then I came out of a seminar one Thursday afternoon and there he was, waiting on the worn marble steps of the humanities building – exactly where I had expected to find him three years before, almost to the day.

He was the same as I remembered him, except that instead of jeans he wore well-tailored grey slacks and a quietly expensive shirt and his shoulders seemed broader and he exuded quiet confidence.

He was confident, all right.

He came towards me, smiling, and put his hands on my shoulders, and then he kissed me on the soft soundless *oh!* of surprise that was my mouth.

19

We had a lot of catching up to do, starting with that kiss; we may have set a record, making up for lost time.

Harry took me out for steak and wine. Afterwards we walked, arms linked, and as we passed the darkened shop windows I caught glimpses of our reflections, and I exulted in his presence beside me as the unexpected gift from destiny it was.

We didn't talk much, but he did say he'd left school because he'd been restless, and felt like seeing California. And that he'd come back to finish his degree.

We didn't talk about me at all. There didn't seem to be much to say. It was as though in the years of his absence I'd been frozen like Sleeping Beauty, waiting for him to come back and bring me truly alive again.

I was so heart-stoppingly glad to see him, so joyously aware that my feelings for him hadn't changed, it didn't even occur to me to ask him why he hadn't said goodbye, or to wonder how he'd known where to find me that afternoon, or why he'd wanted to.

Eventually we went to my apartment, which was small, dark and shabby, but which was nevertheless all mine, and off-campus.

There was no lush background of throbbing strings to suggest unquenchable passion and undying love, no silvery shaft of moonlight cascading onto the faded counterpane on my ancient and creaking double bed.

But that is where we ended up.

And that night, for the first time, I experienced the intense exquisite magic of being touched and known, and of wanting to reach out to touch and know, with an urgency for which no theory of desire had even begun to prepare me.

Early one morning during those first stunned weeks of rapture, in the languid, contented afterglow of making love, I said, 'What did you do in California?'

'Missed me, did you?' He grinned and kissed my shoulder. And then, seriously, 'Do you really want to know?'

'Umm hmm, yes.'

'Well, I took a kind of crash course in applied mathematics.'

He laughed, thinking of that, and then he propped himself on one elbow and lit a cigarette. He blew thoughtful smoke rings for awhile, and then he said, 'Sure. Applied mathematics. Poker, rummy, bridge, dice once in awhile just for the hell of it. Oh, and lo-ball. That's a kind of bastardized poker they play in a crummy little town near Oakland, but it's very profitable if you know what you're doing. Oh, and any other game that came along.'

'Profitable,' I echoed, tasting the word. Its implications hit me and I gulped. 'You – gambled?'

'Umm, that's right, hon, got it in one.' He dragged deeply on his cigarette, smiling to himself. 'You're shocked,' he added amiably, shaking his head, chuckling.

The light was behind him, limning his head and his broad shoulders and his tousled hair like a halo. His eyes were hooded, shadowed, and his mouth full, caressing his cigarette.

He looked like nothing so much as a dissolute angel and my heart caught in my throat, remembering him, wanting him again.

I flushed with desire and anger.

Harry was way ahead of me and looking back over his shoulder with amused contempt, the way he seemed to be too often, ever since he'd come back to school. He could bite me and gobble me up and spit me out, and all the while I was helpless watching him do it, hating him for it, but powerless to do anything but love him so much it was a physical pull deep in my gut.

'No I'm *not* shocked, Harry, why should I be?'

I looked away from him with an heroic effort, and rearranged the sheet, drawing it up around my naked breasts as though for protection.

Lots of people played cards, for God's sake! I played

21

cards myself, my whole family did, nearly every Sunday afternoon while I was growing up. Dad had taught me how to play five card stud and pinochle and pontoon, and mother had tried to teach me bridge – which dad always said, indulgently, was a woman's game.

And dad played what he called 'serious' poker too, with men he'd known for years, men with whom he did business, the manager of his bank, our dentist.

They'd come trooping into our house some Saturday nights and there'd be pretzels and peanuts sitting out in little dishes on the mahogany sideboard in our dining room, and plenty of cold beer. Mother would make herself scarce, and tease them afterwards when she gave them toasted cheese sandwiches and coffee before they all went home.

There'd been plenty of card playing on campus too, all the years I'd been a student. The girls in the dorm played canasta, and you could see bridge foursomes in the Student Union snack bar whenever it was open.

There, with their books stacked in untidy piles beneath the square functional tables, the players would be rapt in concentration over their games, ignoring the blare of the jukebox and the exasperated tray-rattling of the busboys who were trying to get rid of them to make room for the sandwich and coke crowd.

But Harry had said 'profitable', and none of the card-playing I'd ever seen had been that. I don't know what stakes the Student Union bridge fanatics were playing for, but I doubt it was ever very much. And at home we'd played for buttons or pennies – to make it interesting, dad said – and his poker circle had kept to a strict pot limit which I think was something like a dollar. The girls in the dorm had played for cokes from the vending machine in the lobby.

So 'profitable' was probably just another of Harry's colourful exaggerations, I thought, an emotive word chosen specially to make me admire him for living dangerously in the big bad world, to make me feel provincial.

Harry was not larger than life, I thought to myself; he was not! He was, in many ways, just like everybody else – millions of people who played cards for relaxation when there was nothing on TV.

After all, he was a serious student, a gifted mathematician who'd started university with two scholarships and a part-time job just so he could make something of himself.

I squared my chin and looked directly into his eyes.

'That's great, Harry, I'm glad you showed a profit. But what I meant was, what did you do in California for eating money?'

He laughed out loud. 'I told you, Libby. Poker, gin, bridge – Old Maids, for Christ's sake! I played *cards* for a living.'

'I don't believe that,' I whispered. My squared chin betrayed me and began to quiver slightly.

'Oh *baby*, you *are* shocked.'

He grinned again and reached out for the edge of the sheet and gave it a little tug; I gripped it more tightly around me. I was so mad I felt like slapping the smirk off his face. I sat there, fuming.

'Come *on*, Lib, grow up.' he said finally. 'People do gamble seriously, you know. Some win, and some lose. Smart boy like me, nice polite hometown boy – why shouldn't I be a winner? Long as I wear a clean shirt and say please and thank you, why the hell not?'

He cocked his head playfully to one side, and dimpled, and my heart did a quick tempo watusi. Christ, he was serious. He was serious, oh God Almighty Christ he was serious. My heart seemed to stop, and grow cold.

He really believed what he was saying. He – he saw himself as a bona fide hustler, like Paul Newman in that film, or like Clark Gable on a riverboat, looking big.

23

It was exactly as if he'd told me he drank a bottle of gin before breakfast every day, or that he'd tried codeine for a headache and had ended up with needle marks all down the inside of his arms.

Gambling, if it wasn't a sin, was at least a sickness. People got hooked on it, and couldn't stop, and it may as well have been leprosy for the impact it made on me that morning.

My heart went out to him, but at the same time he seemed suddenly unclean. I didn't want him to touch me and yet at the same time I wanted him, wanted to be wrapped in him, consumed, the way we'd been when we were making love.

'Harry,' I said softly, forcing compassion and understanding and sympathy to win over the horror and the stubborn, relentless desire – for how could I feel that for a guy who'd just told me he lived among a shadowy world of creeps and borderline gangsters in filthy, smoky rooms? 'Harry,' I said urgently, 'you *can* stop, can't you? I'll help you.'

'Why should I?' he asked just as softly, cutting across my desperate attempts to help him. 'Answer me that, pretty girl, why should I?'

I swallowed hard. 'Well Harry, school—'

'Well Libby, school,' he mimicked. 'Of course, school. But I have to pay for it, or most of it. And playing a successful session of five-card draw is one hell of a lot more pleasant, and lucrative, than clearing tables in a canteen. Wouldn't you agree?'

'But when you *lose*, Harry—'

'I don't lose, Libby. I win, or I break even, and if I don't win or break even I go back to basics and figure out why not. And I never, ever make the mistake of trusting to luck. I'm not hooked on *gambling*, Libby, I'm hooked on winning. There's a big, big difference.'

'You mean – you play a system?' I asked slowly. I'd seen a movie about a gambler, some guy with a foolproof system for winning at roulette. He ended up a big loser at the end of

24

it, hitching out of Las Vegas with nothing more to show for his time than the shirt on his back. This was after he'd sold his car, and lost the only girl he'd ever loved. My world was in ashes.

'There's no such thing as a system, Libby,' Harry said. 'Winning depends on skill and a good memory and a close knowledge of the odds.'

'I don't understand,' I said helplessly, pleading with him to tell me something I could understand, something that would fit somewhere in my world and made sense.

'I know that, sugar,' Harry said. 'So I'll try to make it easier. Say I'm sitting in a poker game – say, seven card draw. If I start with two pair, I know that the odds against getting three of a kind for a full house in one draw are – ' he did a rapid calculation in his head – 'eleven to one against. They call it gambling, but at its most skilful and careful it's really applied mathematics, see?'

'Well yes, but I still don't—'

'Oh shit, Libby, I know that! And you probably never will. They just don't run the world that way in Lemonade Springs, Montana—'

'No, they sure don't! And they don't run it that way anywhere else either! Even if you do win all the time, or most of the time, what about the poor suckers you're winning from? Even if *you're* not sick, Harry, you're making a profit from somebody else's sickness!'

'Finished, Saint Joan?'

'Oh, don't be so damned sarcastic! You're ugly when you're like that, did you know? Sometimes I feel like the real you just goes away somewhere to make room for this other you, the smirking, detestable, contemptuous person who doesn't even know about the simple ordinary values most of us live by, let alone care about. Oh hell, I don't know what I feel any more. . . .'

He sighed and smoothed my hair, and I turned my face into the palm of his hand and began to cry.

'Honey, don't,' he said. The real Harry said that, the one I recognized and loved and thought I knew. The scholar, the Harry who teased me so gently, oh so gently, because he'd known me all those years ago and he'd come back to me, and I *still* wasn't old enough to drink a legal beer.

'Harry – win or lose, how can you square it with your conscience? Please, just tell me that.'

He sighed again. 'I don't even try, Libby. It's essentially very simple. I found out that the world shakes down to winners and losers, and that if it isn't me winning money from suckers who can't win and can't leave a card game alone, it'll just be somebody else.'

'Sure, but you could say the same thing about pushing heroin—'

'Oh no, Libby, *that* I could not!' He looked and sounded genuinely shocked. 'Let's get this straight once and for all, right? Heroin addicts die—'

'And compulsive gamblers ruin their lives and the lives of everybody around them, their families, their kids—'

'Libby,' he said patiently, 'if you took that analogy far enough, you could say that anybody who owns a bar is guilty of turning people into alcoholics, or that anybody who supplies damn near anything might be indirectly guilty of wrecking other people's lives. And if you thought *that* one through long enough you'd end up sitting on your hands forever.

'Listen honey, I don't force people to play cards at gunpoint. But I'm not about to start turning them down when they're hot for a game and the price is right. Why should that be any different from selling someone a car which he then proceeds to take out and smash up? You see the point, don't you?'

I couldn't see that. By that time I couldn't really think clearly at all; the feelings Harry had aroused by telling me he'd made himself part of what I could only imagine as a sleazy, unsavoury world were so mixed up and tangled I couldn't even begin to separate them, examine them, marshal them into any kind of order.

'Harry, gambling isn't even *legal*,' I said weakly. That was a kind of last gasp at trying to get him to see it my way, but it didn't work.

He shrugged. 'Sometimes it is,' he said evenly, 'and sometimes not. But don't worry about that, sweetheart. I keep my eyes wide open, and I know what's what.'

That was meant as an attempt at reassurance, but it didn't reassure. It only lead me further into a labyrinth of emotions, one of which was fear for him, what would happen to him. It was all wrong, what he was doing, but I couldn't make him see it; I couldn't help him, I was locked out.

'Harry, I don't like it,' I said wearily.

'I know that,' he said gently. 'But you're making too big a deal out of the whole thing, believe me. Listen, in a few years' time I'll probably be heading up a distinguished group of research chemists, but in the meantime I've got to make a living, and I've chosen the easiest way I can think of to do it. Honey, I know what I'm doing.'

He knew what he was doing.

He tugged at the sheet again and this time it came down around my waist. He leaned forward and took one of my breasts and then the other into his mouth until my conscienceless nipples hardened. My arms went round him, and I was lost.

That lasted for all the time it took, and when it was finished, as I emerged from the roller coaster glow of sweet giving and sweet taking, Harry whispered, 'Okay, sweetpea?'

I nodded numbly and smiled up at him. Oh, everything was okay, yes, yes.

Afterwards, reason returned, and I knew with stunned and absolute clarity that I would either have to accept what he had told me, accept Harry totally for what he was, or give him up. I knew with equal clarity that I couldn't bring

27

myself to do either. I told myself I was taking the whole thing too seriously.

He had come back to Iowa to finish his degree, and we had met up again by merest chance and fallen into bed together. It was one of those things that happen to people sometimes, like lightning striking twice in the same place.

I was young and gullible and transparently in love, and he'd been trying to impress me with his worldliness, talking about his gambling. It would pass, or he would go away, the way he had the first time, and the issue would pale into insignificance against my four-star heartache.

So I brushed my teeth and rinsed my flushed face with cold water; then I went into the kitchen to make coffee.

Harry didn't go away.

He enrolled for the autumn semester, bought his text-books, found a part-time job in the library, and moved in with me, and it was glorious.

Apart from an occasional bridge game in the Student Union snack bar, he spent most of his leisure time with me. We studied together. He brought me flowers. He borrowed a car and took me out to every hotel within a radius of twenty miles that boasted a dance floor and a halfway decent band.

I am tall. I'd always thought myself clumsy and awkward, lucky to have come of age in an era when couples stood apart, gyrated separately to the rhythmic insistence of a rock backbeat, and called it dancing.

Harry was taller still, and he didn't dance that way.

The first time he asked me to waltz with him I stammered, terrified, saying, 'Oh I can't, Harry, I never—'

'Come on, honey, try it with me,' he said, pulling me up, smiling into my eyes.

And when he took me into his arms I fitted there and I took flight; I was magically graceful, moving with him, following his lead as though I'd known the steps and turns all my life, as though he'd held me like that forever.

That Christmas I wrote to my parents to say I wouldn't be coming home. I told them that as it was my senior year, my last at university, I had a lot to do, a lot to prepare for. They accepted that, reluctantly, and mailed me a huge box of presents and a large cheque.

I didn't mention having Harry, or walking in the snow with him and having snowfights and building snowmen, and racing him home to the warmth of the apartment and the joys of bed.

Sometimes we played a game together, a game I invented that was intended to make light of the fact that I knew almost nothing about him. It was an attempt to find out more, to place him in the context of a personal history, a past.

'You were found in – a moses basket. . . .'

'Naw!'

'Um sure, why not? On the steps of a monastery, wrapped up warm against the softly falling spring rain, with a tear-stained note pinned to your blanket: "Please look after my beloved child, for I no longer can," signed by your mother. And the monks, perceiving your academic genius at an early age, abandoned their plan to bind you to their celibate community—'

'Just as well.'

'Um! Do that again! Where were we? Oh yes. And sent you forth into the world, a free spirit, to revolutionize science.'

Or:

'Maybe you're the unacknowledged love child of a Balkan prince and a famous ballet dancer. Yes, that's it! And you spent the first years of your life backstage, enchanting the entire company, until at last your mother's failing strength forced her to entrust you to an honest woodsman and his gentle wife, and you were raised in their cottage deep in the forest.'

Sometimes, depending on his mood, Harry would respond

29

to my fantasies with a slow dreamy smile, bringing fingers gentle as whispers to my lips before he silenced them with a kiss.

Other times he turned away abruptly. 'I told you Libby, my folks are dead. Would you please just drop it?'

'Sorry,' I'd say softly, meaning it, rubbing his shoulders, smoothing away the hard knots of tension I could feel there, loving him; more determined than ever to be mother and father to him, sister, lover, and friend.

And that's when it really began for me, with Harry.

2

By the time spring came I was flying high: I was deeply in love, not yet twenty, finished with college and ready to conquer the world.

My parents drove east to attend my graduation ceremony, and they made a little vacation of it. They rented a suite in the best hotel in town and stayed for several days, during which time they made much of me and took dozens of snapshots for the family album. When I introduced them to Harry they were pleased to meet him.

But when I told them that instead of coming back to Montana for the summer I planned to go directly to San Francisco to take up the job I'd been offered there, and that Harry was transferring to a university in northern California, parental attitudes shifted markedly.

Harry ceased to be 'one of Libby's college friends', or even 'Libby's steady date'. Instead he came under much closer scrutiny as a serious contender for a great deal of Libby's time and attention, and even a possible candidate for her hand in marriage. The job I'd been offered was very much a side issue.

In fact, of course, I hadn't been offered a job, not in San Francisco or anywhere else. Like thousands of others, I had earned a Bachelor of Arts degree in English and journalism from a good but unremarkable university, and what I did with it would depend on luck, initiative, and my willingness to commit myself to a career – roughly in that order. It wasn't as though I'd qualified as a brain surgeon.

I'd made up my mind to work in advertising or public relations if I could; there were bound to be opportunities to

do that in San Francisco. And that's where I was going –
with Harry.

My father tried hard to conceal his mid-Victorian sensibi-
lities behind a suave façade of successful businessman and
man-of-the-world. But I could tell it was all he could do not
to ask Harry if his intentions were honourable.

Dad could accept my determination to make a career, and
to do it in San Francisco. That was fine with him; I was
'modern', and that was only to be expected. He was even
proud of me for going further at school than he had, for
finishing a college degree.

But I was still only a woman, his only daughter at that.
My brothers could do more or less as they liked, but getting
married would be central to my life. And if he had anything
to say about it, I would be married in white, to a man who
could and would look after me.

My mother was small and plump and pretty, still justi-
fiably proud of her slim ankles and her excellent legs. She
projected an image of intense and yielding femininity.

She could brim with sentimentality, her view of the
milestones in a woman's life – courtship, marriage, birth –
as kitsch as a picture of two kittens on a hearthrug playing
with a ball of yarn.

Underneath the image she was tough, pragmatic, and
fiercely realistic about damned near everything, particularly
about men and women, marriage, and money.

It wasn't that she expected me to get married, or not to
have a career if I did, or anything of the sort. As it happened
she had built a career of her own alongside my father's, and
in many ways she had been the steel sinews behind his
considerable success.

She was flexible on the point, and not at all protective.
She would cheerfully have accepted my being kept in style
by a Bolivian tin billionaire, and/or my building an empire
of my own. Or any permutation in between.

It was just that if I was going to have a man permanently

32

installed around the house who needed pushing, then in her view I should get behind him and push. And she hoped, loving me, that it would be worth the effort I put into it.

That short period of my parents' getting to know Harry was full of event, and it fixed certain of their impressions of him as firmly as chicken sets in aspic.

On the second evening of the visit my father took the four of us out to dinner. With transparent heavy-handedness he said, 'You two'll see a lot of each other, out in California.'

'Oh, not necessarily,' I said, gesturing nonchalantly with my salad fork. 'I'll be working, after all, and Harry will be studying.'

Harry nearly choked on a mouthful of wine.

It wasn't at all clear to me whether I'd opted to take my chances in California before or after Harry decided to transfer his course credits to San Francisco State University. I'd tried not to think about that too much because in spite of the fact that he seemed to care for me a lot, he'd shied away from making any kind of commitment to our future together.

Once we decided we were headed for the same place, however, we agreed to share an apartment – just as we'd been sharing my apartment throughout the previous two semesters.

If my vaguely reassuring answer to my father's question didn't satisfy him, at least it diverted him. He turned to Harry.

'You're going to study, eh? Didn't you graduate with Libby?'

'Actually sir, I didn't,' Harry said. 'I had to take three years off to work.'

My father nodded, pursing his lips in and out the way he always did when he was pondering something.

Later that evening Harry invited him to a friendly session of pinochle and gin rummy, and dad rocked back and forth on his heels and said he'd be glad to show him a thing or two.

Mother and I went back to my apartment.

33

'Is this really what you want, honey?' she said, almost before I'd closed the door.

'Is what what I want, mother?'

She gestured vaguely, her gold filigree bracelets jingling expensively on her plump arm, her brown eyes darting worriedly over the threadbare carpet and hideous furniture in the living room. 'This. . . .'

I laughed and hugged her. 'No, of course I don't! I'll be able to afford a nice place once I'm working. You can come out to see me. We'll go shopping.'

Her eyes lit up briefly at the prospect, but then she shook her head.

'No, I mean you're – ah – sleeping with him, aren't you? With Harry. I mean, is that what you want?'

She glanced towards the bedroom door and sighed, and it struck me Harry had been right. It had been quite unnecessary for him to remove all traces of his occupancy from the apartment in anticipation of my parents' visit.

'Your mother will probably figure it out anyway,' he'd said. 'And your father won't want to think about it at all.'

I had insisted, and he had complied, but he had been right.

Mother said, 'Libby?'

'Yes?'

'What – what was Harry doing, when he wasn't in school?'

'He told you, mother, he was working. He went to California, and he worked.'

'Sure, but what was he doing? He seems real smart, I just wondered.'

'Oh I don't know. Odd jobs, waiting on table, stuff like that I guess.'

She gave me a shrewd look. 'For three years?'

I shrugged and went into the kitchen to make coffee, and we talked about other things.

34

The following evening my father said he felt too tired to go anywhere. He said he'd rest up in the hotel while the three of us went out. I thought nothing of it; dad never was much of a reveller.

Harry borrowed their car and took us to a real down-home greasy spoon café on the wrong side of town, where we ate fried chicken with our fingers and propped our elbows on the formica table.

Afterwards we drove to a gin mill on a country road in the middle of a cornfield, where we drank draught Schlitz with the local farmers and danced to the jukebox music until they closed the joint.

My mother had a ball.

'I can see what you see in Harry, honey,' she told me the next day at lunch. 'Why, he's what you'd call a walking party all by himself, and he sure can dance. But you be careful sweetheart, okay?'

Then she confided, eyes dancing with mischief, that at the card-playing session a couple of nights earlier, playing head-to-head rummy against Harry, my father had lost eighty-seven dollars.

Harry and I drove to California in the car we bought.

It was of doubtful pedigree and it ate gas and leaked oil, and every hundred miles or so we had to pull off the road, get out, and clean its spark plugs.

But it was a convertible, low-slung and foreign and red, and its engine made a wonderfully powerful noise revving up, and it suited the raffish California feeling of the raffish California people we would presently become.

We kept the top down most of the way, across the plains and over the Rockies and through the desert, and with the June sun beating down on us and the wind in our hair, we sang all the songs we knew about the Gold Rush and the pioneers in covered wagons.

We came into San Francisco early in the morning, just as the mist was lifting from the bay.

As we approached the lyrical arch of the Golden Gate Bridge, gleaming in triumphant splendour, defying gravity against the deep blue sky, my heart caught in my throat.

It was a symbol, a magical omen of youth and freedom and laughter and happiness yet to come, the gateway to a cornucopia.

The apartment we rented was on the second floor of a turn-of-the-century house that perched gracefully and precariously at the top of a hill, at the top of the world.

We furnished its big square rooms with cane and bamboo and teak from the oriental-import warehouses near the docks, and we curtained its light-loving windows with green plants suspended in raffia baskets. It was home, and it was marvellous, perpetually filled as it was with air and sunshine, warmth and love.

Harry enrolled in the summer session at the university, and I was hired by Metcalf Jones Public Relations Consultants, Inc. and landed in clover, although I didn't realize it at the time.

They took me on as a trainee account executive. It sounded good, but it didn't fool me.

I could type, and they knew it. I knew the alphabet, of course, and so I could file things. I could operate the liquid process duplicating machine. I could even change the fluid in the damned thing which, being messy and smelly, was a particularly nasty job.

And I could make drinkable coffee.

These useful if menial accomplishments would keep me low man on the totem pole in the luxurious penthouse suite of offices occupied by Metcalf Jones for a very long time, I felt sure.

I didn't really mind. They were paying me well, and everyone was very nice to me, and besides my career came a poor second to my life with Harry.

He was still gambling, as and when he could find a reasonable game, and I was still uneasy about it and he knew that.

I tried to ignore my qualms, to gloss them over for both of us by teasing him, insisting he should wear a brocade waistcoat or an arm garter, or smoke big cigars when he announced he was going out to play.

When those remarks drew cold blank looks from him I stopped making them.

And he continued to dress for card games as conservatively as if he was going to a part-time job: dark slacks, white shirt, casual jacket.

It *was* like a part-time job, in a way. He worked at it as if it were; after all he didn't believe in luck. He sat in the living room on evenings when we weren't going out, or when he wasn't going out on his own to a game, committing long tables of odds and percentages to memory.

He was studying too; I could see that. And whenever he spent an evening poring over his huge, incomprehensible textbooks, I drew a mental sigh of relief. This was the clear, honest way to his future. Perhaps, though I didn't dare articulate it then, even to myself, *our* future.

Harry never said exactly how much he won playing cards, and I didn't ask him. I figured it must be a lot though; he paid for nearly everything we bought together, in cash.

He kept careful track of his winnings in a pocket ledger he carried, and he made his entries as dispassionately and soberly as if he was keeping track of his wages as an undertaker's assistant.

There was little doubt that he knew what he was doing. All the same, I began to be intensely curious about his gambling – where he played, and with whom.

Gambling was illegal in California, the only exception being Lake Tahoe, a town on the Nevada border – a plush resort set in the magnificent natural surroundings of the Sierra Nevada mountain range where the idle rich could

37

swim and sail and sunbathe and generally hang out in considerable comfort when they weren't squandering portions of their fortunes in opulent casinos.

Harry didn't go there to play lo-ball poker, I knew that much. For one thing Lake Tahoe was too far away for commuting; and anyway he'd already told me he played poker across the bay, in a town on the outskirts of Oakland.

'I'd like to go with you some evening,' I said to him, smiling, nonchalant.

He looked at me as though I'd struck him. He blanched. He recovered quickly, fine poker player that he was. But I had seen.

He laughed, and traced my face with his fingers. 'I wouldn't dream of dragging you over there, sweetpea. You'd be bored out of your skull within fifteen seconds, anybody in their right mind would if they weren't in the game.'

'I wouldn't, Harry, I promise. I—'

'Honey, there's nothing to do there but drink beer and watch a bunch of suckers losing money. Listen, I'll tell you what. We'll go up to Tahoe for a long weekend. We can waterski and you can play the slots – all right? You'll love it there.'

He put his arms around me and held me close; I nestled against him, and we kissed.

And as far as Harry was concerned, that was the end of it. I tried to forget it, and I didn't ask him to take me with him again.

But what had begun as mere curiosity – a desire to flesh out the venue of his card-playing in my mind's eye – blossomed into a need to see it that was almost an obsession: I started to visualize the poker rooms across the bay as sinister dangerous places where it wasn't safe to go. Why else would Harry refuse to take me there? Harry wasn't the super-protective macho type, and I wasn't Little Annie Fannie, so what was the big deal?

38

I'd led a moderately sheltered life, yes, but I was intelligent and independent and resilient, able to deal with situations. I had to know where he went so often, where he spent so much of his free time; I had to see it for myself.

But I had no clear idea where 'it' was. 'Across the bay' could mean almost anywhere within a radius of fifty miles; and it was uncharted territory. I worried about the problem for weeks until the solution – so obvious, it had been staring me in the face nearly every weekday from nine to five – presented itself.

There was an old guy at the office who should have been retired, but who worked in our firm as a sort of superannuated office boy, running errands and carrying heavy boxes and occasionally making simple repairs to the telex machine and the typewriters. He was a gambler, and whenever he found anyone who was willing to listen he loved to talk about horse race betting, his latest killing or unlucky near-miss at the tracks.

It dawned on me that I'd avoided him whenever I could do so without giving offence. He was harmless enough, even pleasant; but for me he was a shuffling, time-diminished object lesson in what an habitual gambler might so easily become in the struggle to support his habit. I realized that in spite of all the apparent evidence to the contrary, I was afraid deep down that Harry would end up that way: a man who had to work at a time in his life when his contemporaries, having led sober and prudent lives, were free to potter in their back yards, cultivating roses.

But one morning I asked him, very casually, if he ever played cards.

'Sure, when I can find a game,' he said, winking at me. 'Not much action, though, unless you go across the bay into the boondocks. The stakes get pretty high over there, some places.'

'Really?' I smiled at him encouragingly. 'Where?'

He told me.

'Couple of fleabags in a slum is all they amount to. Big rooms with lots of tables, folks hunkered around them as though their lives depended on it. High stakes but no class, and not a breath of fresh air for miles. Me, I prefer the ponies.'

The following Saturday morning, on the pretext of a shopping expedition, I took the car and drove across the Golden Gate Bridge; it wasn't hard to find the neighbourhood, once I knew what I was looking for.

It was infamous. I'd heard all about it; I'd even driven through it – eyes front, car doors securely locked – on my way to somewhere else.

It was one of the worst of the ghettos which people like me, to our everlasting shame, could read about in our morning papers and discuss earnestly over our impromptu, oh-so-laid-back dinner parties, and do nothing about.

The main road was not that unsettling; that was the part I'd already seen; it was lined with warehouses that bulked huge and bleak against the mocking brilliance of the California sky.

But the little streets behind them were permeated by a palpable air of weary defeat.

There the poorest black people lived in shabby houses in terrible poverty; on nearly every street corner there was a bar where brawls and stabbings were commonplace.

I must have driven around for nearly an hour, taking it all in: the sleazy gin mills with their night-snazzy neon signs faded and filthy beneath the brazen blue blue of the sky and the spanking freshness of the scudding white clouds, with their familiar names – *The Top Hat*, *Bop Alley*, *The Bon Ton*, the *Smooth n Easy*; the fly-blown glass expanse of store-fronts, most of them abandoned; the broken wooden planks of front porches of the over-crowded miserable houses; the knots of scrawny little kids playing in the streets.

I had intended to park the car and get out and take a

closer look, perhaps even to press my nose against the smeared window of one of the buildings that looked like it might have housed a card room, like a starving urchin gazing into a bakery, so I could bring it into painful searing focus. When it came to it, I couldn't bring myself to do that; I didn't have to. I had seen enough.

All I could think of as I drove back across the bridge, my eyes filling with helpless tears, was that the city morgue would have been less depressing.

And I thought too, how on earth could Harry go there? He was fastidious almost to a fault, and he loved beautiful things: flowers on the dinner table, Mozart, warm clean well-lighted rooms. And he cared about people, I knew he did.

None of it made sense.

Once I'd reached San Francisco and the safe affluence of Ghiradelli Square – the measured elegance of the old-time chocolate factory turned shopping district – I stopped and parked, got out and made a leisurely tour of the stores and galleries; I drank a coffee and then I bought a scarf, gay and bright and floaty and expensive, which was tendered in a smart striped bag emblazoned with the name of an exclusive boutique.

It was a blue silk flag, I thought, proclaiming that I had gone shopping after all, among my own kind, where I belonged. It was an arrogant gesture, mixed with guilt; I had spied on Harry behind his back. Worse than that, the blue silk scarf had cost enough to feed a family of five for nearly a week. But what good would it have done that family if I had not bought the scarf? I couldn't fight city hall; I couldn't abolish poverty single-handed.

Harry need never know where I had been; I need never tell him. But when I got home, Harry wasn't fooled. He took one look at me and put his arms around me and asked me what was wrong. I tried hard to smile and say, 'nothing, nothing at all,' but my face crumpled and I leaned into his embrace and sobbed.

41

'Say, you didn't dent the dream machine did you?' And then, when I began sobbing harder, 'Oh honey, I don't really care! It's only a car—'

'No! No, Harry, it isn't that. I – I saw it,' I said, choking, wiping furiously at my eyes with clenched fists, like a child.

He frowned, puzzled, concerned. 'Saw what, hon? What did you see? Where were you?'

He held me close again, I pulled away so I could look into his eyes. 'I – I went into – into Oakland. It was – oh Harry, it was awful!'

He knew then where I had been; he smoothed my hair and kissed the top of my head.

'Did you go into one of the clubs?' he asked quietly.

I bowed my head. 'I didn't have to,' I said. 'I just drove around for awhile.' I shrugged and shuddered.

'You shouldn't have gone there, Libby. I never meant you to go there.'

'Harry, I'm not a child! *You* go there, don't you?'

He sighed. 'Sure, hon. Sure, I go there.'

He tensed, defensive; I could feel the muscles of his shoulders bunching up through the thin cotton of his shirt.

'And don't think I don't care about what goes on in that neighbourhood! I'd change it if I could, you know that. Meanwhile that's where they play lo-ball poker, where they run the only marginally legal game in town for anything like decent stakes. That sure beats hell out of working in a snack bar, humping dirty dishes.'

I nodded slowly, then looked up at him again and his eyes softened when I said, 'Harry – is it – is it safe down there? I mean. . . .' I bit my lip, ashamed of myself.

It was a thoroughly cowardly question, typically feminine, rooted deeply in the wholly womanly concerns which bound me to my sisters back to the primordial archetype, stripped of the veneer of civilization. If me and mine were safe, to hell with the rest of the world.

'It's okay, hon, really it is. Safe as any other place if you

42

go about your business and don't try to mix it in the local bars. Anyway, the local people don't go near the lo-ball rooms; far too rich for their blood at the stakes we play for. But I'd – I'd change all that, if I could,' he said. He was perfectly sincere, and somehow wistful.

After that Harry never talked about poker, or the clubs where he played, or the people he met there.

If I asked him about it he answered me reluctantly, almost curtly, as though that part of his life was something he had sworn on oath not to discuss.

It wasn't as though he was ashamed of it. It was rather that he knew I'd never accepted it, and that he didn't want us to quarrel about something he had no intention of changing. So far as I knew, he never discussed it with anyone else either.

It remained an area Harry chose to keep apart from the rest of his life. There were other areas like that, particularly his past, which he never discussed. I didn't know where he'd been born and raised, and in what circumstances. Nor who his parents had been, what they'd been like, how they had died, who had looked after him then. I didn't even know if he had brothers or sisters.

His secretiveness worried me deeply at times; it seemed to me to go beyond the natural human need for privacy. My occasional tentative probes were always deflected. They bounced off the opaque surface of Harry's impenetrable shields almost as though I hadn't asked them.

I made up my mind to stop digging. I would wait for him to trust me. I accepted patiently that it would take time.

It became easier as time passed to come to terms with it. He'd been orphaned, badly hurt at a time when most children were protected and cherished. It certainly wasn't as though he was hiding any deep dark secrets; it was just that trusting came hard for him. I would have to be patient, to

43

love him all the more to make it up to him. And there was so much we did share it was easy to be patient. As for loving him, I could no longer imagine life without him.

I moved through that summer in a ring of glorious light, light that swirled and spangled in loops of exuberant brilliance until it settled, glowing, binding Harry and me into a close safe circle where we ate cracked crab and sourdough bread in bed on Sunday mornings, getting crumbs and mayonnaise all over the place and not caring. We wandered into Chinatown long after dark, blinking in the glare of the blazing neon Chinese characters on signs that beckoned us into fragrant and mysterious restaurants. At weekends we drove south to Carmel and Monterey, or north into the redwood forests to Crescent City, delighted with the panorama of hills and sea, the picture-postcard grandeur of the Pacific coast. We made love, fusing closer and closer still until the light that surrounded us became one incandescent white-hot flame.

The abrupt arrival of torrential rains signalled the end of the San Francisco summer. Harry came in very late one Saturday night from playing cards and kissed me awake.

'Libby, we're getting married,' he said.

I sat up in bed and rubbed my eyes. 'Just like that?'

'Don't you want to?' He sounded hurt.

I hadn't really thought about it. Oh, well, I had – but it wasn't for us.

Marriage was real, marriage was earnest; marriage brought children and a future people tried to plan for them as carefully as people could plan anything. And I was by no means in an old maid's race to the altar; given my generation, and my mother's thoroughly unpressurized attitudes to my marital future, I'd probably never feel the frantic urge to marry.

I felt that I was as committed to Harry Franklin as I was ever likely to be to anyone, but Harry was young too – two years older than I was – and when I thought about it hard, really gave it my full attention and tried to bypass the springs of emotion that kept me buoyant every time I looked at him, I knew that there were niggling doubts about the long-term canter into maturity.

There was his gambling, for a start; our conflicts over that – and they'd nothing to do with money, because Harry was as good as his word and did win consistently – had never been resolved. They were moral, or ethical, or, I don't know, social I suppose; whatever their origins they were difficult to point to and wrestle with and come to terms with. Most especially since Harry refused to discuss the matter.

So there was that. And there was his sudden offended silence, his withdrawal, whenever I tried to get him to open up about a childhood which had obviously caused him considerable pain. He was a long, long way from letting me in.

But I was half-asleep. I merely said, 'Harry, why bring up marriage *now*?'

'If you don't want to marry me, Lib, just say so.'

'Some proposal.' I yawned.

'I'm serious, Libby. It's time. I won a bundle tonight.'

'Oh, that's great, honey! Harry – can we talk about it in the morning?'

He flung off his jacket, threw it over a chair and stood beside the bed, unbuttoning his shirt cuffs. I was awake enough by then to see that his face was white with strain and tiredness and anger. He was hurt; I hadn't meant to be flippant, but he was utterly serious, and that's probably the way I sounded.

'The trouble with you,' he said tightly, 'is that you're too eager. Now do you want to marry me, for God's sweet sake, or don't you?'

I opened my mouth to speak and closed it again, I went hot and cold; I felt precisely the same exaltation mixed with dread I remembered feeling the first time a boy asked me to go out with him, to a junior high school dance.

45

I knew, even on that glorious night when Harry made his abrupt proposal, that there were reasons – real ones – why I shouldn't consent to marry him, or why I should at least wait awhile before I did so.

I also realized – and I remember feeling quite astonishingly philosophical and mature at the time, given the hour of morning – that I might wait forever and not be any the wiser about my decision, whichever way it went.

Marriage was a legal contract, legally binding, with legal obligations attached to it. But it was made, by ordinary people in our culture and our time, from the heart, for no good reason, for no *reason* at all. If a couple got lucky and their marriage prospered and they were happy together, they could always rationalize their choice after the fact. And they frequently did. But the legalities and obligations of marriage were so inextricably interwoven with sentiment and sex and the sheer ornery vagaries of human emotion they were often invisible in, and quite inseparable from, the whole tangled mesh.

What came most clearly into my mind that night – the analysis came later – was something my mother had said to me years before, when we'd been talking about love and marriage. She'd said, 'Honey, nobody in his right mind would buy a house because he liked the colour of the walls in the living room, or because it had a cute front door. But people get married every day for sillier reasons, and then they find out that marriage is every bit as binding as a mortgage. That's the trouble with marriage.'

And I'd asked her, 'So – how can you be sure when it's right? Have you been happy with dad?'

She smiled, more to herself than to me, and she put her arms around me. 'Sure I have! We ironed out a few wrinkles – like him remembering my birthday and stuff – and over the years I think I've livened him up a bit. And we've worked together, and had you kids and a real nice life. The main thing is I never tried to change him, not in any important way, but then I was pretty sure I wouldn't want to, when I married him. That's a little like buying a house too, when you think about it. You wouldn't want to pick one with major structural faults. I mean, going back to that, you can always paint your living room. But when you pick a man you more or less have to take him as you find him.'

It meant that if I wasn't sure I could live with Harry's gambling until death did us part, I should resolve it with him or accept it before I burned my bridges.

But that night when Harry asked me to marry him – more or less asked – I put my heart right on the line and let my mind go fly a kite. I did want to marry him. I did. Harry was – exotic; he had come out of nowhere, from a background that wasn't sure and planned and settled. And life with him would never be dull. Harry was exotic.

I said what I said. I said, 'Harry, I do want to marry you, honest.' And I met his eyes so he could see the love in mine flowing out to him.

And very stiffly, not ready to be mollified, he said, 'That's white of you,' and looked away.

But I was fully awake by then, fully alive; my heart had made its maverick unreasonable choice. I got up and opened a bottle of wine, and we stayed up until dawn making plans.

Harry didn't want me to tell my parents.

'I can't get married without telling them,' I protested, aghast.

'Sure you can. You just do it, and then tell them.'

Okay, I thought, here was my first chance to insist on standing my ground as an about-to-be-married person, maybe even a chance to register a gentle protest against the airtight compartments of Harry's life – or at least a chance to deliver notice that he sure as hell wasn't going to be allowed to divide *my* life into airtight compartments.

'I'm not going to do it, Harry,' I said firmly.

'One good reason why not?' he challenged me, eyeball to eyeball.

'It would break their hearts.'

'They'd get over it. Look, they don't like me, Libby. I'm not the type of guy they had in mind as a son-in-law.'

'That's not true. Anyway, I know my mother likes you. She told me she did.'

He conceded that with a shrug. 'Even so, they'd expect to dance in here and take over, make it a big production number with a cast of thousands. I was hoping we could keep it simple.'

He sighed, and I remembered guiltily that he didn't have folks to tell about getting married or anything else he did, let alone to care if he was happy. Mine probably seemed overwhelming just by existing. But getting married was important, and they loved me. I'd have to tell them.

My father was curiously detached about the whole thing, and it was more than an illusion created by a poor telephone connection to Montana.

He said very little, but what he did say sounded distant with an unmistakeable edge of hurt indifference. When he told me he wouldn't be able to take time off from business to come out for the wedding I had to fight back quick hot tears.

But if my mother had lingering doubts about the wisdom of my marrying Harry Franklin, she was perceptive enough to realize it was far too late to express them. And she was graceful enough not to try.

She came to San Francisco, clapped her hands in honest delight when she saw our apartment, went shopping with me for a dress, paid for it and pinned it up and hemmed it, fussed over Harry, and wept in the office of the Justice of the Peace who married us.

Then she took us out for a sumptuous Italian dinner in North Beach, and even Harry was disarmed when a miniature tiered wedding cake was carried to our table with a reverent joyful ceremony at the end of it.

★　★　★

It was two or three weeks later I discovered I'd been wrong about Metcalf Jones Inc.

They were a small firm, well-established and prosperous; they'd got that way by hiring good people and making full use of their talents. They had no intention of allowing me to languish indefinitely behind a typewriter.

One Monday Michael O'Neill, one of the youngest and most energetic of the account executives, stopped by my desk as I was steaming out a particularly dreary press release to ask me if I was ready for a real challenge.

Michael was something of a whizkid at Metcalf Jones, all charm and polish and city manners but still with a certain open-faced Irish boyishness that shone through. He'd masterminded several successful political campaigns – that was his speciality in the firm – and the downfall of more than one smitten secretary. As the newly-minted Mrs Harry Franklin I was immune to Michael's sexual magnetism, though not to his audacious confidence. I liked him.

I smiled. 'I think so,' I said. 'Yes, I'm ready.'

'It's quite a challenge,' he said. 'You've heard of Mirrani Vineyards?'

I nodded. Mirrani was one of the classier outfits among the winegrowers of the Napa Valley. Harry and I bought our wine in the supermarket on Saturday mornings, mainly in big cheap jugs. Mirrani vintages did not come in big cheap jugs. I said so.

'That's one of their problems,' Michael said thoughtfully. 'They've approached us because they intend to increase their output, which naturally means expanding their markets.'

I switched off the typewriter and began to pay closer attention. I took a deep breath and crossed my fingers in my lap.

'I don't know much about wine, Michael,' I said.

I'd been honest. He smiled down at me, his eyes were very blue.

'You will,' he said.

And by the end of that week, I did. I read every piece of bumpf, every leaflet, every book I could lay hands on: on grape growing, the winemaking process, the Napa Valley and its legendary combination of receptive soil and climate and vines that produced consistently drinkable and even great wines.

I dug out all the statistics I could find on wine sales and wine consumption per capita across the country.

'They're not too encouraging,' I said to Michael. 'Americans don't appear to be great wine drinkers, unless they live in California or New York State.'

'They can be persuaded, Libby, sold on the idea of sharing the bounty of California by buying Mirrani. Sun-ripened, harvested with care, transformed into nectar fit for gods.'

'It isn't cheap,' I said, chewing the end of my pencil.

'Neither is bourbon, darlin',' he said.

Meanwhile we ferreted out the names of the chief wine buyers for every large chain of retail supermarkets from Cincinatti, Ohio to Keokuk, Iowa and back again by way of Boston and Philadelphia, so we'd know where to spend the client's money to get the best return. Once we'd persuaded them to grant us the contract, and allocate a reasonable budget.

'We'll hold tastings, of course,' Michael said. 'Small, *chic*, deliberately exclusive affairs for the biggest buyers with the most money to spend. Parties afterwards, perhaps, in an all out effort to show them a good time while they're here.'

'Who'll foot the bills for air fares and hotels and so on, for the out-of-state buyers?'

Michael looked at me long and hard, thinking.

'Their thoroughly intrigued companies, we hope; especially once we've planted the idea that we're holding a major wine happening, and offering them a look-in before the market's taken up by their competitors. If they're reluctant

50

to shell out – and important enough – we'll persuade Mirrani to underwrite at least part of their expenses. They'll fall in love with Mirrani, California, and with you and me. Once they've ordered in sufficient quantities, we'll send them home feeling on top of the world about the project. We'll encourage them to advertise locally, whip up as much attention as possible. We'll hold their hands, fix them up with promotion packages to use in their areas, making sure they'll be able to sell the wine once they've got warehouses full of the stuff.'

'Um. Supermarket promos, that sort of thing?'

'That's it. Women buy most of the booze in this country, after all, along with the meat and potatoes and soap powder. No harm done giving them a little sip of the finest and a friendly smile while they're at it.'

'And then our outlets will run out of wine, and they're bound to reorder.'

'You know, Libby, you catch on fast. And say, I just thought of something else. If we can snag one or two real wine experts, hold a couple of "blind" tastings, challenge the masters to decide which wine comes from the Olde Country, and which from Mirrani, we might even manage to push our California Kool-Aid into the European market.'

'This is not going to be a low-budget production,' I said.

'But it's going to put our client on the map,' said Michael.

I had the time of my life, working on that campaign. I left work late, and came to work early; I learned more in a couple of weeks than I'd learned in all my years at college.

And Harry was marvellous. He cooked, he washed dishes, he cleaned the apartment, he listened to me patiently, excited right along with me, while I talked shop. And his delight that I was happy shone in his eyes.

And he surprised me on the Saturday before Michael and I went to Napa for the first client conference by taking me into downtown San Francisco to select a rainbow of pastel linen and silk dresses – expensively simple, marvellously flattering – so I'd look as good as I felt when Michael and I went off together to meet the Mirrani brothers in his maroon sedan, the colour of claret.

I would have known when we got to the Napa Valley with my eyes closed.

In that gloriously abundant autumn the air was heavy with the scent of perfectly ripened grapes; deep in its heart, along the secondary roads that wound through the valley, the smoky purple fragrance of wines-in-progress was everywhere.

Mirrani's establishment was deceptively modest, invisible from the road, marked only by a crudely lettered plaque above a rural mailbox – 'Mirrani' – at the entrance to the long curving driveway that led to a rambling white house surrounded by old graceful trees.

Behind it stretched luxuriant acres of expertly-tended vineyards, punctuated by brick outbuildings with vast cellars in which row upon row of seasoned wooden casks mellowed the carefully-monitored vintages; and where enormous vats cradled the new wines in the infancy of their flowering.

The Mirrani brothers were the three children of the dark wiry man whose portrait hung in the cellar room in which we talked business; his hands were large, work-toughened, gnarled with veins almost as thick as the vines he worked, hands full of tenderness for the vine cuttings he held in the picture – cuttings he had brought from his native Sicily at the turn of the century.

Mirrani Brothers was a family business, the family art and craft and passion; the men at its head, apprentice vintners from earliest childhood, had inherited their father's legacy. Wine ran where their blood should have been.

Philip, the eldest at perhaps forty-five, though it was hard to tell his age because of his wiry frame and his hair that still curled black and coarse and abundant, was the nominal managing director of the firm. But I had the feeling that the three of them shared that responsibility equally, that their accord was total and complete.

Philip and his carbon-copy brothers, perhaps forty and thirty-five, had been born in the house their father built. Grown and married and with children of their own they lived there still, still together, they and their families in apparent harmony.

They were together too in their determination to put Mirrani Brothers on the wine maps of the world.

I was nervous before that first conference. I had expected it to be a nerve-wracking contest of Michael's and my skills of presentation and persuasion against their old-country conservatism; I anticipated resistance to our judgment about campaign management, and to spending a cent more than they deemed absolutely necessary.

My heart was in my throat throughout the meeting too, during which the brothers took it in turn to pose questions that were – at least at first – very definitely directed at Michael. He'd already warned me that the brothers were unaccustomed to dealing with women in business, but also that they'd get over it when faced with my competence and charm – most of which blarney I wrote off to Michael's willingness to boost my shaky ego in exchange for all my painstaking work.

But I relaxed – and my cynical estimate of Michael's professional integrity shot up several decibels – when he deftly fielded most of the questions in my direction by a deferential nod; and I felt truly wonderful when the Mirrani men really listened to my answers.

They were thoughtful men, cautious men; that was after all how they'd prospered in the very limited market of Northern California, and why they'd decided to expand their operation. They had invested in additional vineyard acreage and built more cellars; and they had invited Michael and me to propose a public relations campaign that would make their considerable investment worthwhile.

They knew it would cost money, and they were prepared to pay it; they were also prepared to trust us, I could feel that. They even saw the charm in my suggestion that it would be fantastic – terrific for their image – if we held wine tastings right there in the room in which we sat around an oaken table, with the portrait of Mirrani Senior looking down, and the fragrance of fine wine pervading the cellars like a distillation of sunshine.

Still, driving home with Michael afterwards, I asked: 'Do you think they'll give us the account?'

He laughed. 'Sure as God gave us green apples, Libby. And a free hand with it.'

He was right. There was a letter signed by Philip Mirrani on his desk two days later, accepting our proposal.

I was in my element with my carefully-researched charts and graphs and lists of names and corporations and a strategy map studded with coloured drawing pins to make sure we'd covered as much territory as possible; making arrangements for hotel accommodation and transport and entertainment for the buyers and experts we invited to California; finding a catering firm that would come up to scratch with sufficient *panache* at the elegant, carefully orchestrated tastings. Working closely with the art department of the advertising agency Michael chose to design the works of art that became Mirrani's logo and their labels: line drawings of the three brothers, simple honest men, offering the magic ambience of California in a bottle.

Best of all, once the campaign was really underway, was watching the curve of Mirrani's out-of-state sales rising steadily, knowing it had been a resounding success.

I began to feel I was a part of Metcalf Jones, that I'd earned my spurs. My job was not yet a career – not in tenure or specific direction. Not yet. But I was involved, and I loved it. When I was awarded a spontaneous, unrequested salary increase after I'd been doing it for six months, it was confirmation to me that the agency directors knew how I felt about my work – that they were pleased with what I'd accomplished.

That was a couple of weeks before I discovered I was pregnant.

3

'What do you plan to do, Libby, have the baby in your lunch hour?'

It was May and I was seven months along. Harry was in Las Vegas playing in a bridge tournament and I'd taken a few days off from the agency to be with my mother during one of her flying visits to California. We'd been sniping at each other almost since the moment she arrived.

I eased off my shoes, settled back into my chair, smoothed my sprigged muslin maternity dress over my knees, and grinned at her, trying to lighten the atmosphere.

'I guess I could, why not? Dr Felton says most women are fit to go back to the rice paddy within a couple of hours after a normal delivery.'

'Oh sure!' she said, suddenly angry. 'And what about the baby?'

'What about him?' It was sure to be a boy. Harry wanted a boy.

'Or her.'

'Okay, mother, or her. What about the baby? The childcare facilities here are superb, we've already checked into it.'

We'd already found someone in fact, a registered nurse who loved kids and had raised three of her own before setting up a nursery. And the agency had made it clear they wanted me to go on working for them, if I could handle it. Harry was all for it too; he knew how much it meant to me.

Harry and I had established all that almost as soon as we decided to have a baby. Except that 'decided' is the wrong word. We talked about having a baby before we got married; it had been part of the *point* in getting married. But making a deliberate, conscious, cold-blooded decision to go ahead and have one seemed to me to be too momentous a decision to make. My hesitation was certainly greater than Harry's.

Oh, I wanted a baby; I wanted Harry's baby. But he was still studying, and despite our stretches of peace there were still so many mysterious no-go areas about Harry. I loved him so; but it was impossible to confide it to him. *What if the dark, withdrawn, reckless aspects of Harry's life should prevail, and I was shut out completely, and left to raise our child on my own?*

My fears didn't dominate me, but they made the deliberate conception of a baby seem like plunging into a vat of dark icy water from a great height. Somewhere in the labyrinths of my subconscious mind, I told myself it was better to get used to the idea gradually – to allow it to 'just happen', or 'not happen', much as it was easier to ease oneself into cold water a toe at a time.

What actually happened was that we *more or less* planned it. I went off the pill and was fitted for a diaphragm, and though we used it conscientiously – sometimes with what Harry referred to as the 'greasy kid stuff' that went with it – we both knew there was a margin for error. All the same, when we knew that I was pregnant, my cup of happiness was full.

My decision to go back to work after the baby was born, however, had been just that: a decision. And it wasn't an easy one to make. It was discussed, dissected, analysed, considered and criticized endlessly by nearly every woman I knew, and in every woman's magazine and baby care book I read. There were many conflicting schools of thought on the subject, it seemed – so many that for weeks on end I veered chaotically between the determination to combine mother-hood with a career, and abysmal stabs of guilt at the very idea.

At one end of the spectrum there were the 'earth mothers': women whose husbands were presumably settled into promising and secure careers, who declared loudly (and often defensively?) that no *real* woman would even dream of abandoning her role as wife and mother for the doubtful rewards of a paying job, no matter how satisfying. At the other end the almost stridently confident adherents of the theory that the youngest infant could positively thrive in the care of a 'surrogate mother', so long as it was treated consistently with warmth and love. And furthermore that a mother's constant, doting worry and attention could smother a child and make it super dependent. And, as grim corollary, that being constantly on tap for her children turned mothers into whining, boring vegetables more often than not. Between these two extremes were compromises: it would be okay to go back to work when the youngest child reached the kindergarten/primary school/high school/ college/job/marriage stage.

On one level, at least, I had a choice. No matter how I felt about the way in which Harry earned money, the fact was that he did make more than enough of it. The real trouble was that on the level of *what if*, I felt I had no real choice at all. If I were to be alone, it would be far better to be alone with a child *and* a career. Oh, I wouldn't be alone, not ever; Harry wanted a child as much as I did, perhaps more. So I dismissed my fears.

But when it was all set out, mulled over and examined from every angle, I knew I didn't want to have to choose: I wanted both, the baby and the career.

Harry said, 'Honey, given that the baby is healthy, and we can find someone reliable to look after him or her in the daytime when we're not home, there's no reason why you shouldn't go back to work if you want to. I'll help you, you know that.'

He would too; he always had. That was one of the most astonishing things about Harry – or so it seemed to me, whose father would do almost anything for my mother except grab a tea towel to dry the dishes. Perhaps because Harry had never before had a home of his own, he had little sense of the dynamics of role playing. He saw no reason why domestic chores should not be shared between wives and husbands.

He vacuumed and cleaned and laundered whenever he happened to be the one with time to do those tasks. And he did them with equanimity, apparently unaware that many men would see such domesticity as a diminution of their masculinity. And he loved to cook.

So, finally, it was decided. I could be a working mother and the sky would not fall down.

Now here was my own mother questioning the wisdom of all my painful soul-searching, heaving up doubts like big rocks for me to carry.

She said, 'You're going to raise your child by remote control?'

Guilt slammed into my solar plexus, somewhere just above where I could feel the baby kicking every time I sat down, or lay down to sleep.

'Mother,' I said patiently, 'I never expected to close my career options because Harry and I want a family. And surely it's the quality rather than the quantity of mothering that really counts. Why, Dr Felton says there's nothing worse for a kid than a frustrated unhappy mommy—'

'All I hear from you is "Dr Felton says". Tell me, Libby, just how many times has this Dr Felton of yours been a mother?'

Her brown eyes narrowed as though she'd scored a telling point.

I sighed. 'Three. She went back into obstetrics when her youngest was six months old.'

Mother blinked, caught out by a trick, and I felt sorry for her. I tried again.

'Oh mom, you of all people should know all that. You worked—'

59

'That was different,' she said bluntly.

'*How* different? Why?'

'Because I worked right beside your dad to build a business of our own, something for all of us. He worked hard too, very hard, and we had a common goal.'

That came out like the recitation it was, like the Pledge of Allegiance to the flag. It was Olsen family history, sacred source of pride and satisfaction and unimpeachable respectability.

J. Olsen & Sons, Building Contractors, founded by my father in the vanguard of the building boom that put Lemonade Springs, Montana on the map as a tourist paradise; an idyllic retreat for weary east coast greenhorns who longed for the wild unspoiled grandeur of the mountain west. Pure Lone Ranger, but there was money in them hills.

In the beginning J. Olsen was a man with boundless confidence, an A-1 credit rating, two pickup trucks and a pretty wife who could charm suppliers and customers alike and keep a tidy set of books. '& Sons' were two tow-headed little boys who could tie their own shoelaces and make their own beds and sandwiches long before they went to school, years before I was born.

And J. Olsen & Sons had prospered and flourished along with the town: triumphs of ingenuity, self-reliance, der-ring-do and hard work.

One of the boys, the elder, my brother Jim, had become an accountant; the younger, my brother Pete, was a lawyer. Both married local girls, established homes and families of their own, stayed in Lemonade Springs because they'd grown up there. Neither had ever been involved in the family business, though my father's fleet of lorries still carried the legend 'J. Olsen & Sons'.

Harry once asked me why he didn't change it to 'John and Nora Olsen', or 'J. Olsen and N. Olsen', or at the very least, to 'J. Olsen and Wife', to acknowledge my mother's status as his actual business partner. After that, I wondered too, though it never occurred to me to ask. My parents would have been shocked by the suggestion.

Now my mother leaned forward in her chair; hesitantly, with a mixture of excitement and apprehension, she said: 'Libby, you did say Harry's in – Las Vegas?'

'Yes.'

I winked at her, and she blushed.

My mother's Las Vegas was the biggest, most, tantalizing non-stop carnival for grown-ups that ever there was: its midnights bright as noon with solid banks of blazing neon light, its streets paved with dream-dazzle and the people drunk on it, loving it, living dangerously, whooping it up and swanking and staggering from one casino to the next, the odds against their winning not mattering a damn.

It was a deliciously sinful, profligate, squandering, once-in-a-lifetime-what-the-hell oasis of tinsel and glitter – twinkling shamelessly in the middle of the sombre stretching desert, flanked by the brooding mountains of the Funeral Range.

We had gone there together on one of our trips when I was home for the summer, one of the short holidays we took just two girls together, one of the rare occasions when she left my father at home with a freezer full of food.

We stayed at one of the gorgeously vulgar casino-hotels, and she stood thrilled and awestruck for hour after blissful hour in front of a row of nickel slot machines, playing one after another, jumping up and down for joy whenever she won and the coins came pouring out faster than she could catch them. There'd been no one standing behind her to disapprove, and it was marvellous.

That was one of the excursions which, by tacit consent, we never mentioned to my father. When he asked where we'd been we said we'd driven through Nevada, and when he asked what we had seen we answered, almost in unison: 'Hoover Dam.'

Mother's Vegas remained a harmless secret, an interlude

of magically irresponsible pleasure she enjoyed with the same gusto she brought to eating fried chicken with her fingers and dancing in a roadhouse to jukebox music. Las Vegas was a playground to her; she'd worked hard all her life and she'd earned the right to go there. But she couldn't understand why Harry should be allowed to get away with it.

'It seems a funny place for him to be at a time like this, Libby,' she murmured, studying her hands.

I thought so too, though for different reasons.

For the second consecutive year, Harry planned to enrol in the university's summer session, the objective being for him to finish his degree in mathematics. Yet as time went by he seemed to be spending a lot more time playing cards than he did on campus, and the mysteries of his gambling world were deepening.

It wasn't that he was risking our money, the money I earned; he had sizeable credit amount in what he referred to as his 'card stake', and if he did happen to lose in a session, his losses were more than covered.

In fact, though I banked Metcalf Jones' salary every month, it was rarely touched. Harry usually managed to pay for everything we needed out of what he won, and we'd even traded our rakish red sports car for a sedate new sedan shortly after we found out about the baby.

The problem was much more subtle than that, and harder to get at, but what it finally boiled down to was that although Harry's course work reflected truly dazzling academic brilliance, I was beginning to suspect he didn't really give a damn whether he got his degree or not. It seemed a shame. A shame and a waste.

'Why?' he asked, when I faced him with it.

That flummoxed me. 'Well – if you have a degree you can do anything you like with it, more or less. You can—'

'Teach,' he said shortly. 'That's what people do with a degree in mathematics.'

'Y-e-e-s, but you can always go on to graduate school.'

'Sure, I can be the eternal student. What's the point?'

'You can make a fantastic career, Harry. In industry, in – in—'

'I can do that any time, Lib. With or without a degree.'

'But you're brilliant, honey!'

He laughed and ruffled my hair. 'Honey, that and a dime will buy me a cup of coffee anywhere.'

And the subject was closed.

But when he mentioned the bridge tournament in Las Vegas I reopened it. I pointed out that if he took time off to go there he'd miss several important lectures.

'This is *more* important, sweetheart,' he said easily.

'Playing bridge is more important than – than, oh, I don't know, differential calculus?'

'It is, if you get paid to play.'

'Harry, who on earth's going to pay you to play in a bridge tournament? For Pete's sake, bridge is a game for retired army colonels and little old ladies!'

'Is it?' He raised one quizzical eyebrow.

'Well, isn't it?'

'Not if you're playing against four grand masters and some of the wealthiest punters in the States.'

'They play bridge for money?'

He looked ceilingward, exasperated. 'Yeah.'

'Oh.'

'Oh,' he mimicked, amused. 'Look, babe, there's this guy I know. He's stinking rich and he'll gamble on whether the sun's coming up and he loves bridge, but he can't play his way out of a paper bag. So he's offered to back me to play for him, and he's placed a discreet and sizeable side bet on the outcome. If I win, I get a cut. It's very simple.'

I picked up on the 'discreet'.

'Why a *discreet* bet, Harry?'

He blew out his cheeks and sighed. 'Because strictly speaking it's illegal to bet on a tournament.'

63

That really had me wide-eyed. 'What happens if they find out?'

'Who, hon?'

'You know, whoever enforces the legalities of the thing. Whoever it is who forbids people to gamble on it.'

He shrugged. 'It won't be my bet, Libby. All I have to do is play and keep my mouth shut. It's strictly a no-risk shot at some action for me, see? Oh, and a chance to polish my game.'

My mother looked up from her hands and frowned me back into the present.

'Libby, I *said* – it's a funny place for Harry to be right now. In Las Vegas, I mean. Don't you think?'

I'd already given her an edited version of why he was there. I closed my eyes and counted to five.

'Not really, mom. He just went there to play—'

'Sure,' she said hotly, 'to play! Oh, you said it, baby! Leaving you here, pregnant, figuring out ways to go right back to work as soon as they tie off your baby's belly button so he can go right on playing, throwing away money you worked hard for.'

'Oh stop it, mother, it isn't like that,' I said tiredly.

'Isn't it? Isn't it? How do you think they built all those fancy hotels in Vegas? With suckers' money, that's how. They suck them in and they suck them dry, and that's God's truth.'

'He isn't playing with my money!' I wailed. 'And that's *not* why I'm going back to work after the baby's born. Harry pays for everything, mother – the rent, the food, the car – everything!'

She exploded then – subtlety, yielding femininity, even grammar forgotten.

'That's just jimdandy if it's true! So if he's such a

goddamn hotshot why the hell don't he quit horsing around and get himself a decent job?'

That was the crescendo, and after that there were several pulsebeats of absolute silence. I breathed deeply and rubbed my temples.

'That's not really anybody's business but ours, is it, mom?' I said quietly.

'No,' she whispered, ashamed. 'No, you're right sweetheart. It isn't – any of my business.'

She searched my eyes and then she looked away, her face turning towards the afternoon light that filtered cool and green through the plants in the big bay window. In profile she looked defeated, old, and her chin was quivering slightly.

We were both weary of doing battle. I heaved myself out of my chair and went to the kitchen for cheese and crackers, wine and glasses. When I came back she was dabbing at her eyes with a tissue, which she quickly tried to hide.

I set the tray on the coffee table and went to her, caressed her shoulders.

'Let's don't,' I said gently, and she smiled up at me.

'Libby, I didn't mean to interfere, honest. I only – sweetie, is Harry taking care of you? I'm only concerned for you, that he should be taking real good care of you – especially now.'

I kissed her soft cheek and smoothed her hair.

'He is, mother. Honestly, he really is.'

He really was.

In spite of Harry's secretiveness about his gambling, and the occasional uneasiness it caused me – in spite of all the other compartments of his life that were closed to me – I was really and truly happy.

He was a model expectant father. He walked with a lighter step, he smiled a lot. He treated me like porcelain.

He accompanied me on long, healthy walks, and went with me to ante-natal classes, and when I reached for a cigarette, he jumped up to fetch me an apple or a piece of cheese instead. He bought me whimsical, impromptu presents: flowers, or my favourite chocolates. He brought me breakfast in bed, and we read baby-care books together.

Ever since I'd been a skinny, leggy kid with yellow pigtails, I'd thought of myself as coltish, ungainly. All through high school I'd managed to be able to rest my chin on top of the heads of all the boys I knew. Harry had always made me feel good about myself. Skinny became slender, yellow hair was cornsilk, and he was taller than I was.

But while I was pregnant he made me feel like the reincarnation of Veronica Lake and the Virgin Mary all rolled into one gently expanding Sexpot Madonna, telling me over and over again how beautiful I was, how I glowed. He even loved my freckles. And he made love to me with especially reverent tenderness.

We had friends too, all sorts of them, married and single. We had parties to go to and parties to give, plenty to talk about; we had films to see and pizzas to eat on Saturday nights.

Best of all, I had never felt better in my life. I wasn't sick, I didn't faint, and the only days I missed from work were the ones I chose to take from my vacation time. My job was full of challenge and responsibility, and I'd never enjoyed it more – right up until the afternoon of the day I went into labour.

And then, very suddenly, Harry was beside me holding my hand, telling me to breathe, breathe in out that's right that's my girl and Dr Felton was smiling eyes over a mask telling me to bear down, not to bear down, to wait, to rest, to breathe deeply, to bear down.

And Charlotte Louise was born.

'God almighty she's perfect. She's beautiful,' Harry whispered.

'You wanted a boy, you schlump,' I whispered back breathlessly.

Dr Felton laughed.

And I looked down at the top of my baby's head and it struck me she looked just like a little chicken so I whispered, 'Chicken, my chicken,' and I wanted to cry.

And then I dozed off and when I woke up my chicken was all wrapped up and Harry was holding her, crooning to her: 'My baby, beautiful baby, sweetheart mine, my baby.'

'Mine too, Harry, ours,' I said drowsily, and fell asleep again.

4

When Charlotte Louise was two days old we brought her home. We hovered over her for the next little awestricken while, full of new-parent anxieties, and exulted by the joyous conviction that she was the most beautiful baby ever born.

She was certainly one of the most cooperative. She slept through the night, she ate on schedule, she seldom cried and never without reason.

When she was three weeks old she smiled, really smiled, for the first time; and Harry knew without a doubt that she was smiling for him and him alone. That's when he started calling her Charlie, and the name stuck.

Charlotte Louise was daddy's girl, Harry's Charlie.

When she was three months old and still no bigger than a minute, I went back to work.

But in spite of my earnest research and all my soul-searching theorizing – and Harry's complete accord with my decision – I experienced unexpected qualms about the rightness of trying to combine motherhood with a career.

They came into sharp uncomfortable focus during my first visit to the Napa Valley, and the Mirranis – a few weeks after I returned to the office. I felt like a brittle uncaring imposter, sitting in the meeting. I ached for the soft joyous burden of Charlie in my arms, snuggled there, close to my heart. What on earth was I doing sitting in a winery a full fifty miles away from her?

That night when I got home Charlie was sound asleep. As Harry and I stood together beside her crib, enraptured, I ran one hand very lightly over her padded rump so as to touch her without waking her.

'You miss her a lot when you're away from her, don't you sweetheart?' Harry whispered gently.

I nodded, and tears began to stream down my face. Harry held me against him, supporting me as he walked with me back into the living room and sat me down; he knelt by my chair, and held my hand.

'Honey, Charlie's fine. You know that. . . .'

'I know,' I whispered. 'But sometimes I feel guilty about leaving her, and – other times I feel – just plain jealous of whoever's with her when I'm not. I'm sorry. . . .'

'Shh, sweetpea. You're tired, and feelings like that are perfectly natural. But it isn't as though you're away all the time. She knows you love her, and you and I know that the times we're together are marvellous for the three of us. Now come on, darling. First one to the kitchen gets to heat the milk for hot chocolate. . . .'

Over the months that followed, with a lot of help from Harry, most of my lingering doubts about leaving Charlie to go out to work were dispelled.

Sometimes, if I had an off-day or it was raining or a client was impossible, I'd wish I'd opted to stay with her and sing lullabies and play pat-a-cake full time. Those days came less often; finally they all but stopped.

The ways things were, Charlie was visibly thriving; and if I missed some of the drudgery of full-time motherhood, I knew I wasn't missing any of the joys. I had it both ways, and so did she.

The care Charlie received at the day nursery was first rate and unfussy. She was the youngest baby there, and for a long time she was the only girl. She watched the older babies and children with bright inquisitive eyes; she copied them and learned from them. At nine months she began to say simple words, extending her verbal range beyond 'mommy' and 'daddy' to include 'cookies' and 'milk', and greetings and farewells; at ten months she began to string the words she already knew into short sentences, and to add

69

to them. She could hum the signature tune from *Sesame Street*; and she could pull herself up on the furniture and lurch determinedly from sofa to chair to my lap, radiantly pleased with herself.

Charlie wasn't at the day nursery five days a week, either – not with Harry as her adoring father, blessed with a highly flexible university schedule. Whenever I knew I'd be late coming home, or he didn't have a lecture to attend, Harry picked her up early, or kept her at home with him all day.

He fed her and changed her and sang to her and played with her toes and laughed with her; he even watched kids' programmes on television with her. He revelled in it.

It was a marvellous arrangement; when Charlie wasn't with other kids, or with me, she was with her daddy or with both of us, the three of us a family.

As for Harry, he was delighted that he'd be involved with Charlie at every stage of her development. As for me, there was no danger of my turning into a martyr-mommy, shrivelling up with resentment at having to abandon a career I had only just begun.

That was thriving too.

With the success of Mirrani Brothers' campaign to become a force to be reckoned with abroad, other vineyards approached the agency, eager to jump on the profitable bandwagon. I was asked to handle most of them, at least long enough to get each new campaign rolling. When I was assigned a small cubicle in which to work – nothing fancy, but boasting a window and a telephone all for me – Michael O'Neill began to refer to me teasingly, proudly, as the resident wino of Metcalf Jones.

Harry and Charlie and I had everything, and everything we had was shared, and it was marvellous.

And oh the fun he and I had with Charlie. Homely, humble ordinary things like taking her into bed with us on Sunday mornings and feeling the warmth of her wriggling little body between us, completing our circle. Or smiling to one another over her downy head when she learned how to pull her father's reading glasses off, and knew that it was naughty, and that she could get away with it.

Harry and I laughed when people said to us that babies grow so fast that before we knew it Charlie would be walking and talking and then she'd be off to school and getting married and having babies of her own.

We knew it wasn't true.

It was, though. Before we knew it, Charlie was nearly a year old.

One morning that spring my cocoon of perfect happiness received an ugly jolt.

It was a Sunday and the sun was streaming through the kitchen windows. Harry and I were sitting at the table after breakfast, Sunday-peaceful, lazy, finishing our second pot of coffee. Charlie had wandered off to the living room, dragging Raggedy Ann behind her by one battered cotton arm, humming to herself.

I smiled after her. 'What should we get her for her birthday, Harry?'

'How about a trip to Europe?' he said.

He stirred sugar into his coffee and studied it while it dissolved.

'A trip to – oh Harry, be serious!' I laughed. 'Charlie's going to be *one* year old, not twenty—'

'I am serious,' he said.

I licked dry lips and waited for elaboration.

Charlie was happy, Harry was happy, I was happy; we were happy.

The pattern of our lives would change, of course, as Charlie grew and Harry finished his degree and found a job. As and when we decided to have another child, other children. As and if we decided I should take – or not take – a

71

couple of years' break from my work, while Harry's career got started.

The finer points of our future would depend on too many unpredictable variables to plan inflexibly; but its broad outlines were firmly fixed in my mind. And it had never occurred to me to include a European tour – except perhaps as an idea for a family holiday, shimmering in the distance when Charlie and her as yet unborn brothers and/or sisters were old enough to appreciate it.

'And I'm not talking about a three-week excursion,' Harry said suddenly, startling me. It was as if he'd read my thoughts. 'I want to get the hell out of here for good, before it's too late. I'm tired of sitting in sleazy poker rooms and—'

'Too late?' I swallowed a mouthful of coffee with difficulty.

'I'm getting nowhere fast, Lib. I'm sick of it.'

'Oh honey,' I said, thinking I understood at last, 'I know school's a grind, but—'

'I quit school a couple of semesters ago, Libby. I just didn't bother to enrol.'

'You what!'

His mouth was tight, and his eyes were full of bleak, cold, distant strain – some shuttered and unutterably lonely misery I couldn't touch or soothe.

'Yes,' he said.

'You never told me,' I whispered.

'No.'

I put my hand over his in a clumsy gesture of attempted comfort. My mind spun while I tried to figure out what to say next.

Finally, tentatively, watching him, I said: 'Maybe you could, ah – find a job or something.'

'I tried that, but I didn't stay with it long. It wasn't as profitable as poker.'

'What were you doing?'

72

'Selling encyclopaedias door to door.'

I swallowed hard, and looked away.

'Yeah,' he said.

For some lunatic reason, I suddenly felt it was up to me to be immensely cheerful.

'Oh sweetheart, you'll find something better, you know you will!' I said. 'Just give yourself a little time, look around . . .'

I trailed off. It was the wrong thing to say. It sounded tinny and false, like Minnie Mouse in the middle of *Macbeth*.

Harry must have thought so too. He gave me a cold look and jerked his hand out from under mine. That galvanized me into anger, which was an improvement over shock.

I straightened my shoulders and glared at him.

'Harry, I'm sorry, but this is all pretty sudden, and it doesn't seem very reasonable. I mean, how can we uproot ourselves just like that? Charlie's only a baby, honey! She needs—'

'A daddy who's harnessed up from nine to five like a donkey to a cart, well and truly insulated from risk by pension plans and fringe benefits,' he recited flatly. 'Oh, no doubt that's what any right-thinking father should be prepared to give her. Or should I say what *your* father—'

'Leave my family out of this!'

'If only they'd *stay* out of it! Ever since I met that tight-lipped—'

'Hey, watch it, Harry!'

I scraped back my chair abruptly, stood up and swept out of the room.

Harry angry was a lot more understandable than Harry totally withdrawn, but I thought I'd better give him a few minutes to simmer down and collect his thoughts.

I took a few minutes for myself while I was at it. I went into the bathroom and rinsed my face; I studied my reflection in the mirror. I looked white and sick, and I was trembling with the vibrations of the bewildered shocked confusion I felt.

Could I really have been so blithely oblivious to Harry's unhappiness while I made up my own lifeplan for our happy-ever-after? Apparently, yes.

I leaned on the edge of the sink while I struggled to compose my features into a semblance of serenity before I went to the doorway of the living room to make sure Charlie was okay.

She was fine, chanting to Raggedy Ann that 'this pig-gy stayed h-o-m-e', so absorbed she wasn't aware of my presence. I tiptoed away, hoping with all my heart that all us little piggies would stay home where we belonged, where we'd been so happy; praying that Harry's dissatisfaction could, please God, be a passing phase.

I went back into the kitchen and closed the door. Harry was sitting where I'd left him, staring moodily into the middle distance, drumming the fingertips of one hand on the table.

'Harry . . . ?'

He sighed deeply. 'Yes?'

'What – what would you expect to find in Europe that you can't find here?'

'Oh Paris, Rome, Venice, London—'

'Harry, please. Please, just tell me.'

He sighed again. 'Right. Okay. In Europe I might, just *might*, have a shot at some real action.'

'What kind—'

'Gambling action,' he said tersely, 'what else? That's what I'm best at Libby, gambling. Surely you've noticed.'

'Honey,' I said softly, 'I don't think they'd let us into a foreign country if we told them that. Customs and Immigration laws are pretty strict no matter where you go.' I smiled, and tried to make a joke of it. 'If they asked you for your occupation and you said gambling, they'd think you'd fallen right out of your little tree, and all your little coconuts with you.'

He didn't laugh. 'Do you know anything about it?' he said.

I sat down and poured another cup of coffee.

'Well, I think we could get in as tourists anywhere in Europe, with temporary visas of – I don't know – it depends – maybe three months. And they might renew them once, twice. But after that I don't think we'd be allowed to stay unless one of us could show we'd found a *job*, and a work permit to go with it.'

'No problem.'

'But honey, they wouldn't let either one of us accept a job in any Common Market country unless we could prove we weren't displacing a citizen from working.'

'Nicely said, babe, still no problem.'

My shoulders tensed and I leaned forward, desperate to get through to him.

'Harry, there's a graphic designer at work who's got a wife and two kids to feed who came back from England with his tail between his legs because their Home Office wouldn't give him resident status as a freelance. And he had something like 20,000 dollars in signed contracts to show them.'

Harry shrugged, unconcerned. 'He should have put himself on somebody's payroll for a while. Shame he didn't figure that out.'

'Harry, how—'

'Lib, I know this guy who actually did it. He was in England too, in London. That's where the real action is by the way. *Very* high stakes. Worth playing for, you know? Anyway, all he needed was some dude to say he was doing essential work and was indispensable and blah blah blah, and he got his work permit and his visa one two three. Once he was in, he was in.'

'And he's still there?'

'No, but that's not the point! It was all on the up and up,

perfectly legal, no hassle at all. He went there to gamble but he really did have a job. Paid taxes and everything.'

'What happened?'

'He lost his bankroll, so he gave up and came home. He's a rotten gambler, though. But I'm not, don't you know that by now?'

'Harry, I—'

'I want to go, Lib. I want to see all the places I've only read about. Not rushing around with a camera strapped to my back, but *really* seeing them, feeling the – just feeling how it is to be there for awhile. Christ, hon, I don't know. I just want us to go, get out and find that there's something else to life than our stale little rut in northern California. . . .'

'Would you – would you rather travel light, Harry? I mean, would you rather go by yourself, be on your own for a while?'

It was painful to ask him that, but I felt I had to. It was possible he'd figured it all out as a plan for one, something he'd really rather do alone, a kind of search for himself. Maybe he'd been hoping I'd be enough in tune with him to sense it, and offer it to him gracefully.

Harry shook his head incredulously and reached for my hand. He kissed my palm, my wrist; he smiled at me with his dreams shining in his eyes.

'Honey, baby, how could you even *think* a thing like that? What do you think I'd have, if I didn't have you and Charlie right beside me, soaking up the glorious ballgame right along with me?

'Libby, I know how much you love your job, and how good you are at doing what you do, and believe me I'm proud of you. But you can pick it up again whenever you want to, now you're established, now you've proved yourself.

'You can afford to take a real vacation if you want to, sweetpea – you know, trip the light fantastic with Charlie Girl and me for a while. . . .'

Harry was still holding my hand. I looked down at it,

entwined with his on the table, still breathless and knocked sideways by his bombshell.

I told myself I should have seen it coming. Not the specific plan to take us off to Europe, but something – some sign I hadn't cared to notice because my own vision of our future had always been so smugly and securely set.

There'd been more than one. Over the months I'd shut my eyes to the persistent hunch that Harry was cutting lectures, spending more days at home with Charlie than he normally did; that his thick textbooks were gathering dust on his desk, unopened.

'Libby,' he said softly, 'I've got enough bread stashed away to get us there and back again, to keep us in reasonable style for six months or so, *and* something left to play with.'

'You have?'

He nodded; he was perfectly serious. 'I've been dreaming about this for years, Libby. Planning for it. . . .'

I was no adventurer, and never had been; I was conservative, prudent and careful, imaginative enough about dreaming up gimmicks for promotional campaigns but pretty thoroughly straight-arrow in making real-life decisions – conditioned by a rock-steady and secure childhood – with the exception of marrying Harry because I was wildly in love with him, and producing his child.

I resisted his wild plan of upping stakes and carrying us off to foreign parts; I didn't carp about it, but I did try to examine it from every side, looking for fatal flaws I was sure must exist within it.

Harry was very patient; he understood me very well.

Finally I realized that there was nothing to keep us where we were, all other things being equal; when I'd got that far, when I finally jumped over the stile and came down on the side of accepting Harry's plan, my acquiescence began to turn into enthusiasm.

I had never been anywhere except Montana, Iowa, California, Wyoming, Nevada. There was more world than that, and we were very young and strong and resilient – able to adapt to what we might find out there with courage and laughter.

As for my commitment to my job, Harry hadn't underestimated that. In fact, he'd got it just right. I enjoyed what I did, and I did it well. I could cheerfully have gone on doing my job in San Francisco for many happy years. But it was not, had never been, would never be, my life.

Harry was that, Charlie was that, the family we had made was what I really cared about. My mother, despite her spitting and scratching and chafing about the untold potential dangers of Harry's gambling, would have done exactly as I did: she would have put in with her man, for better or for worse.

Harry's patience was rewarded handsomely; I began to be almost as excited about going to Europe, to England, as he was. Not the least of my excitement was derived from watching his. Watching his eyes come alive as we made our plans in a way I hadn't seen his eyes alive more than half a dozen times or so since he'd been nineteen years old and burning to isolate all the peaceable uses for atomic energy.

Half a dozen times or so, I could count them without taking my shoes off: the day we got married; the day Charlie was born; the day she smiled into his eyes for the first time; the day she came out with her first exuberant 'Da da!' The rainy day we'd gone out shopping for a Christmas tree when she was six months old. And the day after that, when we decorated it, and Charlie waved her arms in wonder, trying to capture the coloured lights we'd strung on it – the lights we could see reflected in her beautiful eyes.

I brought my notions of contentment into line with Harry's programme for the future: contentment was the three of us together, just that. It was nothing to do with familiar places or routines or set patterns or settled expectations of where we would be or what either of us might be doing in ten years' time.

And the rest was easy.

We put the car and most of the furniture in storage; we took out passports, we bought air tickets.

I arranged my one concession to prudent, pedestrian, prosaic commonsense by making my own very private arrangements for the nest egg I'd built up since I'd been working. It was more than enough to bail us out if Harry discovered he'd miscalculated.

If it came to the point where we needed to use it, I would have to broach the subject delicately and with enormous tact to save Harry's pride. That was a bridge I would cross if I came to it, and I devoutly hoped I never would. The important thing was that the money should be there. Intact, and gathering interest, at inflation-linked rates.

As my mother had always said, there's no such thing as leftover whisky or leftover money; if we didn't use it, there was absolutely no harm done. It wouldn't spoil or disappear.

When it came to explaining our plans to the outside world, I made up a shocking tarradiddle; it would have been an outright boldfaced lie, except that I didn't see it that way. It was no one else's business, and harmed no one: I said that Harry had been offered an open-ended teaching contract in London, and that we'd be living there indefinitely.

I had no idea what an open-ended contract might be, or even if there was such a thing. Neither did anybody else, it seemed. No one questioned it, not even my mother. And it was far, far simpler than telling the truth – especially to my mother, who was relieved to hear that Harry had a job at last.

One of the last things we did before we left was to go shopping. Charlie and I didn't need much – although Harry insisted on buying things for us; the most spectacular item was a stunning full-length evening dress of emerald green velvet which he bought for me because he said it deserved me.

Most of the shopping was for Harry. My Harry of the dark slacks and white shirts and casual jackets. Invisible Harry of the sordid lo-ball poker clubs needed quite a lot.

And glory be if he didn't look magnificent in evening dress, complete with ruffled shirt and cummerbund and shiny black patent leather shoes.

Harry had really come out of his closet.

5

Getting there was not half the fun, though it was touchingly obvious the airline had done its best to make the twelve-hour tourist class flight bearable.

The stewardesses smiled a lot. The pilot treated us to chummy anecdotes through the loudspeaker at the fore of the cabin. There were nearly continuous offerings of pre-packaged plastic trays of food. There was coffee, tea or milk, booze for the jittery.

There were earphones through which we could listen to the soundtrack of the film that was shown mid-flight, or to music from one of four available channels.

We had everything but leg room, packed as we were three abreast in the seats nearest the windows, four abreast in the island in between, with two economically narrow aisles to accommodate the almost constant traffic of staff and restless passengers moving back and forth, including Charlie tod-dling into everybody else's way.

I had flown before, from home to college and back again in the summer, at Christmas. They were longish flights – four or five hours – conveniently and painlessly endured with the aid of a paperback novel or a nap.

This was something else. Charlie was uncharacteristically fractious and fretful, wet and/or hungry most of the time; reading or napping was out of the question.

And when Harry finally got her off to sleep by rubbing her back and patting her padded bottom, we were triumphant. Twenty minutes later we were hustled out of the plane when we landed for refuelling in Chicago, searched and metal-detected with all the rest of the London-bound passengers.

God knew why: we'd been searched before we boarded in California. Nobody told us why they'd done it again; the effective result was to render Charlie fractious and sleepless for the rest of the twelve hour flight.

Finally, numbed and stunned by the frazzled, disorientated, crumpled haze of jet lag, we made it.

No, we had nothing to declare. Yes, we were tourists. I looked on dazed, clutching the baby tightly against my shoulder while the uniformed immigration officer stamped our passports and, smiling a welcome, handed them back to Harry.

And then we were standing outside the terminal with our luggage around our feet, waiting for a taxi to take us into London, to the hotel we'd booked when we bought our tickets, two hundred years ago.

'I wonder how people manage to do this all the time?' I asked Harry, yawning. 'You know, politicians, movie stars, David Frost. . . .'

He grinned at me and reached out to take Charlie.

'They fly first class, hon, and they travel light. For instance, without old grizzle guts here.'

'It's still twelve hours in a plastic box.'

'They get used to it, I guess. People can get used to anything.'

'Um.' I smiled at him. 'Even hanging.'

The taxi driver was garrulous; Harry was drawn to his friendliness. I don't remember what they talked about, but Harry seemed fascinated – probably as much by the cadence of the man's accent as by what he was saying.

I stared glassily out of the window, absorbing my first impressions of London by a process that was something like osmosis – taken in through the filter of a pervasive sense of unreality which amounted to cultural shock.

We passed along street after street of shabby brick houses arranged in tidy rows, alternating with stretches of modest little toytown shops. Occasionally a soaring modern tower would speed past at odds with its surroundings.

The buildings were smaller and more densely packed together than any I'd ever seen, the area more congested than any I'd known in the generous expanse of the American midwest or the wild vastness of Montana.

They'd been built, I knew, by and for people who lived on what was after all an island of limited space and natural resources; by and for people who occupied as little room as possible while maintaining some semblance of privacy and autonomy in their lives. This was, I'd been told, one explanation for their fabled British reserve.

And except for the large black taxis like the one we rode in, or the red top-heavy double-decker buses I saw, or the lorries, the cars were in scale with the buildings, smaller and undoubtedly cheaper to run than the big beautiful Buicks that gulped petrol and ate limitless miles in the US. I gaped wide-eyed, awed, as their drivers manoeuvred them fearlessly on the wrong side of the road.

I was, or should have been, prepared for most of what I saw. I'd known lots of people who'd been to London. I'd read about the British; I'd watched Benny Hill on cable television.

But I was shattered, poleaxed. Hours before – maybe years before, or centuries before – I'd accepted the leather passport case that was my co-workers going away gift, I'd been handing over my precious houseplants to my best friend, far far away in San Francisco.

Suddenly, without warning and without a real transition, I was in England, and the English were swirling all around me, real.

And deep down in my heart of childish hearts I'd expected something very different. My notions of London – just the solid ancient syllables: Lon-don. Londinium – were culled and cherished from history courses I'd sat through in college and from the novels of Charles Dickens, whom I'd loved since I was ten.

My London was peasoup fog and cobbled streets; steely dauntless Elizabeth I, calmly defying the blackguards who locked her in the Tower; it was coffee houses and frock-coated gentlemen in horse-drawn broughams; it was crenellated castles, and Little Nell doing her brave best to look after her profligate grandfather, and Miss Haversham living with her mummified bridal dress and her petrified cake. And all of that was blended and homogenized in a kind of underlayer of expectation without any regard to historical fact, order, logic, or even simple common sense.

Harry and I laughed about it later. He confessed he'd felt something like the same thing that first day, in the taxi speeding us from the airport.

He compared the feeling to a tenderfoot's proconceptions about the American West: no matter how cosmopolitan a traveller might be when he got west of Kansas City for the first time, it was only natural to expect to see a few cowboys and Indians dotted about the landscape. The Chamber of Commerce in Lemonade Springs had sponsored an annual summer rodeo since the year the town was founded, just to satisfy that yearning and keep the tourists happy.

And so, Harry promised, we'd be tourists in London too, and do things up right just as soon as we caught our breath. He'd brought the three of us across the Atlantic, and for the moment that seemed to me like a breathtaking achievement. He'd work out the rest of it later; meanwhile he'd do his best to coax me into his dreams by easy stages.

It was more than enough.

And it was Harry, who'd always been the dreamer, who'd always been the one to take flight while I was desperately trying to find the brakes and landing wheels, who organized everything; it was he who became the competent and practical half of our team. That time became, in retrospect, the happiest in my life with him. I loved him more than ever as I relaxed, and allowed myself to trust him completely.

The hotel where we'd made our reservation turned out to

be in what I recognized later as the better end of Bloomsbury, a neighbourhood graced with private gardens and tree-lined squares, elegant collonaded houses, literary ghosts.

It was small, tucked away in a quiet cul-de-sac. Its lobby gave off an air of faded splendour, its carpet thick but threadbare, its armchairs old and solid and well-worn, heavy curtains at its floor-length windows.

We were greeted with deferential courtesy by a reception clerk who spoke in whispers, dressed in a dark suit and an impeccably conservative tie; we were ushered to the creaking lift with smoothly invisible efficiency by a porter who in his operatic uniform might have been a relict of an earlier and more leisured century.

He unlocked our door and deposited our luggage in the room with a smooth economy of motion that suggested long practice. When Harry tipped him he bowed slightly, smiling his thanks, and his glance lingered gently on Charlie drowsy in my arms.

'Afternoon tea is being served in the dining room,' he said. 'But if you prefer to take it in your room I shall be happy to arrange it for you.'

'Thank you,' Harry said gravely. 'I think that would be best. We just flew halfway around the world, and I think we all feel a little tired.' He glanced at me and smiled.

'Sandwiches and cakes and a pot of tea, sir?'

'Yes, thank you. And two whiskys and water, with ice if you have it, and a glass of milk.'

The man bowed again and closed the door noiselessly behind him as he left; I stood there holding Charlie, trying to take everything in.

The room was furnished in heavy mahogany: huge double bed, a writing desk, a clothes press, a cot for Charlie. And from a later era, but thoughtfully, a portable television and a small hot plate where we could heat bottles of milk and jars of the baby food we'd brought with us in sufficient quantities to last until we got our bearings.

85

There was one long window, the curtains in a fabric similar to the stuff they'd used in the lobby, dark blue to match the carpet.

It was a comfortable room by any standard, and it was clean; the bed linens were crisply white, the adjoining bathroom immaculate.

But the curtains were only partially open, and it was dark, sombre, and it made the apartment we'd so recently left seem palatial by my memory's comparison: so airy and light had it been, so full of living plants and love and memories, that I felt suddenly desperately homesick.

Harry sensed that; he took me and Charlie in his arms, sweetly patient and protective, sheltering us both. 'It's a good hotel, honey. I checked it out,' he said.

He led us to the window, his arm still tightly around my waist, supportive. He drew the curtains back as far as they would go. Sunlight poured in over the circle of our little family, adrift but hopeful in the ponderous obsolescent opulence of that foreign hotel bedroom from another century.

'Now, about these curtains,' he said, laughing. 'Remember latitude and longitude?'

'No. . . .'

'Your eighth grade geography teacher would be mad as hell to hear you say that, hon. Anyway, it doesn't get dark at this latitude in the summertime until very late – 10 o'clock, something like that. I'd expect most hotel windows to be draped like this, in case the travel-weary crave a little early shut-eye.' He yawned.

I laughed, tired and confused but shiny-eyed with love and gratitude for his concern, his thoughtfulness, his willingness to understand and tackle a world that seemed so strange and alien, so different from the only world I'd ever known.

I felt safe and warm and cherished, and my fatigue seemed to lift.

'Say Harry, that guy who showed us up here could be a butler straight out of an English movie. Do you think he's Sidney Greenstreet?'

'Doubt it, sweetpea. Anyhow, it's safe to assume he's not from Sioux Falls, South Dakota, ma'am. . . .'

The porter returned a few minutes later, pushing a trolley laden with fancy little sandwiches like the ones my mother sometimes served to lady friends she wanted to impress.

There were cakes too, and the milk Harry ordered for Charlie, and two glasses, in each of which one melting cube of ice floated on a generous shot of scotch, and a pitcher of water we could add to taste.

I giggled. 'Do you think they could spare the ice?'

'Only just. The English regard it as a barbaric Yankee way of ruining good booze.'

And of course there was a pot of tea, flanked by a silver sugar bowl and a small pitcher that matched it, containing more milk.

I frowned at it. 'What's this for?'

'To put in the tea,' Harry said.

'Why would anybody do that?'

'We wouldn't, but the British like it that way.'

'Quaint,' I said. We laughed together, locking eyes.

Charlie had a ball, chawing and crowing her way through bits of chicken and bread, slurping lustily from her trainer-cup of milk, blissfully unaware she was seven thousand miles away from home.

And Harry told me the story about John Montagu, 4th Earl of Sandwich, who ordered slabs of meat brought to him between slices of bread so he wouldn't have to leave the gaming tables for his meals. And another about an American bridge player who had big plates of spaghetti brought to his table during tournaments, less from hunger than from his determination to distract his opponents while he ate it. And it occurred to me that Harry's attitude to me in relation to his secret life had undergone a major sea change.

He told those stories easily, as though he could share them freely, now I'd shown willing to follow him halfway around the world while he pursued his dreams.

That made me so happy I glowed; seeing that, Harry glowed too. And Charlie, seeing us so happy, laughed with us and clapped her hands.

We devoured all the sandwiches including the cress that garnished them, and the cakes too, sitting tailor fashion on the bed with Charlie propped on pillows between us.

And then Harry closed the curtains and settled Charlie in her cot. And Harry and I, suddenly too exhausted to do more than pull back the spread on the double bed, fell asleep fully dressed except for our shoes.

I woke up several hours later. For a moment I forgot where I was or how I'd come to be there.

But then I turned my head and saw them.

Harry's bedside lamp was on, its shade carefully tilted so the light wouldn't disturb me.

He was lying on his side, with Charlie curled up against him. He was feeding her from her bottle; the guidebook he'd been reading upside down on the blanket he'd thrown over us.

'Hi,' he said. 'Where you been, sugar?'

Still half-asleep I touched Charlie's soft cheek and then Harry's, slightly rough with a shadow of beard, and smiled. 'Right here all the time, honey.'

'Um. Dreaming about food, I'll bet.'

'How did you know?'

'I was just thinking of making inroads on Charlie Girl's supply of baby custard.' He grinned and his dimples dimpled, and my heart turned over. I knew where I was, and I was glad.

'Ah,' I said. 'Baby custard. Not too filling but very

nourishing. No additives, all pure ingredients, puts hair on baby's chest.'

'You must mean dimples, hon. She's a girl.'

I yawned. 'She got the dimples from the milkman.'

Harry laughed. 'I'll be damned! Thought you'd never admit that.' He leaned across Charlie's plump accommodating fragrance to kiss me. 'Think you could finish feeding ol' hairy chest while I go out and kill us a buffalo?'

'Isn't it too late?'

He shrugged, and glanced at his watch. 'Naw! They don't roll up the sidewalks of London at 7.30 p.m.'

'Where would you go?'

'Sweetpea, even foreigners have to eat. There must be some place open where they sell the kind of junk food that made America strong.'

I laughed and pulled Charlie and her bottle to my side of the bed while Harry sat up and put his shoes on, preparing to brave all the sprawling strangeness that was London, fearless in search of food for himself and his mate. My hero.

I sang to Charlie and nuzzled my face in her spun-gold curls while she finished her milk, and then I eased out of bed, holding her, and put her into her cot.

She was asleep within seconds, smiling to herself, arms and legs flung anyhow in baby abandon, in rapturous satisfied security, warm and dry and fed and loved.

I reflected on that while I bathed in the old-fashioned bath, leaning back to admire my toes as I lifted one foot and then the other out of the fragrant bubbles I'd used so liberally.

Charlie had her head on straight. She was a zillion miles from base camp, but so what? She had mommy and daddy to hug and kiss and feed her. What more could she possibly want?

I would have my head on straight too. I thought dreamily about Harry and how much I missed him already. Oh, I'd married a man in a million.

Not a man whose limited and blinkered imagination provided us with a split-level house and an eye-level oven. Not a man with a pension plan.

Not a man with a pension plan, not a man with a pension plan. I made up a song about it, and sang it softly in the fragrant steam of my bath.

> Not a man with a pension plan,
> Waitin' for the gold watch,
> Doin' what he can,
> Grey-faced and knuckled under
> Mowin' the lawn on Sundays,
> Slurpin' beer from a can,
> A man who never dreamed,
> An also-ran.

Not a man who would turn to me in anguish in twenty years' time, accusing me of cramping his style and dousing the burning hopes of his youth, of fixing him to a card of routine just as firmly as a dead and fading butterfly.

Not a man who would drop dead of a heart attack at the age of forty-five in the arms of his secretary, pitifully caught in the act of proving he was still up to it.

Oh no. I had a man of vision, a man of soaring imagination. A man who'd thought nothing of pulling up stakes and flying his little family through the wild blue yonder, across the width of an ocean and far away from home, because doing that was a necessary part of making dreams come true.

Harry had the style and courage to do that even though he'd taken on what the world called commitment – as though a wife and child were cement that fixed a man's feet in mud and kept him mired there while he keened for the stars.

Harry had been brave enough not to let that happen, in spite of what the world might think. He'd dared to shake his fist at convention, to shed it like a dead skin.

Finally I noticed that the skin of my fingers and toes was beginning to pucker. I got out of the bath and dried myself, thinking lazily about which – if any – nightgown I should wear.

I was pretty steamed up, in a mood to give Harry a real hero's welcome when he came back.

Eventually I decided that the extravagantly insubstantial peignoir of tissue-thin ivory silk he'd given me the night before we left for London was sexier than bare skin. When he walked in I was lounging luxuriously on his side of the bed, leafing idly through his guidebook. He was carrying a white plastic shopping bag, looking very pleased with himself.

I smiled at him real slow.

'I missed you,' I said.

'Did you now? I see you kept the bed warm.'

'Always.'

'I brought you something nice, babe.'

'I knew you would.'

I made big vamp eyes at him and fingered the lace border of my peignoir. He sat on the edge of the bed, placed the carrier bag carefully on the floor, covered my hand with his and helped me.

'You're going to love what I brought, hon. We'd better get it while it's hot.'

'Um.'

He laughed softly. 'That too. But first. . . .'

He picked up the bag and very slowly, with the teasing artistry of a stripper, he revealed its contents.

I stared unbelievingly as he brought out two styrofoam cartons, fresh confirmation of Harry's magic powers.

'Honey,' I whispered, 'where in hell did you manage to find a Big Mac?'

'At the sign of the golden arches, where else?'

'*Here*, in London?'

'Sure, why not? I thought you'd be pleased,' he said. 'I got these too.'

91

'Milkshakes?' I was wide-eyed.

'Yup. Oh, and a big coke carton jampacked with crushed ice for English root beer, which I got from the barman downstairs.' He grinned as he drew another item from the bag.

'It's a bottle of whisky,' I said.

'Sure, hon, English root beer. Oh, and one more item.'

He reached into the bag again, and with the panache of a magician bringing forth a rabbit from a hat, he produced french fries, salt, ketchup.

'Harry, I can't believe this!'

'Aw, hon, it's no big deal. I didn't want you to be homesick on our first day in Fat City, is all.'

There was no question of feeling homesick that night. I was safe and warm, cherished and loved. It was more than enough.

6

We had been warned, preparing to come to London, to expect plenty of rain. But it was fair that June, hazy with humidity early in the mornings, the sun high and hot in clear blue skies as the days progressed, the light seeming to last for ever in the soft mild evenings.

Harry and I bought a gaily-striped pushchair for Charlie, and together we wheeled her through the centuries as we came to them.

We went to Westminster Abbey and winced with the rest of the Americans when we realized we were walking on Shakespeare's grave; we followed a Beefeater through the Tower; we drank warm bitter beer in garden pubs, and jostled for position in the crush outside Buckingham Palace to catch a glimpse of the Changing of the Guard. We were unabashed gawping gee-whiz tourists.

The neighbourhoods I'd seen on the way from the airport had seemed cramped and mean, but the landmarks and monuments of central London were massive and majestic – so much larger and more permanent than the people who lived and moved among them.

I had never in my life seen anything to match the towering splendour of the Marble Arch, or the soaring majesty of St Paul's, or the grand gracious sweep of the Serpentine through the ripe green elegance of Hyde Park.

Until I went to England, the oldest buildings I'd ever seen were the Spanish missions that dotted the California coast south of Monterey.

The clapboard houses of the American midwest had been built within living memory, most of them, and Lemonade

Springs' most venerated edifice – the courthouse in the town square – was erected in 1902.

There were places in the States that were old, of course, places like Boston and parts of New York and Philadelphia that had been there since the American Revolution, or even earlier. But London had been there for ever and ever, with a history stretching so far back it made every place I knew or knew of in my own country seem raw and new and rough, as though it had been run up in a hurry yesterday morning.

London was ancient, its bones and sinews overlaid and juxtaposed haphazardly with impermanent layers of importation and technology, a constantly fascinating cosmopolitan conglomerate of antiquity against the up-to-date; an onion I could never unpeel.

We must have made a charming picture: two clean-cut and healthy American kids, corn-fed and courteous to all comers, wheeling their plump and beautiful storybook baby. Everyone we met, from the cleaning ladies at the hotel to the man who sold us fruit from a stall in the street outside, seemed to take honest delight in our enchantment with everything we saw.

And in that idyllic honeymoon period of suspended responsibility, the living was easy.

We might have found a cheaper place to stay, but Harry insisted we stay where we were. Most of our laundry was done for us, food was cooked and served as and when we wanted to eat it, our room was cleaned and aired.

We could afford such luxuries, Harry insisted, at least until we'd got our bearings and decided what we intended to do about staying on. And I thought, so be it: I felt as though I'd been given the key to the most marvellous city in the world; I fell in love with it and all the people who belonged to it. I wanted to belong to it; I didn't want to leave, ever, and I said so.

Harry was pleased. He said I'd caught Ye Olde Fever. He admitted he'd caught it too. Next thing we knew, he said, we'd be buying up chamber pots and using them as planters. Meanwhile Harry wasted no time in making his presence known in the gambling world he'd come to conquer; when we'd been in London ten days or so he began to go out on his own, in the afternoon or early in the evening.

'To look up the friend of a friend of a friend,' he explained, laughing, leafing through the pocket ledger he'd carried for so long, now containing a section devoted to names, addresses and telephone numbers he'd painstakingly collected from people he'd played cards with in California. His success in making contacts seemed amazing; I was convinced he'd gained entrée to the London gambling scene by some masterful and mysterious feat of legerdemain.

'I thought it would take months,' I said, impressed when he told me, about three weeks after we landed at Heathrow, that we'd been invited out to dinner.

'It only looks impenetrable from the outside, sweetpea,' he said, smiling. 'You know, exclusive and closed and very ritzy. But the whole shebang is about money, after all, here just as much as anyplace else only more so. And nobody's about to turn away new talent, especially if it's backed by a greenback bankroll.'

'These people you've been meeting,' I said hesitantly. 'They think we're rich?'

He laughed and ruffled my hair. 'Sweetie, *all* Americans are rich, didn't you know that? It's something about the shine on our gen-u-wine leather shoes.'

Weeks earlier I would have worried, even carped and argued with him. We weren't rich, far from it; furthermore the hotel and all the services provided were costing us a minor fortune. But I had made up my mind not to rain on Harry's parade, and I didn't. When it came right down to honesty time, I didn't want to.

He'd told me before we came that we had enough money to last six months in comfort. We were, as advertised,

95

comfortable. We had legal visas for three months; we could renew them at least once without jumping through too many hoops.

We were having the time of our lives, and Charlie was blooming. We'd even discovered that we didn't have to change her brand of baby food. We were young and in love; we had everything going for us. Best of all, for the first time since I'd known him, Harry was clearly prepared to open one of his most important secret compartments and include me in. And the inclusion I'd dreamed of and been denied for so long inspired in me the heady conviction that I had died and gone to heaven.

Finally, of course, there was the satisfying cache of cash I'd squirrelled away in my American bank account; my mother had told me never to go anywhere without a hanky and the fare home.

We could always go home. But this was our chance to go forward, Harry's way, with Harry very firmly at the helm. There was something about that that spoke to my conditioning, that went far deeper than the layers of liberated self-reliance I'd acquired by going to college, and later on to work.

Harry was my man. He was the one who was supposed to hunt the buffalos while I tended the garden and kept the home fires burning. It just happened that he'd latched onto the notion – lunatic or not, I still wasn't sure – that he could do that playing cards. Maybe he could. Anyway, I'd promised him his chance to find out.

Harry's first and most important contact in London, soon to become his buddy and staunch ally in that small small world, was Andrew Lyle; it was he who had invited us out to dinner.

I was so excited and nervous I was beside myself: our first invitation from a real Englishman in London, my first opportunity to meet someone from Harry's erstwhile secret world.

By the time the day came, and we were dressing, I was so wound up I had an attack of stage fright mixed with panic. What if Andrew didn't like me; worse, what if he didn't approve of me? What if Harry wasn't proud of me, if I let him down or disgraced myself, and he was sorry he'd taken me along, and decided he would have to exclude me after all.

Charlie was bouncing in her cot, staring at us with big round eyes over the top of the wooden rails. I kept blowing her nervous little kisses, wondering what the hell we'd do if we didn't like the look of the babysitter the manager had promised to send bang on the dot of seven.

That was silly; the man had promised us a responsible girl, a student or perhaps even a young nurse. Instead I went back to worrying about Andrew, trying to reconnoitre the situation before I found myself in the middle of it and woefully out of my depth.

'What's he like?' I asked Harry, trying to sound casual while I rummaged indecisively through suitcases, selecting and rejecting and debating about what to wear while I rooted around for the travelling iron.

He shrugged, fixing the pewter cufflinks I'd bought for him into his snowy white-on-white shirt. 'He plays bridge, among other games.'

'For money?'

'Sure, when he's lucky. I've decided already that young Andrew depends too goddamned much on luck though. I'd like to have a shot at getting him to see things my way. We rate to make a pretty good team if I can get to him, get him to stop betting on the gee-gees and other high risk ventures.'

'The gee—'

'He plays the horses, Lib.' He sighed.

'Oh. Well, ah, where does he get his money?'

Harry was doing a windsor knot. 'His father's a bean merchant.' He grinned at himself in the mirror.

'Bean—'

'Beans means brass, babe, bread, spondulicks. You know, money. Andrew's old boy owns a couple of mills or something, up north.'

'He stakes him?'

Harry chuckled and shot his immaculate cuffs through the sleeves of one of the casually elegant jackets he'd bought in San Francisco: a conservative blackwatch plaid with a pure silk lining.

'Maybe the old geezer pays him to stay away.'

It was beginning to sound like Andrew was the ne'er-do-well of an escapist Regency novel. I blinked, and mascara stung my eyes. I reached for a tissue, determined to salvage thirty minutes' careful artistry.

'Why would he do that?' I said, nonchalant, unfazed, unshocked and unshockable.

'Oh tootsie baby, how the hell should I know? Maybe his mommy sends him an allowance, or maybe his girlfriend's rich and hooked on him, or something.'

'Um. Is his girlfriend coming with us tonight?'

Harry laughed. 'Not likely. From what little he's told me, she doesn't approve of his frivolous pastimes, not to mention 99.9% of his friends. I doubt she's good for a packet of smokes.'

I felt quite weak with all the input of new and unexpected information; it was more than I'd bargained for. But I abandoned the inquisition there in favour of getting ready to be seen by Harry's side.

He looked gorgeous. His jacket caressed his broad shoulders as though it had been made for him, and his fair hair was so artfully tousled in its expensive new style it would have made any red-blooded woman want to walk through it barefoot. His dimples, courtesy of his genes, were more irresistible than ever.

I had already rejected an embroidered cotton skirt and a camisole top as too casual, several of the outfits I'd worn to the office as too business like.

I wondered, folding the outfits back into the suitcase, how my co-workers were getting along without me at Metcalf Jones. I felt a sudden intense flash of longing to know, to be included again in the furious skulduggery of the latest campaign.

I pulled out of that one double-quick. Hadn't I come halfway across the world to stand by my man? And wasn't he delivering the goods? Wouldn't any of the people I'd worked with in California be more than happy to jettison their nine-to-five number for the chance to have the time of their lives in London, England?

Of course they would.

I went back to deciding what to wear. Finally I settled on the chocolate-brown silk dress I'd found in a North Beach boutique while on my pre-marital shopping spree with my mother. It was low-cut, back and front, unwaisted, with a dark brown satin sash at hip level. The bodice was inset with creamy cobwebby lace that sat peek-a-boo fashion over the swell of my cleavage, and the same lace edged the full sleeves that fluttered around my elbows.

'Very *thé dansant*,' the salesgirl assured us when I tried it on, and my mother sighed with pleasure. 'And by the way, a genuine article from the period.'

Mother nodded. 'Hon,' she said, 'it must be. It's just like the dresses they used to wear to tea dances in the afternoon. You've got to buy it.'

'Where on earth would I wear it?'

'You'll think of some occasion,' she said. 'You can't just leave it here, you'll kick yourself later.'

When we got home, mother altered it for me so it slithered and slunk over my flat belly and the slim curves of my pre-Charlie hips, and it shimmered all the way down to the hemline that fluttered around my knees.

But until that evening in London I had never worn it. It was hardly suitable for wearing to the office, or even to wine-tastings in the Napa Valley, certainly not out for a pizza or to the movies with our friends. Not even to the moderately swank event that was Metcalf's staff Christmas party.

I'd seen plenty of fashion features about the resurrection of the '20s and '30s 'looks', and so had all my girlfriends. But I, like them, had little if any wish to stand out wildly in our crowd. There was sure to be some smartass – even in laid-back super-cool California, or maybe especially there – who would have wished us 'happy Halloween' if we did: the look *was* a costume, after all.

Nevertheless my determination to get back into the dress after Charlie was born had kept me to the straight and narrow of post-natal exercises much more effectively than any of Dr Felton's earnest and eminently sensible lectures could ever have done.

And it had finally come into its own: it was just perfect for my debut – stomping, as it were, at the Savoy.

Harry watched me getting dressed without saying a word. When I'd put on my double rope of real pearls and slipped my sling-back beige satin pumps over my sheer tights, I wriggled across the room to him.

He whistled long and low. 'Holy *smoke*, baby,' he said. 'All that meat and *no* potatoes!'

I snuggled up to him and arched my back in an exaggerated tango stance. Charlie shouted with glee and clapped her hands, watching us from her cot. Harry said I looked like a million dollars, and I glowed.

The sitter was punctual, crisp in her blue cotton skirt and white blouse and sensible flat-heeled shoes, efficient. She presented her card of introduction without being asked for it, and she listened carefully to my earnest, slightly anxious, bedtime instructions.

She had a cap of curling coal black hair and eyes to match, and a mischievous and beguiling smile that lit up her face and made me realize how pretty she was. And how young she seemed, though she was perhaps nineteen or twenty, a year or so younger than me.

Without seeming to stare, she took in my outfit with a discreet glance of covert admiration. When I grinned at her in open complicity, woman to woman, she blushed and then grinned back.

'You look super, Mrs Franklin,' she said.

'Thank you,' I said.

And then Harry and I said, almost in unison: 'We've asked them downstairs to send you up a tray later on.'

'Oh, and please watch television if you want to,' I added quickly, gesturing towards the set. 'And if you get sleepy, feel free to stretch out on the bed. We, ah, might be late.'

I glanced at Harry, and he nodded.

'Depends,' he said to the girl, shrugging expansively. 'We're going out with a business associate, you see, and I've no idea what he's planned for the evening, or even where we're going.'

'We'll call you, to let you know,' I said. 'One of us will.'

'It may be, ah, *very* late,' Harry said, 'when we get back.'

The sitter took all that in her stride, nodded confidently, smiled calmly. 'Don't worry, we'll be fine.'

She held up the bulging briefcase she'd brought with her.

'When the baby's asleep I'll probably work. Unless of course,' she added sheepishly, 'there's something tempting on the telly.'

'You're a student,' Harry said.

'For my sins. I hope someday to qualify as a barrister.'

Harry whistled, impressed. 'Pretty heavy going,' he said.

'Well – sometimes,' she said.

She laughed, and then she changed the subject, turning us neatly back to the business at hand.

'Enjoy yourselves and don't worry,' she said firmly. 'Charlie and I'll be fine!'

She was holding the baby in the crook of one competent

101

arm as she ushered us out, smiling, telling us once again not to worry; when we were standing in the corridor, she turned her attention to Charlie.

Charlie glanced at me with supreme indifference out of solemn unblinking eyes, and then she smiled up into the young woman's face and gurgled with pleasure, reaching out greedy baby fingers to touch the fascinating stranger's shining curls.

And I felt a pang of such intense jealousy, hearing the door close softly behind us as Harry and I walked away, it was all I could do not to go back, snatch my baby out of the girl's embrace and clasp her to my heart.

That shook me. I'd never felt that fiercely about leaving her in all the eleven months of Charlie's endlessly absorbing existence on the planet.

In the lift, empty but for Harry and me, I turned to him and smiled nervously. 'They'll be all right,' I whispered softly.

He took my hand and squeezed it lightly; his palm was damp.

'Of course they will, hon,' he said. 'Felt a little odd, though, didn't it? Almost as though we were the girl's guests, being politely shooed out so her baby could get some sleep.'

I looked up at him and blinked, astonished. 'You felt that too?'

He laughed down at me. 'That poor girl thought she was never going to get rid of us. For a minute there I got the distinct impression she thought she might have been hired to babysit the three of us for the evening.'

'Stage fright,' I said solemnly. 'First time out in Fat City in our Sunday best.'

He grinned and pulled me in for a squeeze. 'We'll get over it, hon. We're gonna knock 'em dead.'

7

Andrew Lyle was waiting in the lobby, smoking a cigarette in short nervous puffs, watching the lifts.

When we emerged he came towards us, walking quickly, addressing anxious apologies to the neutral mid-space between Harry and me, soft-spoken in an accent I later learned to identify as West Yorkshire overlaid with the genteel patina of English public school.

'Sorry, I'm afraid I'm a bit early. I was about to, ah, ring the room.' He coughed behind his hand. 'Caroline's awfully sorry she couldn't come out with us this evening, and she hoped she'll meet you both, er, very soon. . . .'

He was tall, nearly as tall as Harry, though with none of Harry's exuberant confidence. Andrew was too thin for that, and his narrow shoulders seemed hunched in his expensive looking grey suit. His eyes were grey too, and restless. And although his hair was brown, it looked grey as well.

And for some reason his nervousness at the prospect of meeting Harry's wife was so obviously greater than mine at the prospect of meeting Harry's new friend it was palpable, and I wondered why.

Anyway it was reassuring; I liked Andrew at once.

How or where Harry had managed to connect with him was, and would remain, a mystery. It didn't really matter; no doubt he was one of the friends of a friend, one of a series of Harry's contacts from the carefully annotated, scrupulously maintained black book Harry carried.

So be it: my first gambler (unless I counted Harry) and an Englishman at that. And a guy who seemed so taken with

Harry, presumably on sight, he'd decided to show us the town – or at least to take us out to dinner.

I offered him my hand and murmured 'hello', but Andrew stood uncertainly, grey all over, diffident and dejected, hopeful and eager-to-please all at once, nervy as a thoroughbred at the starting post, and at a loss for words.

Harry rose to the occasion magnificently. He grinned and put his hand on Andrew's arm, man-to-man, which seemed to steady him considerably. He darted Harry a grateful smile as he took my proffered hand and shook it, then beamed me a lopsided grin.

'You must be Libby,' he said. 'Welcome to London.'

'And you must be Andrew,' I said. 'It's great to be here, and lovely to meet you.'

There didn't seem to be much any of us could add to that, and there was a moment of three-way beaming and body language to show how glad we were to be there in the lobby together, and then Harry said 'Shall we?' and offered me his arm, and the three of us walked out into the mellow golden light of the summer evening. Harry hailed a passing taxi and handed me into it while Andrew spoke to the driver.

In the taxi Andrew seemed to unbend a bit, making small talk, chuckling and nodding his approval as I recounted all Harry and I had seen and done so far in London, and then the small talk drifted gradually away and Harry began some earnest discussion with his friend across my perfumed bosom, dissecting a knotty problem he'd had with a bridge hand or something. I wasn't really listening; Andrew responded with enthusiasm, however, and for the moment I was more or less forgotten.

I didn't mind. I sat back contentedly, flanked by my escorts, feeling beautiful and wealthy and carefree and luxuriously comfortable as the big black Metropolitan cab purred and rumbled and growled along the London streets.

I was on the inside looking out, pampered and cherished; I felt the buoyant bubbling urge to wave discreet salutes to the ordinary mortals walking on the pavements beyond my shining chariot, and to the harassed drivers trapped in snarls of traffic as we sailed majestically by.

Harry was feeling pretty good too. I knew that when he sat back and put his arm around my shoulders, his discussion with Andrew suspended or forgotten, and mimed me a kiss. I kissed him back with my eyes, remembering what he'd said in the lift: we were going to knock 'em dead. And I was so proud of him for getting us where he'd wanted us to be, so proud to be by his side, I loved him more intensely than ever.

We stopped for drinks at a pub Andrew knew, in an impossibly narrow alleyway in the heart of the City. It was old he said, and still featured its original mullioned windows and charred beams and oak bar. And it was much too far off the beaten track to be in any tourist guide.

'We must start you as you mean to go on,' he said, winking at Harry, then smiling at me. 'They make the best Pimm's in London here. You'll like that, Libby.'

And when Andrew fought his way through the crowd of laughing, chattering people, bearing my silver goblet with its elaborate fruit garnish, his pleasure was plain when I clapped my hands in delight. My feeling of belonging escalated until I felt like singing.

We dined at a restaurant so grand it was legendary even in Montana, certainly in San Francisco, in a dining room that might have been a set from some lavish '30s musical: all plush and gilt and chandeliers and thick carpets that rolled back to reveal a highly polished dance floor. And a raised dais where I expected to see Lester Lanin waving his baton.

And a *maitre d'* who obviously knew Andrew and was glad to see him, and who escorted us personally to a table where we could see and be seen by everyone else in the room.

And waiters in white jackets who advanced in a close

105

respectful phalanx to hold our chairs and hand us enormous tasselled menus, and to place thick snowy linen napkins on our laps.

And to hover, bowing slightly from the waist, while we ordered. And to hover, lighting cigarettes, replacing ashtrays, bringing wine and filling glasses, serving, anticipating every need; doing damned near everything, in fact, but eating for us.

I had never experienced such a splendid distillation of everything I'd read and heard about service at its finest, tales of dining out in an atmosphere of such precise and careful near-perfection that the act and its execution approached the shimmering pinnacle of fine art.

It wasn't as though I'd been working third tub in the laundry all my life, or that I'd come straight from a hayrick carrying a cardboard suitcase. I knew which fork to use, which glass to sip from; I'd eaten in more than one elegant restaurant. I'd even organized a couple of grand soirées in San Francisco, as part of my job. Here, however, the whole performance was so well-coordinated and disciplined and beautifully timed it was positively balletic; I almost expected the entire dining room staff to take up positions for a soft-shoe chorus, or to burst into song.

Harry was impressed too; in face he was awed, and perhaps slightly overwhelmed. He hadn't come off a hayrick either, and he had beautiful table manners; he never chewed with his mouth open, and he was famous in a modest way among our friends for being able to eat spareribs without getting his fingers greasy.

But when we were seated at our table he leaned towards me and whispered: '*Ho*-ly Christ!' I think it was the silverware that got him.

At home, even in restaurants where full silver service was provided – or at least attempted – nobody gave a damn what you did with it, so long as you didn't stab anybody.

Here, enough implements surrounded each place setting

to make it possible to repair a small car. I had the uneasy impression that the hovering waiters were going to watch us all with beady eyes, to see who got it right. And that they would then award marks on a scale from 1 to 10.

When the entrées were served Harry surveyed his tool kit for a moment and said to Andrew: 'Nice place.'

And here Andrew showed his mettle, proving himself a superb and classy host. He shrugged and smiled, swept most of his cutlery to one side, and attacked his smoked salmon with the knife and fork that was left.

'I hoped you'd like it. It's marvellous for its theatre value, the food's not bad, and most evenings the band's quite good. The waiters are awful snobs though. Somehow I always expect one of them to slap my wrist for eating ice cream with my coffee spoon.'

I laughed, remembering a rather elegant dinner party Metcalf Jones had given for some important European vintners, at which I'd seen a French wine master *premier classe* pick up his *escargot* shells with bits of French bread, and dig out the snails with a toothpick. Class of the highest order, as in 'those who know the rules are free – and often quick – to break them.'

However Harry, rather perversely I thought, consumed his entire dinner – from parma ham to cherries jubilee – using the silver in correct sequence (skipping sets which did not apply) with the unhesitating precision of an open-heart surgeon. That was Harry all over: throw down a glove and he'd pick up a pair, every time. It wasn't that he thought Andrew's gesture was meant to put him at ease in case he didn't know his p's and q's; nor was it one-upmanship. It was simply that if Harry didn't rise to every challenge and meet it, he felt he had failed.

Harry wanted full marks from the waiters. That made me sad. I gave the matter a mental shrug and forgot about it. Harry was Harry, and would remain so.

After dinner we danced. I was whirled first in Andrew's

courtly, arm's length embrace, and then in Harry's, close and practised, smooth, where I fitted so well my feet seemed not to touch the floor, and I wanted the music to go on for ever and ever.

It was Harry's turn when the band struck a tango; we performed it with such passionate, if restrained, intensity that when it was finished, me swooning in his arms, gazing up at him through half-closed eyes, there was a smattering of applause.

After that I danced with the two of them more or less alternately, and when it was Andrew's turn I gave him equal time. I flirted with him just enough to make him feel good, following samba foxtrot waltz two-step, and some homogenized rock rhythm that was tame enough to accommodate the more dignified couples on the floor.

Through it all I felt like Mrs Gotrocks, filthy rich and gorgeous, languorously certain that at any moment one of my charming escorts would challenge the other to a friendly duel for the privilege of drinking fine champagne from my size eights.

Finally I drifted off to the ladies' powder room, which was everything it should have been: fragrant hand soap, tinted mirrors, a uniformed attendant who called me madam when I tipped her. When I glided grandly back to our table my swains were in earnest conference over brandy.

'Andrew was wondering where you'd like to go next, sugar,' Harry said.

'There's more?' I laughed a silvery southern-fried magnolia laugh and batted my lashes. 'Oh my.'

Harry swirled his brandy. 'Sure is, toots. They don't roll up the sidewalks here at sundown.' He dimpled at me. 'Andrew suggested we might like to look in at his club. One of them.'

Andrew looked uncomfortable. 'The thing is, Libby,' he said, 'it's a gambling club, and there's not, well, not a lot for ladies to do there. . . .'

'Ladies aren't – allowed?' I said.

'Oh certainly they're allowed – welcomed, in fact; but most of them are, ah, players, you see. Or else they're with someone who's playing. Wives and, er, girlfriends don't usually like the atmosphere. Caroline hates it.'

'Oh well. . . .'

I looked at Harry for my cue, but he was watching one of the couples on the dance floor – the man bald and portly, the woman in cerise ruffles and stiletto-heeled shoes that were too small for her – who were in the various tortured postures of an attempted rhumba.

Harry was tapping his toe in time to the music and I felt, or thought I did, the pressure of his foot against my instep, rapping out some cryptic code.

'Oh well,' I said again, 'whatever. . . .'

Andrew picked up his cigarettes and put them down again and worried the packet in an intricate pattern on the tablecloth, then picked it up again and opened it and drew one out. A waiter materialized and flicked a lighter; Andrew drew smoke deep into his lungs.

'May I be excused?' he said. I nodded.

He left and Harry turned to me.

'What say, hon?'

'Andrew didn't seem too ecstatic about the prospect of going to his club,' I said.

'He's trying to kick the habit.'

'What habit?'

'Roulette.'

'Oh.'

'Well, do you want to go or not?'

'What do you want to do?' I said.

He dimpled. 'Honey, three guesses and the first two don't count. Do you realize I've just been invited – no, *we've* been invited – to have a crack at the real high-class action? We're on our way, sugar!'

He hunched forward, excited; his eyes were dancing with

109

light. 'Sweetheart, listen. Andrew belongs to just about every club, casino, nightclub and back-room cribbage circle in town. So when the man invites us to walk right in with him' – he shrugged expansively – 'what do *you* think?'

I thought Harry was talking in riddles, and it made me nervous. This was the man who not ten minutes earlier had held me in a tango embrace so hot it sizzled my bones and fired them with the imperious desire to melt into him right there, right then – without even bothering to stop to find the nearest available bed. He was my beloved husband, the father of our child; I had never felt closer to him than I had since we'd arrived in London.

But he was waiting for my answer to his conundrum; and as the seconds of my honest confusion ticked by I could feel him retreating from me into an opacity so thick it was frightening. The excited light in his grey eyes seemed to dim and go flat, and I went cold.

But suddenly he came back to me, so abruptly my insides felt as though I'd just been spun around a hairpin bend at ninety mph. He smiled, took my hand, and kissed it.

'Come on, babe, what do you think?' he asked gently.

I swallowed. 'I thought you didn't want to be involved in casino gambling. You – you called the games they play. . . .' I searched for the words, and he waited, still smiling. 'You called them mug shots, where the odds are always with the house.'

He laughed – warm, genuine. I breathed; I'd got it right.

'Yes,' he said. 'Yes, of course they are. But a lot of the people who play them will play *any* game, don't you see? And I can hardly find high-stakes card games by wandering down Petticoat Lane looking for takers, can I hon? The thing is that by getting into the casinos I can round up all the wealthy mugs within a radius of two hundred miles. They're more or less gathered there together, like housewives at the January sales.'

I smiled at that, and nodded.

'Right,' he said. 'I can't just waltz into a high-class members-only London casino without an invite, can I? I mean, it isn't like Vegas, where any yahoo can wander in off the street with his complimentary silver dollars from the Bide-a-Wee Motel.'

I laughed out loud; it was so apt, so precisely Vegas in a nutshell. Harry laughed with me, and the tension dispersed.

But we hadn't quite finished. We had established that Harry definitely wanted to go with Andrew to his club(s). We had not established whether or not Harry wanted me to go too. We hadn't hammered out chapter and verse of my involvement in Harry's new venture. Up till then I'd never so much as watched him at a friendly game of three-card brag. And although I'd anticipated inclusion in Harry's gambling world once we got to London and the big time, once the venue of his games was presumably a lot more presentable than the terrible neighbourhood in California where he'd played lo-ball, I was still unsure how to respond.

Lord knows Andrew wasn't keen on having me go there with them, stammering on about his own girlfriend's distaste for the very atmosphere of the place. So was I supposed to say yes I'd love to go, or was I supposed to demur, plead a diplomatic headache and ask to be taken back to the hotel? After I'd graciously insisted that Harry and Andrew should go on without me, of course.

There was nothing for my dilemma but plain English.

'Harry, do you want me to come?'

He shook his head and smiled. 'Libby, honey, I've spent several minutes trying to find out what *you* want to do.'

'Well,' I said earnestly, 'I hate to sound naive, but this is brand new territory and I don't know how you feel about my going. Before, in California, you didn't want—'

'Sweetheart, I know,' he said softly. 'This is a different ballgame, honey, a scene I'm proud to have you see – and to show you off in. How about it?'

111

I grinned, exhilarated. 'Of course I want to come,' I said. 'Wouldn't miss it for the world.'

'That a girl,' he said, grinning back. He glanced around at the couples poised on the dance floor waiting for the next number.

He rose and extended his hand to me. 'May I have this dance?'

I lowered my lashes and flashed him a flirtatious smile.

'I should love to, thank you,' I said demurely.

He took me into his arms and whirled me onto the floor as the musicians launched into a shamelessly romantic waltz.

I felt giddily, crazily happy; I was the enchanted princess of every fairy tale that was ever written, and Harry was the handsome prince, and we would live happily ever after.

We were laughing softly together as we went back to the table, just in time to join Andrew as he was in the act of sitting down. He stood up again, and held my chair, and signalled to the waiter for another round of brandies.

'You two look fantastic out there,' he said, beaming at us both.

Harry laughed. 'I think I'll keep her on,' he said. And then: 'Say Andrew, Libby decided she'd love to come along and watch us while we win a fortune. If you hang on a mo' I'll just go out to the lobby and call our sitter, and then we'll be all set.'

When he'd gone I picked up my liqueur glass and sipped drambuie, and smiled at Andrew. 'Harry's a wonderful father,' I said.

He nodded, obviously uncomfortable, playing with his cigarette packet.

'Eh, Libby, are you sure you won't be – well, bored? I meant it when I said that Caroline won't go near this club, or any of the others. She says gambling's a shocking waste of money. . . .' He shrugged. 'I suppose she's right.'

112

He lit a cigarette off the one he'd already got going, thwarting the waiter who appeared, genie-from-a-bottle fashion, with a lighter already cocked and ready to fire.

'We could hear some jazz or something instead, go to a nightclub. . . .'

Poor Andrew, pussy-whipped by the formidable Caroline even in her absence, not able to take his pleasures freely under the constant friction of his Caroline-induced guilt. Well, Harry could teach him a thing or two about that, and maybe he would.

'I won't be bored,' I said gently. 'I really want to go.'

We sat in silence for awhile, watching the couples on the dance floor, until Harry reappeared, crossing the room in long confident strides.

Women glanced up as he passed; more than one pair of feminine lips parted slightly, watching him; I could almost hear the sighs, I could almost feel the heat behind them. It gave me immense pleasure, really shivered my timbers when Harry put his hands lightly on my shoulders and leaned down to me, caressing my ear with his mouth. As though he'd chosen me just then, singled me out at random and claimed me.

'The sitter says we can stay out as late as we want to, hon,' he said, soft and low. 'Says she's watching a Dracula movie and that Charlie's snoring like an old drunk.'

'This is it?' I said, peering out into the night.

A quiet narrow street of brick buildings, the only light from the show window of an antique shop, a gallery, and all the rest in darkness.

Harry put his hand over mine. 'Wait till you see the inside, doll,' he whispered. 'They tell me there's nothing like it anywhere else in the world. Not the parts we've seen, anyway.'

113

I smiled at him in the dim interior of the cab; his eyes were shining.

No, this wasn't Caesar's Palace; nor was it a lo-ball poker club in the slums on the outskirts of Oakland, California.

In my consumer guide to gambling Andrew's club would be a separate entry, with nothing but a smartly-painted door to mark the spot, a brass plaque to indicate that behind it lay the gateway to Harry's mecca.

I allowed Andrew to hand me out of the taxi, and I took his arm as Harry alighted behind me; I felt grand and royal, attended fore and aft by my retinue, ready for anything, high on Harry's excitement.

We were admitted by a smartly uniformed doorman who smiled and tipped his visored cap; we were greeted and welcomed by an immaculately groomed, jacuzzied, shrewd and charming man who sized Harry up covertly without missing a beat in his repartee, and who signed him in as a guest member. He escorted us personally through the foyer to the large wood-panelled, beautifully appointed room where most of the business was transacted, and bade us enjoy ourselves.

Business is the wrong word, too pedestrian and prosaic for that room. An aura of grandeur hung over the scene like a benediction. I tried to take it in without gawping like Dorothy in Oz.

The oases of light from delicate chandeliers that illumined islands of smooth green baize; the elegantly dressed people clustered around them; the men who presided, white shirts gleaming against dark lapels, dealing cards or spinning roulette wheels with quiet, rhythmic, imperturbable passivity; the ambiance of understated wealth, real and definite and solid; the smell of money.

'This is it,' Andrew said, at my right. His face was radiant, he seemed taller and broader than he'd been before. It was as though that room was his home. He looked at me, eagerly searching my face for a reaction; I suppose my eyes

114

were shining with the wonder of it all. He smiled, delighted. 'Would you like to go through to the bar for a drink?' he said.

Harry at my left held his face impassive, but he was taking it all in even more thirstily than I was, I was certain; and he was undoubtedly just as impressed as I was, vindicated that his expectations of a private London gaming club had more than come up to the mark.

He said, 'Sure, let's have a drink.'

'Libby?' Andrew said, the chivalrous host.

'I'd like that very much,' I said.

I smiled at Harry and took his arm.

We traversed the length of the splendid room, side by side by side – a confident processional of people who mattered – and walked through a high-ceilinged archway and along a corridor to the bar, equally splendid but much smaller, carefully separate from the action at the tables.

No pretty little gals in this joint running around among the players in cowgirl mini-skirts with trays of drinks; no twanging country and western music to set the punters jigging with manaical excitement and suspension of belief, forgetfulness of their real lives as shopkeepers or wage-slaves fifty weeks of the year. Andrew's club was the real McCoy; jumped-up dudes with ten dollars in their jeans for a one-off good time need not apply for membership.

I hoped my stocking seams were straight, was oh so glad the pearls in the ropes of my necklace were real, and that I'd washed my hair that morning. I wondered if the Tur-neresque canvases at intervals along the panelled walls, glowing mellow beneath gallery lights, were originals or reproductions; I wondered even more speculatively about the women I saw gambling, dressed without exception to the nines, and whether the glittering points of light from jewels at throats and ears, wrists and fingers, dazzling richly beneath the crystal prisms of the chandeliers, were refracted courtesy of Cartier or Woolworth.

115

There was little doubt, actually; Woolworth didn't sell jewels like the ones I saw that evening – not unless they squirted water.

It was as though Andrew had been reading my thoughts, and was positively high on delight; he inclined his head to me and whispered mischievously, 'Want to meet a duchess, love?'

Harry heard the question too; his eyes lit up and he whispered across me. 'Where?'

'Hang about, old son,' Andrew said, laughing easily. 'She's usually in the bar. Before or after she's hocked another of the family jewels at the cashier's window. Nice old girl, actually. May have been quite a looker in her time.'

'What should we call her if we do meet her?' Harry asked.

Andrew laughed again and shook his head in mock incredulity, gleeful to have found a friend so innocent that the resident duchess could impress.

My own preconceptions about duchesses in general were highly coloured by the Tenniel illustrations in the Alice books: duchesses were regal beings with the power to order the very roses painted red or white at whim; to have babies who quietly turned into pigs while their cooks went berserk; to shout 'off with their heads!'

Duchesses according to Tenniel looked suspiciously like Queen Victoria: bosomy, substantial, severe, their hair piled high, their wide skirts stiff with crinoline petticoats. I was confident that real-life duchesses, in the twentieth century at least, were nothing like that.

Andrew's duchess had probably married a duke, presumably a rich one, and she was unlikely to be the autocrat of Alice's adventures. I wasn't too worried about what to call her when we met, either: a polite 'how do you do', would cover most introductions, I was pretty sure. Unless I was presented to the Queen of England, in which case I could look it up in Debrett's. My mother had said so, often, though naturally we didn't see much royalty in Montana.

116

Harry seemed less sure. 'Andrew, come on,' he said, 'what should I call her?'

'You call her Mary, Harry. She replaced the duke years ago with a furrier from south London. She keeps the title for fun, and because the furrier was so impressed by it. But Mary'll do fine.'

Mary was impressive nonetheless, and very obviously rich. She was imperially slim, her silver hair elaborately coifed; and she was beautifully dressed in heavy oyster-coloured satin. She wore emeralds in a collar at her throat, set in platinum or white gold, that were so large and shed their green fire so softly in the dimly-lit bar they could not possibly have been anything but real.

And indeed she must once have been beautiful. As it was, only her eyes, huge and green as her emeralds, remained to remind the world of that. It was impossible to guess her age, but the expensively preserved and carefully made up skin of her face and neck looked paper thin and creased like onionskin when she smiled. As she did, luminously, when she saw us come into the bar with Andrew.

She was sitting alone at one of the small round tables – each with its small shaded lamp and vast glass ashtray; she hailed us gaily as we walked through the archway, and bade us join her.

'Tell me, Andrew,' she said, 'who are these charming children you've dragged into our little den of iniquity?'

And she sat, all eyes, her attention riveted, while he told her; she put Harry and me entirely at ease as she asked us in her soft, cultured voice to tell her why we'd come so far from home, and what did we think of London and the English and oh, did we really have a baby? Oh, how sweet.

'What've you been up to?' Andrew said finally, patting her beringed hand.

She shrugged and very casually, with the merest sugges-tion of regret in the moué she made with her mouth, said

117

she'd lost a packet at roulette earlier and was drowning her sorrows.

'I know I shouldn't do that too often. The gambling, I mean. . . .'

Nor perhaps the drowning of the sorrows afterwards, though the only telltale signs of that were the way she kept knocking back the gins and tonics Harry and Andrew took it in turns to order for her, and the tired droop of her hand over each fresh drink, and something desperately sad about the sagging line of her jaw.

And she seemed terribly lonely too, though it didn't seem right that she should. She was such a lovely lady, and a duchess to boot.

We left the bar after her quickly drained fifth gin and tonic since we'd come in. I had to admire the way she handled herself, the way she rose from the table and walked a straight line on Andrew's arm back into the gaming room. God only knew how much she'd had to drink before we got there. She might have been a bit of a lush, but Christ how well she held it.

She and Andrew had decided to gamble together, on whether or not a little ball would fall into a certain numbered slot, black or red: roulette.

Harry and I stood watching for a while, though I lost interest sooner than he did. I was far too busy, mesmerized in fact, watching the rest of the people there, at Andrew's table and the others I could see from where Harry and I were standing.

The men: some young, some old, not all of them dressed to kill but every man Jack of them dressed at least for church, in suits and shirts and ties, their faces etched within the pools of light. The women glittered beneath the weight of finery and jewels.

I wondered idly if the pair of flapping Arabs all in white, gesturing and muttering occasionally to one another, sallow faced and heavy jowled, intent as any of the others at baccarat, were sheiks or sons of sheiks, father and son, or what.

None of the players betrayed by gesture or words above a whisper what fate was dealing out to them or rolling their way.

There was a low murmur of voices in the room, but the dominant sounds were the smart flick of cards, the unceasing spin of roulette wheels.

No, this was nothing like Las Vegas: there was no synchronized neon to split the night sky; no curving driveways where the limousines could swish; no dollar twenty-five cent steaks, no Frank Sinatra, no circus act above the punters' heads. No hoots of sudden joy, no disgusted throwing down of cards and hunched shoulders and quick grim steps away from tables; no ballyhoo, no drama.

In fact, no fun appeared to be being had by anyone present.

I didn't know what went on in the sleazy lo-ball clubs at the end of the world, surrounded by the monster shapes of warehouses and the stink of poverty; but I did know about Las Vegas, and there at least there'd been gaiety, evidence of what-the-hell camaraderie among winners and losers alike.

Even my dad's limited-stake poker games at home had been staged as relaxing get-togethers. Nothing fancy, but fun nevertheless – the men with rolled-up shirt sleeves and pretzels and beer at their elbows, maybe a little friendly bellyaching when one of them was a big loser. Big, big loser – oh yes, maybe five dollars; at carried-away excess, maybe ten.

Oh, Andrew's London gaming club was a new chapter in my lexicon, all right. It was mighty serious stuff, just as Harry had said it was.

I soon found out why.

★ ★ ★

119

'Come on, Lib,' Harry said quietly, touching my elbow. 'I can't bear to watch this.'

'What?'

I looked at him, startled out of my absorption with the general scene, and he nodded very slightly towards Andrew, who was sitting on a high stool next to the Duchess Mary in a semi-circle of roulette players. 'Him. Just take a look.'

Andrew's face was as impassive as the others, as frozen in an intensity of concentration; but the bones stood out in sharp relief against the light from the elegant chandelier overhead, skeletal beneath the pallor of his skin. He looked sick. And the stack of chips on the green baize at his place was diminishing at the rate of knots, even as I watched.

'He's losing,' I whispered, stricken, so sorry for Andrew I had to restrain the impulse to go to him, hug him, comfort him, drag him away.

'You might say that,' Harry said. 'Come on if you want to. I'm going to play a couple of hands of blackjack before I get him the hell out of here.'

'You're – going to play?'

Harry gave me a look, amusement bordering on impatience. 'Manners, babe. Can't go into the store without buying something. Didn't your mother ever tell you that?'

'Some store.'

'Don't panic, hon. I know what I'm doing. You going to watch me do it, or are you just going to stand here gaping like a fish while Andrew does the rest of his bread?'

He offered his arm and I took it, swallowing panic at the thought of Harry ending up as Andrew apparently would, 'doing his bread'.

What if you do, Harry? What happens to us then? To me and Charlie, you, all of us?

I wasn't stupid. I was pretty sure money changed hands in that place pretty damned fast, and that the sums involved were substantial; that the odds were heavily stacked against the punters. That super-ritzy atmosphere hadn't been established and maintained by people who gave money away. On the contrary, they raked it in, in big green spendable stacks. The people who came here had money to burn. They burned it, and came back to burn some more.

And in spite of all his bravado, and all his years of careful keeping track, the new clothes and the plane tickets and the hotel – the sure promise there'd be more to come – Harry didn't have all that much bread to 'do'.

Panic rose and choked me. I got a quick take of Charlie crying, waking up in that strange hotel room with a strange girl sitting there watching Dracula. Charlie crying for mommy and daddy while mommy and daddy were waltzing into a fantasyland that was one hell of a lot too rich for daddy's blood.

I was stuck with two choices, both bleak: I could walk out, get into a cab, go back to the hotel and shake with terror until Harry came in. Or I could stay with him and watch while he flexed his muscles among the big boys for the very first time.

There was a third possibility: that Harry and I could leave right then, together, and go back to the hotel to talk the whole thing over. Surely that would be the most sensible, rational, loving thing to do. Maybe I could persuade him that it was time to go home.

I stiffened, balking as we walked away from the roulette players, about to suggest doing that before it was too late. It was crazy, unthinkable, that I'd staked my entire future, my baby's future, everything, on fifty-two pieces of cardboard and the way they fell in response to wordless nods from fools.

Harry sensed my fear. Maybe he could smell it beneath the expensive perfume I'd applied so liberally. Perhaps he could see it in my big scared googly eyes.

He glanced briefly at the nearest blackjack table, hungry for action but resigned, before he walked me back into the bar, seated me at a table well out of earshot of the three or four already occupied, and signalled for drinks.

'What is it, sweetpea?' he said.

121

'I, ah – can I have a cigarette, Harry?'

'You don't smoke, remember?'

I hadn't, since my pregnancy; it was something I'd flaunted smugly nearly every time Harry lit up. But I wanted that cigarette desperately.

I grinned nervously and shrugged. 'I fell off the wagon, I guess,' I said. Harry smiled, lit one and handed it to me.

'Okay sugar, out with it,' he said.

I took several quick drags and coughed, and placed the cigarette carefully in the ashtray.

'Well, what happens – if Andrew loses tonight? I mean, if he – ah, does his bread?'

'Nothing, honey. Why should it?'

'He won't have any money,' I mumbled, skirting the issue, reluctant to broach what was really on my mind. 'He did say he has a system, though,' I added hopefully.

'Oh sure, I told you,' Harry said, chuckling. 'He's got this trust fund or whatever, which I suppose means a hefty dollop of cash into his bank account on the first or tenth of every month, regular as the moon shines. I think they carry him on the strength of that all over town. Mind you,' he added, 'I haven't actually asked him to spell it out for me. It'd be presumptuous.'

I nodded, picking up the cigarette again.

'Honey, I think I know what's bothering you,' Harry said. 'We don't have a safety net like Andrew's, and you're afraid I'll get in over my head, right? Isn't that it?'

I studied the cigarette. The waiter brought the drinks; there was a four second reprieve while he set them down in front of us.

'Libby?' Harry prompted.

'It isn't that I don't trust you, Harry. It's just that – well, what if you *do* get in over your limit? By the look of things out there it wouldn't be too hard for J. Paul Getty to do that. . . .'

He smiled and touched my glass with his.

'Relax, Lib! Sweetheart, do you honestly think I intend to go a bundle on a few hands of pontoon dressed up and known as blackjack?'

'No, Harry, no. It's just this place and the casual way the people seem to throw their money around. I know you know the rules and the stakes and the risks and all that, and the odds, but still. . . .'

He leaned back and sipped at his drink, thinking.

'Baby, it's okay, really it is,' he said gently. 'I know it's overwhelming, that you've never seen anything like it.' He grinned, and reached out for my hand. 'Neither have I, we both know that. But I do know the odds, and I always limit my stake, and I'm sure I know what I'm doing. These are just folks out there, hon, give or take a few diamond bracelets. Come on, sweeheart, watch me while I show 'em how it's done, okay?'

I watched, sitting on a high stool next to Harry's at one of the tables among the green baize islands, studying his face, his square beautifully shaped hands, the businesslike demeanour that set him apart instantly and definitely from the others seated there, one in particular who fascinated me.

A young woman immediately next to Harry on the other side, young though her eyes were not; her right arm firm and rounded in a flimsy sleeve of trailing dusty rose chiffon; her right hand at the end of it a graceful limpid instrument for placing bets, pushing chips forward with languid carelessness, caressing the cards dealt to it, pausing unflinching as the dealer won from her, time after time after time.

She didn't care, didn't give a damn that she was losing, it was obvious.

I would have wondered why and watched her longer, constructed a past for her, perhaps a future, above all a present so bleak she was seated there past midnight, splashing her slender fingers through expensive chips as though they were eddies of water in a stream, if Harry hadn't nodded to the dealer then: *Yes, I'm playing*.

I knew the rules, or vaguely. My father had explained pontoon to me, had demonstrated the game and once had even won my pocket money as an object lesson at our kitchen table, one Sunday afternoon when I was ten.

Two cards to player, two to dealer, face card and ace a perfect hand, total twenty-one, pontoon, blackjack; twenty-one a winner no matter how it comes; twelve or less takes another card until player holds a total of twelve or higher; stand on twelve for safety, anything over twenty-one is bust, sorry honey, you lose. Another hand?

Harry wasn't losing. Hand after hand, as though by magic, Harry won: ace, king; ace, queen; seventeen and dealer, forced to draw to twelve, went bust.

A string of indifferent hands, chancy: fourteen, fifteen, twelve. Harry played correctly every time, and with every appearance of being as indifferent as the others. And I watched the stack of chips in front of him grow taller and taller, like Little Black Sambo's stack of pancakes.

My excitement grew with them until it was a feeling very like a sexual turn-on, until my focus narrowed to the chips and Harry's moving hand as though they would move in rhythm for ever, as though I never ever wanted them to stop.

They did stop and I was bereft, so close, so very close to orgasm I looked up, flustered and ashamed, afraid the dealer may have seen it.

By then Harry's chips were so numerous that picking them up and carrying them across the splendid room to the cashier's window might well have seemed a vulgar act, garish, showy and smacking of braggadocio and Vegas. Harry managed it with style by handing most of them to me. I put them in my evening bag. It wouldn't close.

The cashier was as impassive as the dealer had been, counting out banknotes, but he registered us I could tell, and he appraised us too and allowed himself the shadow of a smile of approval when he looked at me. We'd be remembered, he seemed to be saying.

As we walked away, Harry handed me a sheaf of bank-notes and gestured towards my bag.

He grinned impishly. 'Buy yourself a hat,' he whispered.

'How much is here?'

'Five, six hundred pounds. I didn't really count it.'

'A thousand *dollars* . . ?'

He nodded. 'You a believer now, babe?'

I took a deep shuddering breath. 'Harry?'

'Hm?'

'Ah, what would have happened if' – I bit my lip – 'if it had gone the other way?'

He shrugged, amused. 'It didn't.'

'But what if it had? They don't know here, that – you'd be good for it. What would they have done?'

Harry chuckled and took my arm. 'I guess they would have shot me in the kneecaps, just like on TV. Oh, not here, of course. Bad for the image, but—'

'Harry! Oh Harry, for God's sake don't say that! It isn't true – is it?'

For all I knew, it was, or something near it. All that window-dressing had to be paid for, and a gambling debt was not negotiable, like a car loan or a mortgage. And the territory, at least in literature and films, was strewn with tough guys and quick reprisals.

'Harry . . . ?'

He relented. 'Honey, I was only teasing. Now relax, enjoy yourself! If I'd lost they would have carried me on Andrew's say-so, that's all. And it's highly unlikely I would lose, or at least not very much. Just think of this place as the runway of a carnival, somewhere to come for a little warm-up before or after the main event. My total stake this evening was twenty pounds, hon.'

Andrew materialized, smiling sheepishly, walking towards us a little uncertainly; he looked like he'd been through a wringer.

'How'd it go, champ?' Harry said.

Andrew shrugged, palms up; he managed a weary smile. 'I lost.'

'Do tell.'

Andrew's face collapsed. He looked wounded, exhausted. 'I was winning at one stage,' he said quickly. 'Actually—'

'Actually you should have quit then,' Harry said.

He sounded waspish and pedantic, like a teacher whose exasperation with a dull pupil has got the edge over his patience. But then, to my relief, he relented; he smiled and Andrew looked relieved, as though he'd been reprieved if not forgiven.

'All right, sport,' Harry said easily, 'go settle up with the tallyman, and then what say we all go back to our hotel. We've got some whisky.'

The sky was streaked with pink, and the rumble of the taxi jarred against birdsong and the cosy rattling of milk floats as we rode back to Bloomsbury.

The sitter was yawning and dishevelled and muddled with sleep after a night spent stretched across our hotel bed in her stockinged feet. She rallied when Harry paid her, tipping her generously; she offered to come again any time, and she thanked us as she left.

Andrew admired the still-sleeping Charlie in her cot, then stared into the amber depths of scotch as he and Harry engaged in a low rumbling monosyllabic discussion of their plans for later in the day.

When he'd left, I asked Harry how much Andrew had lost in his roulette session.

'Two thousand five hundred pounds,' he said.

I gasped.

Harry nodded thoughtfully. 'Going to have to take that boy in hand.'

After that Harry and Andrew were virtually inseparable. Harry met him nearly every afternoon, joined him at one of the numerous gaming clubs to which Andrew belonged and to which he nominated Harry, and to all of which Harry was admitted and welcomed with open arms.

There they played backgammon or, together, bridge; both were excellent players, a formidable pair. They began to talk of entering tournament play, as partners or members of a team.

Harry began to drum up interest in serious poker too; those games were held very privately indeed, for stakes so dizzyingly high I could only imagine what they might be – I never asked – in smart pied-à-terres or luxurious hotel suites lent by one of the punters as a venue.

In the evenings, unless a game became an all night marathon, as sometimes happened, Harry and Andrew came back to the hotel to pick me up and take me out.

I was waiting, with shining hair and manicured nails and soft summer dresses, scented and smiling and glad to see them, euphoric at being privy to their excited telling of the doings of their day, delighted at the fun Harry and Charlie had together while he played with her and put her to bed and told the sitter – one of the succession of conscientious, totally reliable girls from the agency that had sent the first one – that we might be very late, coming back.

Dinner might be anywhere, so long as the restaurant was expensive or fashionable or unusual or diverting. Afterwards we might go to a discotheque or nightclub. More usually we went to a casino or a club, where some of Harry's businesslike attitude began to penetrate to Andrew.

I could feel that it took a monumental effort of self-control, but Andrew began to curb his worst excesses at roulette, trying hard to copy Harry and succeeding – limiting his stake and memorizing odds and playing the chancy mug shots cautiously and just for fun, as Harry did.

Usually it would be morning, or very nearly, when Harry and I got back to the hotel. A handful of hours when we could fall exhausted into bed and tumble into sleep before

Charlie crowed the sun up, ravenously hungry for her breakfast and raring to go. I didn't mind that I was usually the one to get up with her. My euphoria kept me going like a miraculous drug.

As the new man in town, Harry acquired considerable cachet wherever he went; and he gained momentum as his skill and careful judgment was broadcast via jungle telegraph. Andrew gained much-enhanced status and respect in the night-blooming world he inhabited, for having discovered him; and their emergence as a complementary team was the event of the summer.

I was their mascot.

Intriguing, Andrew said, to the dozens of men to whom he introduced me, his friends and cronies; most of them married to spoilsports, Andrew said, carping nagging whiners who were determined to put a stop to their men's folly; frustrated and bitter when they found out they could not, withdrawn into uneasy purdah in the cloisters of their separate lives.

Not I, though. I floated in a delicious bubble of suspended animation, surrounded and swept by a distillation of the rumble and smell of London taxis and laughter and nonstop entertainment and the sweet sounds of homage paid constantly to my round-eyed awed acceptance of all of it as it came; holding a very special spotlight all my own.

Above all, always, next to Harry. Making him proud of me.

8

Charlie's birthday was celebrated quietly but with ceremony in the third week in July.

Her party was intimate but festive; the guests were Harry and me and Andrew. We sat on the bed in our hotel room with Charlie in the middle, in the place of honour. We grownups smiled in sentimental complicity when Harry brought out the pink-frosted cupcake with its single lighted candle and placed it carefully before the birthday girl.

We laughed as she clapped her hands and cried 'Pret-ty!' And we moved like greased lightning when she scrambled towards the tantalizing flame, to help her blow it out before she burned her fingers.

We toasted her in champagne as she attacked the cake and her presents: a jigsaw puzzle and a story book from Harry and me, and from Andrew a larger-than-life stuffed rabbit. It was a whole lot bigger than she was and she eyed with frowning suspicion until Andrew, shy and awkwardly tender, cajoled her into touching it by crooning to her: 'Big bunny *likes* you, Charlie, he wants to be your friend!'

When she chortled and gurgled and, christening it with cake crumbs, encircled as much of the rabbit as would fit in her embrace, Andrew was unashamedly delighted; he leaned forward to kiss Charlie's forehead.

'You know,' he said thoughtfully, straightening, looking at Harry and then at me, 'you should really have a flat.' He looked around the room. 'You're awfully cramped in here, especially Charlie.'

I looked round as though I was seeing the room for the first time. It was true. After nearly two months in London,

Harry and Charlie and I were still living like gypsies. Our suitcases standing open, spilling half their contents; we tripped constantly over the ever-proliferating paraphernalia of Charlie's babyhood that covered almost every available surface and most of the floor: her toys and books, the mountains of laundry we sent down with the maid every day, the crisply folded stacks of diapers and vests and dainty dimity dresses that came back to us every afternoon.

I looked at Harry. 'He's right,' I said.

He nodded. 'It's not a home,' he said.

Especially not for Charlie. Harry and I had been far too engrossed in our non-stop social whirl to notice or to care that we were bursting out of its confines. But then we hadn't been confined to the room day in and day out, the way Charlie was.

While Harry and I were out on the town being wined and dined and generally whooping it up, Charlie had been eating most of her meals out of jars labelled junior baby food – sitting in her pushchair or on somebody's lap. And while she was still too young to play with other kids, she hadn't even *seen* many since we'd been here. We took her out every day to the park, but if she did occasionally strike up a tentative acquaintance in the sandpit, it was with a child she was unlikely ever to see again.

Even the conscientious, competent, kindly sitters who looked after her nearly every evening were a parade of new faces; we were seldom able to get the same girl on two consecutive nights.

After all the thought we'd given to establishing a secure routine for her in California, we'd been positively cavalier in the way we'd disrupted it.

'Sorry,' Andrew said suddenly, coughing into his hand, 'I didn't mean to—'

'It's okay,' I said quickly.

'No, Libby, you don't understand. I went about this clumsily. I should have come right out with it at the beginning.'

'Come out with what?' Harry said, smiling at him.

'Well,' Andrew said. He paused to light a cigarette. 'I know a guy who owns several properties near Marble Arch, lucky beggar. And he, ah, told me he's got one vacant. Or rather, I asked him. Sorry, I—'

'Andrew,' Harry said, laughing, '*never* apologise. Believe me, your friends don't need it, and your enemies won't believe it. Now, out with it man.'

'Well okay. I've never seen the place, but it's a good address and it's central, handy for taxis late at night and so on.' He grinned.

'Um,' Harry mused. 'But our tourist visas expire in August unless I come up with a job, and all our furniture and stuff's still in California, so—'

'Oh, he's willing to rent month to month. I asked him! And it's furnished, of course; they all are.'

'All?' I said, incredulous.

Andrew grinned and relaxed a little. 'Mostly. Something to do with a law they pushed through parliament. It makes it easier for landlords to get tenants out. I don't know the ins and outs of it, but – that's the way it is.'

'Is the flat very expensive?' I asked.

'I, ah, didn't think to ask him the rent,' Andrew said, shamefaced. 'Though it'll be less than he normally asks, of course. . . .'

'It's bound to be cheaper than this hotel,' Harry said, 'modest though it is.'

I grinned. 'Amen.'

There was the rent, and the room-service meals and snacks, the laundry, and the valet service that kept Harry's suits and most of my dressy outfits in a constant state of readiness – on top of the sitters for Charlie, and the fancy dinners when it was Harry's turn to pop. And the taxis, telephone calls, tips, incidentals. It added up fast.

'As for finding a job,' Andrew said, 'you will find one, Harry. After all, we're both working on it.'

131

It was as if Andrew couldn't bear the thought of having to part with Harry; it was like listening to a small boy who, anxious not to lose his baseball coach to another school, another team, vows to keep him where he is by sheer force of will.

'I could ring him now,' Andrew said eagerly. 'He told me his estate agent could let you see the place any time. . . .'

'What say, Lib?' Harry said. 'Shall we give it a try?'

The flat consisted of the ground floor of what once had been a rich man's London residence, built in the nineteenth century to accommodate a large family and a full complement of servants. Its two square high-ceilinged rooms were accessible from the landing. The first overlooked a small walled garden (neglected, choked with weeds), and had probably been the drawing room in palmier days. The second, adjoining and connecting, had probably been the library; it overlooked the street.

I could visualize the rooms as they might originally have been, statements of their inhabitants' gentility and considerable wealth: the drawing room overstuffed and cosy with aspidistra and mantel ornaments, the library a bastion of Victorian masculinity. Not my taste, certainly, but having the virtues of consistency and comfort. All trace of the original was gone. What was left in its place undoubtedly had the original owner spinning in his crypt.

Whoever owned it had bought the place as an investment, had carved it up with breathtaking ingenuity and furnished it anyhow, the better and sooner to realize the rental income it would yield. There was a basement below it, a second and third storey above. It was a big house.

The ground floor drawing room had been converted into a sitting-dining area, defined by a formica-topped table and four kitchen chairs at the far end of the room; the nubbly beige three piece suite at the other. The kitchen was assembled in a partitioned alcove in a corner, with a cooker cheek by jowl with a refrigerator. Small, like the one my father used in his garage workshop for cans of beer. There was a sink, scratched linoleum defined the space. The bathroom was a tacked-on back extension accessible through a short corridor, partitioned at an unnatural angle off the sitting room, just far enough away from the cooking equipment, such as it was, to satisfy whatever passed in London for building regulations. The second room was furnished from the contents of somebody's attic with a double bed, wardrobes, night tables, and two lamps that wouldn't have passed muster as pitch-penny prizes at a county fair.

The agent who showed us through the flat was middle-aged, balding and running to fat; he followed us around as we surveyed the place. Every few seconds he glanced at his wristwatch, as though he had some urgent appointment elsewhere.

'My client doesn't normally rent to couples with children,' he said when we were finished looking, standing in the middle of the sitting room poised for negotiation or, I devoutly hoped, departure.

'Your client is a personal friend of mine,' Andrew said politely but with an edge of crisp authority I'd never heard him use.

It worked. 'Oh of course, of course,' the agent said almost obsequiously. 'In this case he's asked me to make an exception, of course.'

But still the agent eyed Charlie with a pained expression as she toddled into the kitchen area to explore. I dashed after her, scooped her up and held her tightly, wishing with all my heart I had the nerve to say that demolition would be by far the kindest fate for the whole sad brutalized building.

He looked at Harry, and flashed him an on/off sort of smile. 'Well, Mr, ah, Franklin, do you think you'll take it? There's never any difficulty finding suitable tenants, I

133

assure you. It's marvellously central, handy for the shops. And it's a steal,' he added as a clincher, glancing genially at Andrew, 'at the rate he's prepared to offer to a personal friend.'

I looked at Harry and he looked at Andrew; Andrew coughed into his hand and said: 'I'll, ah, look after Charlie while you two talk it over, if you like.'

Harry nodded. 'Will you excuse us for a minute?' he said smoothly, smiling at the agent.

The man shrugged and Harry took my arm and steered me into the bedroom, closing the door behind us.

He sighed and whistled softly, looking around at the faded cabbage roses on the wallpaper behind the bed.

'Some steal,' he said, shaking his head. 'Oh, practically daylight robbery at twice the rent we were paying in California. Still, it's cheaper than the hotel.'

'So's the Salvation Army,' I said.

Harry laughed. 'Seriously, hon, you heard Andrew say this is cheaper than anything else we'd find in the West End. And the guy who owns it *did* knock something off the rent.'

'But maybe if we looked for something a little further out—'

'Sweetpea, *that's* no good, not with the hours we keep! Think of the taxi fares!'

'Once the novelty wears off—'

Harry grinned; he was lit from within, incandescent with the glory of his dream.

'Libby,' he said softly, 'we're on a gravy train with biscuit wheels here, don't you know that yet? It'll take quite a while for the novelty to wear off a licence to steal. Listen, we can fix this place up in no time flat! We can paint, shove the furniture around until we have it the way we want it. . . .'

He looked around again, considering. 'And I know there's not a separate room for Charlie, but we can work that out too. And then later on we'll have all the time in the world to scout around for something bigger.'

I knew then that Harry really meant us to stay in London; and that with Andrew's influence there was a high probability he'd be able to come up with a job to justify a work permit and visas for the three of us. That had been his plan, and I knew it. Still, it unnerved me.

He pulled me close. 'Can I tell the man we'll take it?' he said softly into my hair.

We moved in the following day, and I set to with a will; it was make do and mend time, and for the next week or so I went nowhere in the evenings except to bed, exhausted.

I saw the flat as my mother would have seen it: far too small for us, shabby with neglect and ugly furniture; I could hear the echo of the words she'd used when she was alone with me in my off-campus apartment at college: 'Are you sure this is what you want, honey?'

She hadn't meant the apartment; if she'd been with us in London, seeing the flat near Marble Arch, she wouldn't have meant that either. She would have meant: did I want a life bound up with Harry. I had, I did.

And it was up to me to create a home where we could be a family, safe from the incursions of the outside world, no matter how far Harry chose to take us from the charted beaten track of the future I'd created for us in my earthbound imagination.

I didn't allow myself to dwell on the future, rooting myself instead in the here and now of immediate practicalities: I scrubbed those rooms as I'd never scrubbed before, on my hands and knees in jeans and tee-shirt, my hair tied back with a square of cotton. I scraped and scoured and emptied endless buckets of blackened water until the place shone clean. I bought a secondhand cot and a folding screen from a junk shop in the Portobello Road which, with the rearrangement of a wardrobe, made a little room for Charlie within the bedroom. I pulled down the hideous curtains and folded them away, replacing them in the bedroom with new ones, gay and bright, in the living room with green plants in

135

hanging wicker baskets. I stocked the kitchen with as many staples as its restricted storage space would hold; I bought plates and cups and silverware and pots and pans, sheets and towels and pillowcases – things we'd given away to friends in California or stored with the furniture because they could easily be replaced and would have been prohibitively expensive to ship. I rented a television, arranged to have a telephone installed, ordered a daily paper and the delivery of milk. Buoyed by momentum, I took Charlie into the disused garden while I made inroads on the tangled dusty weeds until I'd cleared it.

Meanwhile Harry, out killing buffalos while I homesteaded, came home most nights well past midnight and was careful not to wake me; at midday, ready to go out again with Andrew, carrying his coffee cup, he marvelled at the transformation I had wrought.

One morning he said, 'It's high time I give the punters a break while we paint the joint. What do you say?'

'Oh Harry!' I hugged him, and he laughed.

'After all, we can't have you breaking your pretty neck on a ladder.'

Those days were precious, just the three of us, Charlie being gently coaxed away from turpentine and thick creamy emulsion while I painted walls while Harry painted ceilings.

I fell in love with him all over again, seeing him again in jeans and a checkered cotton shirt that might have been the outfit he'd been wearing the afternoon I met him, and went for coffee with him for the first time.

When we'd painted ourselves out for the day, we held hands in the misty midsummer afternoons, walking down the Bayswater Road, turning right into Queensway (Chinese dried mushrooms, a wok) or, in the other direction, to the Oxford Street department stores with their food halls (Mexican tortillas and taco spices, California wine), things we missed, familiar dinners prepared some-

136

how or other in the kitchen so small we couldn't stand there together, unless we were locked in an embrace.

Our evenings were spent alone, just Harry and me sprawled on the sitting room floor after Charlie was asleep, sharing the remains of the wine we'd drunk with dinner, touching, floating into one another's arms, taking flight.

My doubts and fears about the future receded, then evaporated, bad dreams washed away by the clear light of what I felt for Harry, what I'd always felt for him, and were forgotten.

When we were satisfied we'd done everything we could to camouflage the flat, Harry rang Andrew and invited him to dinner.

'He'll think I died,' he said, smiling at me.

'Nonsense!' I said gaily. 'Tell him to bring Caroline.'

He looked at me doubtfully. 'She won't come, Lib, you know that. Hell, we've never even met her, and we've known Andrew for a couple of months.'

'All the more reason to check her out.'

It would be a start towards getting some sort of social life going – another step towards normality.

We'd done our best with the flat and needn't be ashamed; it shone with cleanliness, gleamed with new paint, glowed with colour. Surely Caroline would appreciate that. Caroline, the elusive aloof counterpoint to all that Andrew most deeply disapproved of in himself: his reckless gambling, his rootless existence; what I had begun to sense more and more as a terrible gulf of loneliness in him. He referred to her so often, and always in terms that seemed to confirm his yearning to be respectable, and no longer alone.

'She's beautiful,' he would say earnestly, late at night in after-hours' drinking clubs, stark contrasts to the gilded glamour of the casinos where his compulsion to play roulette had got the better of him once again in spite of Harry's tutelage. His hands would play with endless cigarettes in the dim light, his hair would be rumpled, his tie at half mast.

'She's far too good for me. She told me when – I'll bet you didn't know I did two years reading law – she told me when I packed it in she'd never marry me. Oh, and she's right, no question. Caroline's not going to tie herself down to a guy who doesn't have the sense to come in out of the rain. She's right, I know it. . . . So beautiful. . . .'

Hooked, and drunk, he would be so near tears I would reach out to touch his hand. 'Oh Andrew. . . .'

And Harry would say, low and sympathetic: 'Say, old man, let's have another drink and split, okay? Things'll seem brighter in the morning, promise.'

Caroline was Andrew's dream girl; I was beginning to think of her as a person who didn't really exist except in Andrew's wistful imagination.

But she did. They came on a Tuesday evening.

And I was shocked by how strange it seemed to see Andrew against a backdrop of homely domestic peace; he was greyer than ever, a shadow who had taken substance for me in the restaurants, clubs and taxis where he was truly at home. Harry had told me, when I asked him where Andrew lived in London, that he had a bedsitting room in Knightsbridge where he slept, when he slept.

'A room with a hotplate?' I had asked. 'I thought he had money, or that his family did.'

Harry shrugged. 'The boy's got expensive hobbies, hon, you know that.'

When I thought about it it seemed appropriate that Andrew should live like that, anonymous and deflated like a ghost when the sun came out, coming alive at night.

He stammered slightly, introducing us to Caroline. She was titian-haired, with skin as pale and flawless as fine porcelain, and so tiny I towered over her.

138

'Hi! We're so pleased to meet you,' I said, feeling that my greeting was too loud, feeling too loud altogether in my peasant blouse and cotton skirt. She wore a snowy-white shirtwaist blouse with a floor-length black velvet skirt, and a plain gold chain around her neck; she was exquisite, and reminded me of a delicate miniature of a Stuart queen.

'Pleasure,' she said softly, offering her hand.

Harry was hearty, starting the ball rolling, rubbing his hands together, offering drinks.

We sat, and Charlie was admired briefly and politely in her nightie and carried off to bed. Dry sherries, drier conversation, filled the space. Caroline admired the table, my masterpiece of cool green cloth and darker linen napkins, fresh flowers.

At dinner her fragile hand kept flying to her throat, and she ate around the garlic sausage in the cassoulet, picked at the green salad and fresh raspberry sorbet, refused a second glass of wine.

After coffee she said, 'I've enjoyed this so much,' and glanced at Andrew, who stood up as though he'd been catapulted from his chair, spilled his brandy down his trousers, and looked mortified.

'We, ah, have to be going,' he said. 'Caroline's got an early start at work. . . .'

'Oh well, sure!' Harry said. 'Well, well, we're glad you could make it – hope we'll be doing this more often.'

Caroline offered her hand and smiled, I smiled, Harry smiled, Andrew looked sick, and they were gone. Harry and I blinked at each other.

'Wow,' I said.

'Wow *squared*,' he answered.

Andrew's hospitality at the Plaza Grill the following Thursday, sans Caroline, was genuine and generous, more than

139

lightly sprinkled with half-guilty apologies. In the end he made a little speech of it.

'Caroline wanted me to tell you what a marvellous time she had the other evening,' he said. 'She' – he coughed – 'lives with her parents, and it's awfully difficult for her to have friends in.'

He was telling us we wouldn't be invited back.

Harry and I, trading compassionate, complacently happily married glances, made it easy for him.

9

Living in a flat was infinitely preferable to living in an hotel.
And even though we'd only be there for a month or so, the
money we'd put into making it bright and clean seemed well
spent. As Harry said, 'The only thing we bought that we
can't take back with us is the paint.'

'You'd want the furniture?'

'We could sell it. You know, gen-u-wine souvenirs of a
London furnished flat: a kitchen table with a gamey leg,
neatly supported on three paperback books, an occasional
chair that lives up to its name by occasionally collapsing.
After all, somebody bought London Bridge.'

'We all make mistakes. Who knows? We might make a
fortune.'

We could make light of its deficiencies, pleased with
ourselves that we'd found a temporary base. Our flight-
weight luggage was empty, our clothes hung in wardrobes
or neatly folded in drawers.

And if there wasn't much space, at least two rooms plus
kitchen and bathroom and a front door that closed us off
from the other flats in the building made it home.

I made the most of it, pleased I had the time in which to
learn something of the rhythm of the British way of life at
first hand.

The greengrocer soon knew us on sight. He was a tall and
still handsome man in his sixties who teased me almost daily
in his shop that smelled blissfully of oranges when I asked
for 'to-may-toes', and chucked Charlie under the chin and
said she reminded him of his youngest grandchild. He
presented her with carefully-polished apples, and he told

me exuberant tall tales of the fun he'd had in Pensacola, Florida, doing his RAF pilot training.

And I drank a mug of tea sometimes with the middle-aged couple who owned the paper shop; they were so taken with Charlie's toothy smile they wouldn't hear of my paying for her ice-cream cornets when I went there to buy magazines.

And when the girl who lived in the top floor flat arrived home one Saturday from shopping just as I did, and insisted on carrying Charlie's pushchair up the outside stairs while I negotiated Charlie and the groceries, I invited her to come in for a coffee.

'Or tea?' I asked, smiling, extending my hand. 'I'm Libby Franklin, and this is Charlie.'

She grinned, and her brown eyes danced. 'I'm Sally Barlow,' she said. 'Welcome to England.'

She came in for half an hour or so; we chatted amiably; I liked her, and I could tell she liked me. She was dark-haired and slender and pretty and about my age, as keen to hear about life in America as I was to hear about life in England.

When I mentioned we'd be leaving London at the end of the summer, she shook her head ruefully.

'Why is it I always seem to meet people just as they're about to leave? I suppose that's what living in London is all about.' And she made me promise to visit her whenever I could.

That evening, over dinner in a restaurant Andrew had chosen for its authentic Mexican cuisine and atmosphere – complete with *mariachi* players – I told Harry and Andrew about Sally.

They exchanged a glance, and Andrew offered me a toast.

'To an ambassador without portfolio, and the friendly natives, and – and hands across the Atlantic, and all that!'

'Hear, hear!' Harry said, raising his glass. And then, smiling at me, 'How'd you like to stay on in London awhile, darlin'?'

142

I drank. I smiled. I was aware of the sparkle of my bangle earrings, the pleasure of being a pretty woman in an expensive restaurant.

'I hadn't thought about it,' I murmured. 'If we outstay our visas, however,' I added, 'they'll have us up as' – I cupped my hand delicately over Harry's ear – '*wetbacks*.'

Harry roared with laughter and provided a quick *sotto voce* translation for Andrew, who laughed so helplessly he spluttered wine.

'No fear,' Harry said solemnly. 'Our tourist visas can be extended for at least another three months without question by the simple expedient of our showing up in East Croydon at the Alien's Registration Office, looking prosperous. No need to sweem across ze border, *senora!*' He winked at Andrew. 'That would give us a lot more time to – manoeuvre.'

I looked from Andrew to Harry; they beamed at me, the Gold Dust Twins.

'A bit more time to find a berth in British industry for my favourite player here,' Andrew said. 'I know it can be done. It must be done subtly, of course.' He smiled at Harry. 'That may take a little time.'

'How do you feel about that, honey?' Harry asked.

I sobered, considering. I said, 'Staying on in London – indefinitely?'

'Oh, pay no attention to my ambitious friend here with his grandiose plans for the distant future,' Harry said carelessly, dismissing Andrew with a playful wave. 'Think of staying on until November.'

Then gravely, seriously, meeting my eyes, 'You do like it here, don't you, babe?'

'Oh I love it, you know I do! Harry, it's the most wonderful holiday I've ever had.' *The six month holiday he'd wanted.*

The Home Office clerk who stamped our visa extensions was courteous but very firm when he told us it would be difficult to extend them a second time. Unless one of us were to be offered suitable permanent employment, he added, smiling indulgent regret as though that was a highly unlikely prospect, we would have to leave Great Britain by the end of November.

November was a dark brown word that belonged to the unlighted future, nothing to do with us. And the present was a portrait of one long perfect day with the sky stretched like a strong blue canvas on which the sun shone resplendent through the wealthy leaves of trees, the evenings delicate pastels that faded to sepia edged with gold.

Late lazy mornings and lingering afternoons, strawberries red as postboxes and rows along the Serpentine with our fingers trailing in the water.

Indulgent evenings filled with splendour and excitement, tinkling glass and sparkling crystal, indifferent fortunes won or lost in a principality of dazzling careless brilliance, ruled by cubes of ivory on green baize, the flick of playing cards.

Coming back to reality was slow and painful, a reluctant process, like the awareness of awakening from an unbearably beautiful dream induced by some powerfully seductive opiate.

I caught a cold from Charlie, I shivered and burned. I went to see Andrew's smart West End doctor at Harry's insistence; I sat and leafed through back issues of *Country Life* in a turkey-carpeted waiting room set about with tapestry-seated chairs and polished tables on which empty vases stood, where bucolic landscapes and desperate sea battles lined the walls, and the sun was an intruder through the casement window.

I was run down, he said, perhaps I should take more rest, oh certainly that, and vitamins as well for a time. I was very thin, too thin perhaps; I should take care.

I took the vitamins but there was very little rest; I was exhausted, trying to lead two lives, not sleeping enough. Reality was brutally exhausting. Evening after evening I was decorative and charming by Harry's side, trying not to stumble as I tripped the light fantastic. Evening after evening I accompanied him to what began to seem like the same glossy restaurant, the same exclusive casino, the same wealthy out-of-town punter's lavish suite of hotel rooms, serving as venue for the same poker session.

I was Don Juan in hell; I was on a glittering treadmill that never lead to pleasure, and never stopped turning long enough for me to jump off.

No one else there with me seemed to notice or to mind; they seemed to have no need or inclination to do anything except eat in restaurants and play cards in clubs or hotel bedrooms. It was as if their lives began at dusk and ended promptly at dawn, that they were actors on an enormous film set, all false fronts and no jelly beans in the general store. The script was a non-starter: conversations, when there were any, never varied.

Night after night I listened politely while Harry and his growing coterie analysed the games they had played, the games they were about to play. Occasionally, as a tantalizing courteous gesture, someone would turn to me to make a general remark about the weather, or to ask after Charlie, or to issue some vague invitation to 'come out to the country some weekend – you must. Fine weather this year, quite remarkable the way it's lasted, you two must have brought it with you. Mustn't waste it, wife and kiddies'd be delighted if you came out to us. . . .'

Those invitations were part of the script, empty lines, content no more substantial than mechanical expressions of generalized gallantry and good will, on a par with bits of business like lighting cigarettes or holding chairs. They were never mentioned twice. They were never specified, date and place and time.

At dawn the playhouse emptied. The pellucid innocent morning sky shamed my burning painted eyes; my artful silken good-time clothes were fancy-dress, an affront to the sweet borning day.

And while Harry slept, held deeply in the dream, I shed my night skin and was there for Charlie, wearing jeans; there for the daily round of shopping and playing in the park, cups of tea and cornets of ice cream, laundry and cooking and the mundane crises of defective power points exposed too near the floor, accessible to Charlie's exquisite inquisitive fingers.

I longed for sleep; I longed for wakefulness; I longed for a return to a life filled with people who talked of anything except their obsessive preoccupation with games and gambling; I longed for the textured fabric of a life that wasn't a rhinestone-studded cardboard imitation of the real thing. I longed for home. Our holiday had gone on beyond its time.

Another holiday surfaced behind my eyes, one my parents planned the summer I was ten; we would go to Wyoming, to Yellowstone National Park, they promised; we would see Smokey the Bear, and Old Faithful the geyser that shot boiling spring water high into the air every hour by the clock; we would eat in restaurants and sleep in motels. I was so excited about the trip I didn't sleep for two whole nights before we left, and when we got there I wanted to stay forever. The holiday was all I hoped; but it ended, as I knew it would.

When we were on our way home, the car broke down in some dusty Wyoming town, and we were forced to stay there one whole week while it was being fixed. My mother made the best of it. She took me and my brothers out to buy us cowboy hats, and to the local rodeo; she made the extra time away from home seem like a bonus treat, unscheduled but all the more delicious for it. So many more nights in a motel with miniature wrapped soaps, so many more meals out.

146

My father took it hard. Day after day he paced up and down, hands behind his back, in the forecourt of the garage where he had left the car. And when we finally pulled into the gravel driveway at home in Lemonade Springs, he heaved a great sigh of relief and turned to mom and said, 'Home sweet home! Never again, eh Nora? Never, never again.'

Mom's exasperation broke through. 'Gol' darn it, John, don't be such a grizzle-guts! No harm done, was there? Business still goin, ain't it? Home not burned down?'

After that, my mother emerged for me as the dancer, always the one to take us out to eat spareribs with our fingers with our elbows on the table, to gasp in contraband delight in Las Vegas when the one-armed bandit paid off and her paper cup was full to overflowing. While my father found excuses to stay behind, with a freezer full of food.

But my mother, teaching me the joy of holidays and pleasures taken gaily, had also taught me to know when to go back to base, back to reality. Knowing when to do that was part of the pleasure, because the base and the reality were home, and sweet.

And I was beginning to realize, with painful insight sharpened by fatigue, that for Harry the tinselled carousel of the high-level London gambling scene might be more real and solid than anything he had ever known.

That the whole shimmering chimera would never fade for him; that he had tasted a drug he would need for the rest of his life in ever-increasing quantities, in order to feel alive. That he would be bitter and empty and burnt-out if it were withdrawn.

I hoped with all my heart it wasn't so, that he would awaken and emerge beside me, shaken but willing to learn to walk on solid ground.

For my sake, for his own. Most of all, for Charlie's. She needed the world's reality, a base and a home. She needed a mother who wasn't poleaxed by fatigue and lassitude, a father who wasn't permanently absent, riding on a rainbow.

147

I sensed that Harry's awakening would have to mean leaving London and going back to California, or at least back to a place where the temptation to embrace the dream would not be always present, always sweetly tantalizing, always available for the price of a taxi.

So I waited for the *deus ex machina* of mundane practicalities to descend; and I thought I saw it coming.

In spite of Andrew's constant lobbying on Harry's behalf, his desperately frenzied attempts to come up with something, anything, that would do the trick and keep us Franklins legally in England – and in spite of Harry's wholehearted cooperation – Harry had not been offered a job.

And we had begun to have money worries.

Harry was still winning, seldom losing, playing as carefully as ever, and for much higher stakes; but our outgoings, always high, had spiralled. And I was fairly certain that although my secret nest egg was intact, Harry's was not, quite.

Caught up in the relentless pace of lights that never went out and music that always played, Harry had hired a Savile Row tailor; had himself measured for handmade shoes; booked weekly manicures and hairstyles from one of the most expensive salons in the West End. These were investments, he said – feverishly, uneasily – digging into his stash.

Finally, to save face for him, there was the man in East Croydon with the ink-stained fingers who had put a deadline on all the insanity in faded purple letters, unequivocal nonetheless:

'The condition attached to the grant of leave to land is hereby varied so as to require that the holder:
(1) Does not remain in the United Kingdom later than 30 NOVEMBER 1983
(2) Does not enter any employment, paid or unpaid, while in the United Kingdom.
For Under Secretary of State, Home Office. Dated.

148

Meanwhile I stayed balanced on the high-wire in my spangled tights, working without a net. There for Charlie, there for Harry.

To keep myself going gracefully I allowed myself to build a dream of Christmas, which I elaborated as lavishly as any gingerbread castle as I went along.

We would spend it in Montana with my parents, cosy and cherished and welcomed and listened to with awed pleasure as we spoke of England in front of the huge open fire in their living room while it snowed outside and the mountains etched white in the distance beyond the warmth.

Harry would play rummy with my dad in let-bygones-be-bygones camaraderie for matchsticks at the kitchen table. They'd drink beer together while mother and Charlie and I bustled around the kitchen, mom slipping stuffed dates to Charlie when I wasn't looking, saying 'aw never mind!' when I caught her at it. Mother and I laughing while we performed our time-honoured tradition of sneaking behind each other's backs to add another teensy drop of rum to the pumpkin pie mixture.

Reprise: 'I'll be home for Christmas. . . .'

Alternately, interchangeably, depending on my mood, Harry and Charlie and I would spend Christmas in California in the flat we would have rented, magically the same one we had left, laughing while we opened our presents, because it was raining instead of snowing. Waiting for the phone to ring and my mother to call out, 'Hey, you guys, where the hell are you with the snow shovel?'

Harry and me reminiscing about our fabulous holiday in London, me praising him to the skies for having given it to us just as he'd planned and promised, painting it as a luminous interlude that would shine in memory long after our grandchildren were old enough to be bored, hearing us tell of it one more time.

Reprise: 'I did my best for you – me and my drum . . .'

Harry under lamplight Christmas night, tackling his

149

thick, incomprehensible textbooks while I roasted pheasant and made vinaigrette for the cold asparagus.

'. . . *ta rump-a-bump-bum – me and my drum*. . . .'

Late one sultry October afternoon when black-bellied grey clouds lowered, and thunder filled the heavy air, Harry came home grinning hugely with suppressed excitement, his arms full of long-stemmed red roses and a bottle of champagne.

I was sitting on the sofa beside Charlie, reading to her – or rather, listening proudly while she read to me. At fifteen months she could at least pretend to do that because she'd memorized most of her dog-eared favourite story books, and could say most of the words intelligibly – or at least they were intelligible to me.

Harry came to us and scooped her up and tickled her, threw back his head and laughed with her, and then he bent down and kissed the top of my head and placed the flowers in my lap with great tenderness before he went into the kitchen for glasses and a towel. Charlie followed him, clapping her hands.

'Red roses for the ladies I love,' he called over his shoulder. 'And bubbly for Mama Bear and Papa Bear, apple juice for Baby Bear, and water for the posies. Then the good news.'

I laughed. 'Harry, what on earth—'

He came back with the glasses. He popped the champagne cork just as the first sheets of rain pelted the windows.

'I – found – a – job!'

'Oh Harry!'

My heart plummetted and my mouth went dry; I took the full glass he handed me; I looked up into his jubilant face and began to cry.

He sat down next to me and pulled me close.

150

'Baby doll, what did I say? What is it?'

I shook my head helplessly and began to sob in earnest. He held me so I was scrunched up against him. I could feel Charlie's roundly plump little leg against my arm as she climbed onto the sofa and began to cry in sympathy. I could smell both of them, Charlie's baby powder sweetness and Harry's salty cleanliness with its backbeat of the subtle cologne he used.

'Sugar?' he coaxed, bewildered.

'Harry, oh Harry, we were going *home* for Christmas! Home, Harry! Oh Harry, Harry. . . .'

His arms tightened around me. 'Shh, shh – sweetheart. We're having a ball here, aren't we? Now come on, dry your eyes and drink up and I'll tell you all about it. Come on, honey.'

'Harry, our visas expire—'

'At the end of November. Sure, I know that! Hey presto, a job, with a working visa and even a salary thrown in for good measure. We're on our way, toots, can't miss!'

I burrowed into him, wanting to hide, wishing with all my heart I could put the whole out-of-focus puzzle of Harry straight, wondering crazily how all my love could save him, wake him up, save all of us. Wanting to go home, wanting him to want it too.

'Harry,' I whispered. 'We were supposed to go home. . . .'

He sighed and smoothed a tendril of hair away from my forehead. 'Honey, we *are* home. Home is any place we are, so long as the three of us are together, right? Oh sweetie, I know it's been a bit rough this last month or so, but this is going to make all the difference. Now come on, hon, let me tell you all about it.'

I drew away a little and looked into his eyes, shining with the dream of it. I wanted to call to him, to shake him gently the way I did sometimes to wake him up in the morning.

151

'Honey, we were going home at the end of November, remember?' I said softly. 'Home for Christmas.'

'Sweetpea, I've got a job here now. I *told* you.'

'Sure, Harry, but—'

'Hey, baby, just listen while I tell you about it, okay?'

He grinned, relieved, fully restored to enthusiasm.

'Well now, where shall I start? The whole thing's more or less connected with computer software, designing video games or some damn thing. American knowhow needed to cover the markets they hope to corner. That's what it'll say on the forms, anyway. . . .'

He chuckled and shook his head. 'Crazy, really, but it looks like it'll work. This guy we know wants to form a team of four to play tournament bridge. The geezer has money to burn, and he really fancies his chances, especially if he can make it sweet enough to get Andrew and me in with him. He knows enough about bridge – just enough, I might add – to realize how good we are. So he's offered to foot the bills for travel, stuff like that, hotels. And he's willing to cover for me visa-wise by putting me on his corporation's payroll. I'll get a nominal salary, and every once in a while I come up with an idea, why not?'

I nodded, still numb. 'An idea – for a video game.'

'Right.'

'Like, ah, Space Invaders?'

'That's it! It's a real kick in the head, don't you think? Can't you just see me inventing a programme complete with moonshots and little green/blue/red/yellow monsters darting in/out/up/down to whoops and screeches?'

'Well. . . .'

He laughed, lit a cigarette, shrugged. 'It's a living. Listen, hon, how about we really celebrate tonight? I'll call the agency for a sitter—'

'Harry?'

'Hm?'

'Could we make it just the three of us tonight, just you

152

and me and Charlie? Maybe we could have a pizza at the place around the corner.'

'Just a downhome family get together, with authentic British pizza, bland as library paste, right?'

'Sure, why not? Charlie loves it,' I said.

He ruffled my hair. 'Sure,' he said, 'why not?'

When Harry's work permit and our visas came through, our passports duly and legally stamped in the same faded purple ink I had counted on as our salvation, my uneasiness about the network of lies and evasions on which the whole tenuous unrealistic scheme was based haunted me for days.

It frightened me badly to have to face what I felt was true – that Harry was so thoroughly hooked on his artificial world, so enchanted by its sorcery he was willing to go to any lengths to make it possible to stay – that there was little or nothing left for me to hope for that might bring him out of it.

The 'job' was so transparently manufactured that he might eventually be found out, of course, and the visas revoked; that might set him free, set us free.

But if that happened he would be culpable, and surely held responsible. That was cold comfort; if that happened, we would all be sent back to the States in disgrace, or possibly Harry would be imprisoned.

There was little or nothing I could do about any of it. I would just have to try harder to make the best of things because, for the moment at least, that was all there was to do.

I also had to face the fact that the blame for what I saw as our predicament was at least partly mine. I had let things slide, trusting to luck and events outside my control to write our happy ending.

I had said 'yes' when I should have said 'no', and far too often. Not to be a nag, not to rain on Harry's parade.

I began to withdraw, to retreat into depression and guilt and ennui; I despised myself for that, but I couldn't find my way out of the maze.

When Harry and Andrew were officially launched on the tournament bridge circuit, I went with them to France at the end of October, to Italy in November.

I saw little of Paris or Rome except the interior of hotel ballrooms, little more of Harry than the back of his head, of Andrew his thin white nervous hands on the backs of thirteen cards.

Harry still looked at me with pride, when he turned to look; Andrew still watched us both with a raw, naked longing, as if he were a kid with his nose pressed against a bakery window, yearning for what Harry and I shared. But the cake on display was cardboard, the frosting plaster of paris. My fragile bubble of happiness was wobbling, its rainbow colours running and threatening to fade away.

More and more often I began to say I'd decided to stay home for the evening. To watch television, to read. To sleep.

'Pace too hectic, hon?' Harry said.

'I'm a little tired.'

'We'll miss you.'

'Your friends'll keep you company.'

'They're your friends too, sweetpea.'

'We don't really have all that much in common.'

'You should learn a couple of card games, you know? You'd be good, I know you would.'

I smiled. 'I don't think so, hon. But maybe some evening we could invite a couple of people here for dinner. . . .'

'Well, I don't know,' he said, considering, frowning.

I wanted to break off a piece of my heart and hand it to him so he would notice me, so he would really look at me and see what was happening. But he was too far away, so far away the aching sadness I felt was too deep for ordinary tears.

154

He grinned and snapped his fingers, inspired. 'Say, why not ring Caroline? She and Andrew haven't been over for dinner since we moved in.'

'She's pretty busy. . . .'

'Yeah. Well what about your girlfriend, the one upstairs? What's her name?' They'd never met.

'Sally.'

'Why not go up and invite her for a coffee, lift a jar?'

I smiled again. 'Maybe I will.'

'Great. But get some sleep, you hear? Don't wait up for me.'

More and more often, I didn't.

And I avoided Sally. I liked her, but I hardly knew her; I could hardly go upstairs and pour out my heart to her. And meaningless small talk was the last thing I needed; I'd had enough of that to last me the rest of my life.

So I brooded, sifting through emotions that frightened and exhausted me; and I tried to think, and got nowhere.

Night after night I stood over Charlie's cot, watching her sleep by the light from the street. Trusting, peaceful, beautiful; night after night I wondered painfully what I was doing to her by doing nothing, wondering where it would end.

One night my thoughts took me so far down within myself they seemed to crystallize at a nadir. I was angry with Harry, ashamed of his blindness and his folly. Charlie would feel that, catch it as though it were some terrible contagious disease. And she would writhe in shame, not knowing what to say when she went to school and the other kids asked her what her daddy did for a living.

I struggled against that. I cancelled it, I hadn't really thought it, it wasn't so, it wouldn't happen. I loved Harry, I couldn't betray him. I had come too far with him for that. Everything would work out for the best; Charlie would be fine.

That night I waited up for Harry, or tried to.

His key in the lock startled me awake. Light was beginning to filter through the plants in the sitting room window; the high-pitched whine from the television announced that viewing time had ended hours before.

I had curled up in what passed for our one comfortable armchair, and I came to with difficulty. My foot was asleep; I stumbled when I got up to greet him.

He was tender. 'Dummy,' he said softly, catching me against him, 'you shouldn't fall asleep in chairs. And especially not that one.'

He made tea and we sat together, talking quietly until Harry thought he'd better get some sleep.

'You come too,' he said, taking my hand.

'Honey, Charlie—'

'Won't surface for at least an hour, sweetheart,' he whispered, pulling me close to him.

There was glory then: pure, untarnished, the one bridge that still stood sound, solidly connecting us.

Winter came in suddenly, the days grew miserably short, the rain was needle sharp. It was cold and getting colder.

Times were getting harder. Harry was irritable about money, critical of the amounts I spent, which was unlike him.

He spent more and more time going over the meticulous columns of figures in his notebook, frowning in intense concentration.

When his token salary cheques began – an amount not quite sufficient to pay the rent on the flat – he paid them into our London account, and he topped up the account with cash, as usual. He was generous, as usual, or as generous as he could be.

But I knew that his original bankroll was low, or even gone; that most or all of our considerable expenses were being met out of his current winnings.

More and more often he asked for the chequebook so he could draw cash at whatever club he found himself in for the evening, and I'd know a dip and swoop of anxiety when I saw how large those cheques sometimes were.

What little I could do to economize was trifling: I washed Harry's dress shirts by hand; I went out with him even less often, saving on sitters and sessions at the hairdresser's. I was saving pennies, it wasn't enough.

As winter deepened I knew I'd have to buy warm clothes to replace a lot of what we hadn't brought with us, or what we'd never owned.

We hadn't needed warm clothes. Charlie had never owned a snowsuit, mittens, flannel nightgowns. I had, of course, through all the fierce Montana winters of my childhood and later, equally intemperate winters in Iowa when I'd been at college. But all of these things I'd left behind.

More alarming still were the exorbitant expenses of Harry's lavish front, expenses he met out of the bankroll he carried around with him in a silver money clip: his tailor, his shoemaker, his gentleman's hairdresser, the lavish meals and drinks and tips, the occasional losses he sustained. I began to say, far too often, desperate to put a brake on Harry's devil-may-care spending, of the wastage, 'Harry, I need some money too.'

These requests were always made in similar circumstances, while Harry was awake but still in bed before his day began, by then established as one of the few times we had together. I resented having to make them, to be forced to think of him as some kind of benevolent sybaritic king, myself as chief petitioner.

'*More* money?'

'Yes. . . .'

'What for? Jees, babe, it doesn't grow on trees.'

'Baby needs a new pair of shoes.'

It never got a laugh.

157

Harry would screw up his eyes against the smoke from the cigarette that was becoming a more and more frequent fixture between his teeth, thinking hard.

'A C-note be enough?'

I thought that was a hundred, but I was never absolutely sure; I stood there at the end of the bed, trying to work it out, trying to figure out if a hundred pounds – if a C-note was one hundred pounds – would cover what we needed.

Harry would drag hard on the cigarette before he stubbed it out impatiently, stabbing it into the ashtray; he would stare at me and sigh, exasperated.

'One hundred quid. Make it last, would ya?'

And I would burn, shamed by the indignity of having to plead for necessities while Harry was out night after night spending cash like Daddy Warbucks.

But then I would look at him, propped up on one elbow in the bed, his hair still rumpled with sleep but his mind already working, ticking, tense, and him already rummaging for his second or third cigarette of the day. My heart would go out to him, I would think: God, if only I could reach him, hold him, open his eyes to reality, then we'd all be safe and happy.

'I'm sorry, Harry. I'll try to make it last as long as I can. Thanks.'

I'd bite my lip, furious with myself for falling into my 'please, sir' act, obsequious and grateful, and always ending with the same anxious line: 'Don't forget to leave it on the dresser.'

'You'll get it, Libby. Say, is there any chance of a cup of coffee around here? Hey, and could you remember to starch the collars of my shirts next time?'

One morning as he peeled off banknotes, his lips working as he counted them out, he said: 'You know, Lib, I would have thought you might have saved a little something all that time you were working. I was picking up most of the tabs at the time, if you remember.'

158

My neck prickled with guilty fear. I could see the close secure column of credit amounts on the most recent statement of the account I'd squirrelled away in California. For one panicked moment I was sure he could see it too.

I shrugged, and smiled at him. 'I wasn't working all that long, before the baby—'

'Long enough. Did you forget your early training in thrift?' He wasn't smiling.

'Harry—'

'That's the way it was, wasn't it? You know, "use it up, wear it out, make it do or do without"? The good ol' American work ethic, reinforced by your good ol' hardworking dad every time your mom bought an extra jar of peanut butter?'

'I spent it on clothes, things for the apartment, whatever. It went, Harry. And please, please leave my folks out of it. *I'm* here, aren't I?'

He levelled a cool measuring look at me, at the frayed jeans I was wearing with one of his worn-out cardigans, at the laundry I was diligently folding on the end of the bed while Charlie helped, patting down the tidy piles and singing.

While Charlie helped, nearly eighteen months old but still being treated much like a butterball turkey – plump and beautiful, good enough to eat – but some kind of non-person who couldn't be expected to be aware of her parents' deteriorating relationship. Surely not aware of what was going on when they wrangled, their differences ever more apparent, even though she'd put her arms around me when I broke down crying when I was putting her to bed and say, quite clearly for a non-person, 'No, no, don' cry, mama. . . .'

I glanced quickly at her, and then at Harry, willing him to realize she was watching, listening, understanding.

But he only said: 'You'd be here, babe. You know when you've got it good. But I'll just bet you saved a little something for the proverbial rainy day.'

I stopped folding laundry and offered Charlie my hand.

159

'Shall we go fix some lunch while daddy's getting dressed, honey?' I said.

'No!' she said. She climbed into the bed and snuggled up to Harry. 'Don' be sad, daddy,' she said, and Harry looked ashamed.

He kissed her with a resounding smack. '*I'm* not sad, princess!' And then he looked at me, chuckling like a department store Santa. 'Charlie Girl here's growing up fast.'

'Yes,' I said evenly. 'Yes, she is. Charlie, want some lunch? Chicken soup today.'

'Soup,' she said happily, climbing off the bed. 'Chick-en soup with *rice*!'

Harry called after me, 'Say hon, don't be sore. I didn't mean it about the dough.'

'It's okay, Harry,' I said.

But he had meant it. He was hoping pretty hard I'd saved some, and pretty sure of getting me to 'fess up and hand it over if he worked on me long enough, no longer able to see any good reason why I shouldn't be willing to ride right along with him on his rainbow, right to the end of the line, taking Charlie with me.

I was damned if I was going to do that. Somebody had to stay on dry land with a thick rope while he skated on thin ice.

But I wasn't always so certain about it; I wavered sometimes.

The day I went out with Charlie to buy the winter clothes we needed, I spent nearly everything we had in the London account. I was sorely tempted to write to my bank in California and ask them to send a draft to cover it. I could simply cash it and use it for as long as it lasted, and Harry would never know how I'd made the money he gave me last so long. He wouldn't think about it. He'd only be aware, and annoyed, if he thought the money he handed over so reluctantly didn't last long enough.

But if I began drawing on my savings, it would only delay the inevitable day of reckoning, when Harry would realize for himself that we really couldn't stay where we were, living as we were; we would have to go home so I could work while he finished school, and he could find a real job too.

And yet a few days after that, petitioning again for money, I felt so bad about how tired he looked I got as far as drafting a letter to the bank after all. A couple hundred dollars wouldn't—

But yes, it would.

Once I started digging into my savings I'd go right on doing it until we really were dependent on what Harry won – minus what Harry lavished in his clubs – until there was nothing left at all.

I tore the letter into tiny pieces and burned it carefully in an ashtray.

There was a pre-Christmas bridge tournament in Brussels; Harry and Andrew were seeded as favourites.

'You've got to come, Lib. It's a long weekend, do you good.'

'I can't, Harry. I'd like to, but—'

'What'dya mean, *can't?* Listen, toots, this is important! Big bucks! We need you there to root for us!'

I looked down at my hands. They were clenching and unclenching with a life of their own, covering my solar plexus, instinctively working to protect me.

'I, ah – Harry – we shouldn't spend that kind of money on sitters right now, and, ah, I think Charlie's going down with something anyway. We can't leave her with a stranger—'

'Oh, that's rich!'

'Harry—'

'That really takes the cake! You've been leaving the kid

161

five days a week for damn near her whole life without giving it a second thought, so—'

'Not when she's sick, Harry.'

'She looks okay to me.'

'Harry, you're only with her for about twenty minutes a day, top weight!'

'So that's it. You don't approve of what I'm doing, do you, toots? That's why you've been turning into old Mother Hubbard while I've been busting my butt trying to make it, isn't it? *Isn't it?*'

I shook hair out of my eyes. 'Harry, this isn't – working out for us, not really. I—'

'You're eating regularly, aren't you?'

I closed my eyes; I felt as though all the barriers that had ever separated me from Harry were knitting themselves into a badly tangled cat's cradle, never to be unravelled except by being torn apart with brutal force. It was like a Chinese puzzle, the kind that imprisons its victim's fingers remorselessly – drawing tighter and tighter still with each desperate attempt to break free of it. I'd had one of those in my Christmas stocking once: a delicate mesh of bamboo strands woven together with infinite patience, endlessly frustrating until I learned that the only way to defeat it and to free myself was to relax while I thought my way out of it.

Cat's cradle. Chinese puzzle: voluntary prisons, harmless games. The struggle between Harry and me was voluntary too, and a game.

But it wasn't harmless. And there was no kindly parent watching fondly over my shoulder, patiently guiding me while I mastered the technique.

I sighed, tired from the effort. 'Damn it, Harry, we can't afford to hire a sitter while we both go to Brussels! Not if we're going to pay the rent and have a halfway decent Christmas, and . . . Charlie *is* coming down with something.'

I started to cry. Harry pulled me to him and caressed my hair, contrite.

'Honey, I'm sorry. Listen, we're going to have the biggest wingding of a Christmas ever, you hear? And in the new year—'

'Harry, I want to go home. It's time to go home, Harry. . . .'

He kissed my cheek. 'We can't leave now, sweetpea,' he whispered, 'not when I've almost made it. We've got to give it a fair shot, babe. . . .'

Harry gave Brussels a fair shot; he and Andrew won the tournament and a great deal of money on side bets.

Harry sat beside me on the bed when he got home, laughing jubilantly, telling me all about it while we watched Charlie eating the marzipan pigs and chocolate letters he'd brought her from Belgium, taking it in turns to make sure she didn't scratch her chicken pox.

10

---❖---

'Wake up, Lib, we've got company.'

I recognized Harry's voice from very far away, invading my dream; I mumbled something and burrowed back into my pillow. He started shaking my shoulder with rhythmic persistence, and I surfaced reluctantly.

'Harry . . . ?'

'Come on, hon, they're waiting for us.'

I groped for his hand, frightened. 'Who is?'

'Some guys I know. They're in the living room, waiting for us. I told them you'd fix us something to eat. Rise and shine, hon.'

Harry switched on the bedside lamp, and I blinked into the sudden light. He was standing there like a prize fighter's second, holding my dressing gown ready for me to get up and shove my arms into it.

The soft flowing dark green velour dressing gown he'd given me for Christmas. Our fourth together, our second with Charlie.

Subdued, much like any other day except for the tree and ornaments and coloured lights, the tinsel and turkey, the telephone call from Montana at the crack of dawn.

My mother. 'Merry Christmas, honey. Gosh, it must be exciting, your first Christmas in England. Is it snowing? Did you get the box I sent?' My wave of gut wrenching homesickness when I heard her voice.

My father's embarrassed joviality, further strangled by Telestar. 'Hope Santa's good to all of you.'

Charlie's carefully coached 'Merry Chrissmuss, gamma. Merry Christmas, gampa.'

Harry's restrained but cordial monosyllables of greeting after three hours' sleep.

Harry and I opened presents sitting on the floor beside the tree I'd hauled from the greengrocer's, with Charlie sandwiched wriggling and squealing with delight between us. We tickled and hugged her as she chewed and crumpled all the pretty wrapping paper, grew sentimental over the fact that this was the first Christmas she was aware of. For a couple of hours we were in our charmed circle again, a family.

Around lunchtime Andrew came by to toast the season, bearing lavish gifts, including an elaborate dolls' house for Charlie that was fitted with curtains and furniture and even pictures on the walls that could be taken down and dusted by the parlour maid, who was dressed – like the doll family she served – in mid-Victorian costume. It was a treasure I couldn't imagine Charlie appreciating until she was at least ten years old.

Then Harry broached the sudden unexpected but essential poker game he and Andrew could not afford to skip, even if it was Christmas, saying 'No rest for the wicked!', dimpling at me in complicity because he'd promised me, late on Christmas Eve while we finished wrapping Charlie's presents and listened to jazz carols together, that everything would be different in the new year.

They were in too much of a hurry to eat a full-scale Christmas dinner, so I offered turkey sandwiches instead. Andrew at first declined, but when Harry said go on, I'm having one, he changed his mind. They ate quickly, and then they went off together.

On leaving, Harry said, 'Say, hon, why don't you give that girl upstairs a shout, invite her down for a drink or something. You said she was good company.'

'She's off visiting her family over Christmas,' I said.

'Oh sure, she would be. Christmas is a big deal in England, right Andrew? Goes on for ever.'

Andrew nodded shortly, studied his shoes, coughed.

'Honey, you're not sore about my going out?' Harry said, low and intimate, halfway through the door, buttoning his overcoat.

'I'm not sore, Harry. Good luck.'

In the dying afternoon I sat down at the table set for two to eat turkey and the trimmings, alone with Charlie delighted to be propped on pillows so she could reach. I lighted the candles, which delighted her further; I polished off the chilled Chablis I'd opened, which did nothing at all to quell the maudlin self-pity that was becoming so habitual.

I played with Charlie on the floor and read to her from the huge book of fairy tales my mother had sent as one of her gifts. I sang 'Jingle Bells' and 'It Came Upon a Midnight Clear' slowly so that Charlie could join in, and felt awful when I saw the puzzled frown in her eyes because I kept swiping at tears.

After she was in bed I broke down and sobbed. It was the first lonely Christmas in my life.

On New Year's Eve there was a party in a restaurant, subscribed by Harry and Andrew and their cohorts and consorts – those who wished or deigned to come – among whom even Caroline appeared for once, exquisite in flowing white chiffon, a vestal virgin, the only woman there I'd met before.

There was a prearranged set menu and unlimited booze, paper hats and cardboard horns that rolled out paper tongues when you blew on them and a lot of drunken *bonhomie* at the tables. The high spot of the evening was Andrew getting up to dance alone to piped *Zorba the Greek* music, while Caroline sat rigidly transfixed, appalled, not knowing where to look when he began to take his clothes off and the Spanish waiter took him aside and asked him anxiously to 'sit down *pliz*, sir.'

Then it was January, dun grey and limitless, and holding no further surprises.

Except for Harry standing beside the bed, shaking my dressing gown matador-fashion, inviting me to charge.

'Come on, Lib, I can't wait all night.'

I sat up and rubbed my eyes. 'Where're we going? What's the matter?'

'Jesus, nothing's the matter. I told you, we've got company and they're hungry; it's very simple. Come on, get up.'

I glanced at the alarm clock and winced.

'It's two thirty in the morning, Harry. Go away, I'm sleepy.'

I tried to sink back into the pillow, but Harry hauled me forward by the shoulders until I was sitting up again; he'd been drinking, I could smell it.

'Harry—'

'Come on, sweetpea. I brought some people home for dinner, just like you told me.'

'It isn't dinnertime, Harry. It's the middle of the everloving night, for pete's sake!'

'Aw, come on, honey, rally for me, would ya?'

Half playfully he began to drag the duvet off the bed. 'Say, hon, do you have the makings for chili? That'd be great,' he said.

I knew when I was beaten; I knew how to walk along the path of least resistance. I said, reaching for my dressing gown, 'Okay, Harry, I'll get up and feed the people. But we'll talk this whole thing over in the morning, all right?'

'Sure, hon, you got it. I just wanted my pals to meet you, find out for themselves what a great cook you are.' He grinned and dimpled, magnanimous in victory. He'd pulled a fast one on me, he'd won. He was pleased as a little kid who'd got away with murder; but he'd be sorry in the morning.

Charlie stirred in her corner and began to whimper.

Harry whirled towards the sound then faced me again, his eyes glowing. He snapped his fingers, inspired.

167

'Hey, tell you what, let's make a *real* party out of this! Let's invite ol' Charlie Girl!'

'Harry don't!'

But he was already across the room, lifting Charlie gently out of her cot and nuzzling her. 'Who's my special girl, hey? You know what's what, don't you, sugar? Ooh, baby, they're going to love you to pieces!'

Charlie looked up into her father's face, wide-awake and laughing and adoring, ready for anything. And that was that.

There were three men in the other room, none of whom I'd met, sitting around the table on which Harry had set out bottles and glasses.

The men scraped back their chairs and stood as we came in, Harry behind me with Charlie in his arms; they began to shuffle and fidget with their loosened ties, their tousled hair, not knowing where to look or what to do or say.

The room was blue with cigarette smoke and there was a faintly rancid smell of booze, as in a tavern; no one was actually reeling, but it was obvious that all of them were well on the way to being drunk.

Even so, they were mortified by the appearance of a woman and a child. They may have been half-tanked but they were English, and if they hadn't actually heard Harry's determined attempts to drag me out of bed and my resistance, they had the wit to imagine it, and sufficiently good manners to try to pretend they hadn't.

I smiled at them, feeling sorry for their discomfiture; they'd had too much to drink and when Harry invited them back, they came. It wasn't their fault he'd prised his wife and infant daughter out of bed to entertain them.

They said, almost in chorus, that they weren't hungry, that I shouldn't go to any trouble, that it was late, that they were just on the point of leaving to go home.

'No no, gentlemen, it's the shank of the evening!' Harry cried. 'My house is your house.'

They sat down again. Harry, dandling Charlie on his knee, the picture of fond indulgent fatherhood, refreshed the drinks all round and put his own glass to Charlie's lips at intervals, so she could taste his scotch and join the party.

He poured a drink for me and brought it to the kitchen; he kissed me with loud smacking noises while I diced onions, opened a tin of kidney beans, browned minced beef, stretched up to reach the chili spice in the rack above the cooker.

'You're one in a million, you know that?' he said.

The party ended as the sun came up; Harry went immediately to bed, staggering a little. He came to shortly after lunch, groaning and holding his head and looking sheepish, pleading for bromide and forgiveness.

'That was a hell of a thing to do to you and Charlie,' he said contritely.

I was restrained. 'It makes for a long day,' I said, handing him a cup of coffee.

'I'm sorry, Libby, I really am. Forgive me?'

'I forgive you. But Harry—'

He held up a hand for peace. 'I know what you're going to say, sweetheart. Don't worry, it won't happen again.' He crossed his heart and smiled disarmingly. 'Promise.'

Light woke me, high glaring light from the overhead fixture in the middle of the ceiling, not the bedside lamp. Before I realized what was happening, Harry yanked the duvet off the bed and I was cold.

'Hi there,' he said. His voice was soft and he was smiling, but there was an ugly edge of menace in it. I shivered, sitting up in bed.

'What time is it? What's the matter?'

'Christ, here we go again. It's about 1:30 and nothing's the matter, why should it be? You sound like a broken record. I just want you to get up and fix a snack for us.'

169

'Us?'

'That's what I said.'

'Harry, you promised you wouldn't do this again.'

'What the hell are you talking about?'

'You said you wouldn't wake me up in the middle of the night—'

'Night? *Night*? I *work* all night, Libby, or hadn't you noticed? I work my guts out, and then you have the nerve to sit there like some prissy suburban housewife, expecting me to keep conventional hours. To make a goddamned appointment before I bring some guys back for a couple of drinks and a few laughs.'

'So your promises aren't worth the powder it would take to blow them to hell!'

He glared at me and took a step or two towards the bed and for a moment I thought he was going to hit me.

'This is different,' he snapped. 'This is business, you hear me? Now haul your ass out there and greet the people. Put a little lipstick on while you're at it, you're looking a little pasty—'

'Business?'

'That's right. After we've had a little something to eat you can crawl right back into bed and get your beauty sleep because we're going to play a couple of friendly rubbers of bridge.'

'Bridge?'

'Bridge?' he mimicked. 'That's right, toots. That's the name of the game. That's what pays the rent and buys the onions around here, and don't you forget it.'

I stared at him open-mouthed. 'You brought people here at this hour to play cards?'

'Sure, why not? It's no skin off your nose. What the hell else do you have to do except make a home where I can invite my friends?'

'It's not so easy, Harry. I'm exhausted most of the time. I need some sleep.'

'You can sleep any time! You've got all goddamned *day* to sleep!'

'Me? And who'd repair the rotten furniture in this place when it threatens to fall apart, and pick up after you and Charlie? You know, there really isn't enough room in this flat for three people, Harry. Come to that, there isn't even enough space to cook a meal here unless you're a gold medal gymnast. And who'd walk miles every day in search of the delicacies you can't live without? Hershey bars, for instance, they're really hard to find. Oh, and avocadoes and artichokes in the middle of the winter, and all the other stuff we need. Stuff I cook but which you're very seldom here to eat—'

'You're a housewife, for Christ's sake, that's your job!'

Once launched, I couldn't stop. 'Struggling against gale force winds with all the groceries draped and disposed around Charlie in the pushchair. It might not be so bad if I didn't get so bone weary I forget how to relax and enjoy my daughter. She gets on my nerves sometimes, you know that? I scream at her and then I hate myself. A couple of times I thought I was going to hit her.'

'You better watch that,' he said tightly.

'Oh sure, I'll watch it. But why should I put myself through a routine like that? For whom? You? Harry, I never see you alone any more, except in bed. And even then, we sleep in shifts. . . .'

'My heart bleeds for you,' Harry said. 'Now would you get up and fix some chow?'

Tears pricked behind my eyes and I buried my head in my hands, trying to force them back. When I looked up at Harry his eyes were flat discs, reflecting nothing. I wasn't entirely sure he'd been listening, or taking in what I'd said.

'But—'

'Shit *but*! Cards are why we have a home to keep, and don't you forget it. And smile while you're at it, would you?' Harry said.

171

I nodded grimly.

It was the hour of philosophy, the hour of Confucious says: *Beware of what you want; you may get it. Take what you want, and pay for it.*

It was a stark moment of clarity when I could see Harry for the complete stranger he was, perhaps the stranger he'd always been. Or the stranger he'd become because I'd gone too far with him into his fantasy, hadn't resisted, hadn't dug my heels in, in time.

And what did that make me? My personal destiny was where it had always been, where I had refused to see it or accept it: I was the only one who could live my life.

But there was no point at all in making brave far-reaching declarations in the middle of the night.

So I let things slide. I made a huge pile of tuna salad sandwiches, past caring that Charlie had woken up and been taken out by her father to be admired. I was even past caring that Harry's buddies didn't file out until the middle of the following afternoon, bleary-eyed and emptier of pocket.

'Harry. . . .'

'What is it? Can't it wait? I'm bone weary, for—'

'Harry, it can't wait, no. I thought you went to somebody's hotel suite when you wanted an all night session—'

'Yeah, well, these guys weren't from out of town, and hotels – if you hadn't noticed – are expensive.'

'So don't any of them have homes?'

'Where the hell are my cigarettes? I don't suppose you bought another— *What did you say?*'

'I said, Harry, why did you bring your friends here? This is our home, Harry. Not a floating crap game, not a twenty-four hour diner, not a nightclub where baby gets up out of bed and does an obliging little tap dance for the company! What kind of life do you expect her to—'

'You're turning into a real shrew, you know that? If you want to know why we didn't go somewhere else it's because

I thought you were different. You're not, though, are you? You're just like all the rest of the whining, moaning—'

'Whose fault—'

'Drop it, I need the bread! Oh, that reminds me—' He reached into the breast pocket of his jacket and pulled out a roll of money and counted off four twenties. 'Before it occurs to you to ask,' he said, handing them to me. 'That should cover the damages.'

'Harry, I—'

'I said *drop it!*'

He walked past me into the bedroom, shedding his clothes as he went. 'When Charlie wakes up keep her quiet, would you? I've got to get some sleep.'

It became a regular event, Harry's showing up with strangers to play games that lasted through the night.

Sometimes he didn't wake me up; more often he did, taking theatrical precautions not to wake the baby – tip-toeing into the bedroom, stage-whispering to me – though more often than not she woke up anyway, and had to be rocked and soothed back to sleep after she'd been passed from hand to hand and clucked over and patted by strange men.

At other times Harry failed to come home at all, with or without company.

The first time it happened he was away for three days, and I was frantic with worry and guilt, sure I'd driven him away, certain he'd had an accident and was lying broken and alone in a high white bed somewhere, too ill to identify himself.

On the third day he telephoned from Brighton.

'Oh Harry, I've been phoning all the hospitals!'

'Aw, hon, you should have known I was okay! It's just that I got stuck in a marathon down here,' he added, laughing.

'God, I was so *worried*—'

'Silly! Now listen, hon. I'll be back some time this

173

afternoon, and I'm trying to persuade a few of these characters to come with me. So make sure there's plenty to eat, okay? These guys are hot, babe, believe it. Say, chili'd be great.'

I formed the syllables of protest; I started to push them out through dry lips. 'Harry, no—'

But then I realized he'd hung up.

Another party was over.

Cigarette butts floated on melted ice in smeared glasses, ashtrays overflowed, plates and crumpled paper napkins were stacked haphazardly around the table with abandoned cups, ringed where milk had separated from the dregs of coffee or tea.

The slate sky beyond the window hinted at snow. The glare of light into the room was merciless, picking out the shabby furniture and the mess, the lingering pall of blue smoke that floated above it all.

I started to clear up, yawning, resigned, then said to hell with it, eased off my shoes and walked into the bedroom and stretched out next to Harry. Charlie hadn't settled to sleep until dawn; I'd get up when she did.

She woke me several hours later, her delighted face peering into mine. 'Deal!' she cried happily. '*Cha'lie's* deal!'

I sat up and swung my legs around off the bed, stunned into abrupt wakefulness. I shook Harry roughly, rhythmically, until he mumbled 'Wha, wha, wha's wrong?' and tried to burrow back into the duvet. I shook him again, until he propped himself up reluctantly on one elbow, shrinking away from me, fumbling for a cigarette and the time.

'Okay, Libby,' he said heavily, sighing, flicking his lighter. 'What's the matter now?'

I stood up and walked to the window, threw back the curtains as far as they would go, satisfied with the grating

rasp of hooks against rod, vindicated by the clean slate light
of afternoon tumbling onto the rumpled bedclothes, furious,
containing my fury between my teeth as I glanced again at
Charlie innocent in her frilled flannel nightgown, her golden
curls an aureole around her baby face, her hands full of
tobacco and cardboard; her father's legacy.

Harry blinked and stared at me. His face was stark against
the light, pale skin drawn tight against bone, and his hair
stood up in dry sleep tufts, and the smoke from his cigarette
curled around his fingers and up to wreath his head.

'Well, what is it?'

'Look at Charlie, Harry. Just look at her.'

She was still standing by the bed, quite still as in a tableau.
Harry glanced at her, rumpled his hair with his free hand and
laughed. His eyes swung to me.

'Well isn't that a kick in the head? Isn't that the
funniest—'

'No. No, I don't think it's funny at all, Harry. It makes me
sick.'

I walked quickly to Charlie and scooped her up, cuddled
her, coaxed her to release her trophies from her curled fingers
with laughter and little kisses.

I threw them at Harry. Cards and crumpled cigarette,
weightless, insubstantial, fluttered down onto the duvet
beside him.

He threw up his hands in mock self-defence and laughed
again, but nervously. 'Hey, don't you think you're overreac-
ting, hon? I mean, Charlie Girl was just having a little side
game, just like her ol' dad—'

'Exactly,' I said.

The word was brittle in the winter glare, clean and sharp
against the chaos.

Harry sighed and drew deeply on his cigarette. 'Okay,
okay, hold your fire. I've got to make tracks here, starting
with a hot bath. So could you bring me a nice quiet cup of
coffee when it's ready, in the bathroom if you don't mind?'

'You got it.'

I turned on my heel, Charlie still in my arms.

She looked up at me and then back over her shoulder at her daddy, big-eyed, quiet, watching, as we left the room, as I closed the door behind us with a soft definite click.

I could hear Harry getting up, stretching, coming round by easy stages to remembering the greeting I'd given him the previous evening when he and several other strangers piled boisterously into the flat. When he stirred the peace of the bedroom where I was sitting on the bed with Charlie, watching the television I'd moved from the other room, by flinging the door open and asking breathlessly for the cab fare from Swiss Cottage.

I had tossed my purse across the bed without a word, without even taking my eyes from the screen where a quizmaster in a green velvet suit was trying to give prizes to people who clearly wanted them, whose faces contorted earnestly while they tried to articulate answers to his questions, who laughed relieved with him when they got the answers right and were given food processors and video cassette recorders and trips to Canada; who frowned in chagrin and disappointment when they got them wrong, or thought of them too late, after the buzzer sounded.

'Lib . . . ?'

'There's money in there,' I said, inclining my head. 'Help yourself.'

Charlie tried to wriggle away from me and off the bed. 'Daddy!' She held her arms out, and he came towards us, his eyes devouring her. 'Princess!' he said.

I held her tightly, looked up at Harry. 'We've eaten,' I said. 'There's stuff for sandwiches in the kitchen.'

'We have company, Lib,' he said softly.

'Again? Harry, that's five nights in a row without let up. Five nights with virtually no sleep. Something's got to give.'

'Poker's my best shot, Libby, you know that. And we can hardly hunker down and deal at any of the clubs. Where

176

else could I have taken them without spending a fortune on a hotel room?'

'Harry, I —'

'Libby, come on,' he coaxed. 'Come on out and fix us some sandwiches – please? Say hello and make them feel welcome, and then I swear to God I'll let you get some sleep, you and Charlie too. Please, Lib?'

I went, I did as he asked, my energy to move at all coming from pure inertia, without reference to any hospitable impulse or the desire to please Harry. But I went.

And somehow, as always seemed to happen in those sessions, despite the solemn singleminded concentration of the players in a poker game, I stayed to dance attendance until the bitter end. And so did Charlie.

There were six men around that table; one plateful of sandwiches didn't last long no matter how high I piled it, and no one was willing to take the last one.

So I made another. Drinks too, from a signal of Harry's as he dealt, his eyes meeting mine then resting significantly on the glasses at each elbow. And there was the fight to fool the little fridge into producing enough ice to last. By emptying ice cubes into plastic freezer bags as fast as they came out of trays.

There was the second wind, the pre-dawn gentlemanly insistence on playing another couple of hands to help the big loser recoup the worst of his losses, Harry's signal for a more substantial snack to get them through it, more urgent than usual because it seemed he was it. Big loser.

I made chili in my sleep; I was getting good at that: brown the minced beef, chop and brown the onion and green pepper, open tins of kidney beans and tomatoes, season with chili spice and salt and pepper, simmer all until Harry leaned back and sniffed the air and said, grinning around the table but speaking to me: 'Say, what's cookin', hon? Hope you made lots!'

Charlie had been sitting on Harry's knee all that time, too

177

young to spoil a poker face by betraying by word or facial expression the cards her father was dealt, but not too young to look up at him adoringly, or to bask in the uneasy attentions of the other players, who were distracted by her presence – by what Harry called his built-in coffee houser – into making mistakes.

After chili there was coffee, tea for those who preferred it, more or less continuously until the end.

Somewhere between chili and coffee I was signalled to carry Charlie off to bed, and I timed my lullabies to coincide as nearly as possible with the five minutes it took the percolator to send its first brown bubbles up to the glass top of the pot.

Late that morning, as always, I faced the clearing up before I slept.

Except I hadn't; I'd said to hell with it and gone into the bedroom to stretch out beside Harry.

So I tackled it on too little sleep, which I knew from bitter experience was worse than no sleep at all.

I switched the television on for Charlie, found the children's programmes; and before I did anything else I poured her fruit juice and decanted the cold cereal and milk that was her breakfast and sat her down in front of it and the television.

Then, with the room spinning delicately for a moment as I surveyed the carnage, I took a deep breath, went into the kitchen, put in the plug, squirted in a practised amount of washing-up liquid, and ran hot water into the sink, fiddling delicately within the visible interior lip of the temperamental ascot water heater with the back of a teaspoon – also a practised motion – to persuade the jets of flame to go up instead of out.

Then the reconnoitre, first for the glasses and sandwich plates. Into the plunge, rinse, and out again, dried and put away in the cupboard above the sink before the rest was tackled, to make room for the rest.

Napkins in the pedal bin below the sink, chili plates retrieved, smeared sickeningly with hardened tomato sauce and clinging bits of dried onion to reproach me for my slovenly postponement of their washing. I broke one in my haste to start the coffee in the middle of the clean-up, shoved it unrepentedly into the pedal bin and returned to the sitting room for cups.

And finally I went through into the bathroom with Harry's mug of coffee, steaming fragrantly, one sugar and no milk, and set it carefully on the wide edge of the tub near the taps.

'Harry,' I said, 'we have to talk.'

'Aw Lib, I'm in the goddamn bathtub, you can see that—'

'And Charlie's in the sitting room, mesmerized by *Blue Peter*. Now's a good time, Harry. For once, we don't have an audience.'

He sighed heavily, took up his coffee, blew on it and sipped it. 'It's late, hon—'

'It's late, yes. It's almost time for you to go out and round up another prayer meeting, and it's almost too late for me to go out and buy some more fodder for the soup kitchen, so—'

'Take it easy, Lib! Back off on the bongos, would ya? My head's killing me.'

'So's mine.'

'Okay, okay, let me finish! My head's killing me, and tonight's a big night with a lot riding on it, so I've got to keep going. But it's rubber bridge, so you won't need to worry about having your beauty sleep disturbed.'

'Now, and calmly, Harry, we have to talk about what you're doing to me, to all of us. Most of all, to Charlie. It's not fair, Harry. It isn't going to work, it isn't working—'

'*What's* not working?'

'The way we live, Harry, I'm trying to tell you. It isn't right, it isn't – working. I'm not happy, Charlie's not—'

179

'Hey, wait a goddamn minute! Charlie's great! Ab-so-lute-ly *fine*, got that?'

'No she isn't,' I said quietly. 'Something ugly's happening here, and it's not something fit for a nineteen month old baby to have to live with. She's—'

Harry fished out the soap and hurled it with great force across the bathroom.

'She's fine!' he shouted. 'Now get the hell out of here and let me finish my bath in peace! Go! Now!'

I turned to go, but as I opened the door anger welled up in me hard and hot and fast.

The bar of soap hadn't hit me, it hadn't come anywhere near me; Harry hadn't meant it to. It didn't matter.

I whirled and walked deliberately to the sink and picked it up from where it lay steaming on the cracked green linoleum. Without bothering to take aim I threw it back into the bathtub with an almighty splash.

And then I went, slamming the door as hard as I could behind me.

I kept walking, out through the crooked narrow hallway and straight through the front door. Coatless, uncaring, unseeing, out and out, and down the chipped stone steps to the street. I didn't even stop to see if Charlie was okay, sitting in front of the television, spooning in her breakfast, dribbling some of it onto her chin.

I remember taking great gulps of air in the deepening twilight and being soothed by the mellow light of street lamps, suspended invisibly among bare branches still etched against the sky, before it gave up the last of its pale winter blue to night and the full fire of stars.

I remember the great rush of tenderness I felt for the lighted windows I could see from where I stood, and for the lives being lived behind them; and I could almost hear, or thought I could, the faint theme music that accompanied the news at 5.45. Though surely I imagined the snap and crackle of newspapers being opened, and the automatic question, 'What's for dinner, darling?' being echoed up and down the terrace in cadences ranging from the comfortable indifference of long years of marriage to the ardent and slightly-embarrassed playacting of young couples imitating what they'd heard their parents say at home.

Dreamily I started walking again, along the long quiet road towards the urgent sounds of evening traffic, listening as I went, until I reached the turning at the corner and was aware of the concrete bulk of the hotel that stood there and, walking on around the corner, the red white and blue neon of the tube stop sign, suspended beyond the row of shops still doing business with the rush-hour trade.

I stopped again in the middle of the flow of hurrying pedestrians, bound for home or friends, the ubiquitous plastic carrier bags of carless Londoners flashing around their knees, strained and swollen with the wherewithal for that night's dinner or slim and important with bottles of wine for hosts, all unseeing and uncaring, locked in private visions of particular destinations, swirling and eddying past me on either side.

Sally Barlow nearly collided with me.

'Libby? Libby, it's me, Sally!'

She took my arm and frowned. 'What are you doing out this time of night without a coat, love? I know they've got businesslike winters in Montana, but this is—'

'Oh hi!' I said. 'Hi, Sally! I was just taking a walk, and I, ah. . . .'

I shrugged, flustered, remembering where I was and why, taking in the fact of Sally's warm wool coat, her matching scarf and gloves, her breath on the air in puffs as she spoke to me, mine as I answered, the gooseflesh on my arms, bare below the elbow where my sleeves ended.

'I, ah, thought I'd run down to get the evening paper, so. . . .' I gestured vaguely towards the paper shop a few doors down from where we stood.

Sally was unconvinced, and concerned. 'Libby,' she said, watching me closely, 'is everything all right?'

'Sure it is! Of course, everything's just fine. I was just, ah, on my way to get a paper. . . .'

'Look, love, here's mine,' she said briskly. I tried to protest, but she said, 'Oh for heaven's sake, Libby, go on, take it and welcome. I read it on the train coming home.'

I took it, folded it carefully and tucked it underneath my arm.

'Thanks,' I said, smiling. But I made no move to turn and start walking back the way I'd come, back to the house Sally and I shared as tenants and, after an awkward pause, she said, 'Well, ah, going my way?' Hesitantly, encouragingly.

'Oh, not just yet,' I said. 'Now I'm out, I think I'll walk on a bit, get some more fresh air.'

She nodded slowly. 'Well then, how about coming for a drink with me? I haven't seen you since before Christmas, and there's still the new year to toast. *And* it's Friday.'

'I'd like that,' I said at once, grinning at her. And then, 'but I don't have a penny—' And stopped abruptly and bit my lip, thinking what a terrible social liar I was. I didn't have a penny on me, not even enough to buy an evening paper.

If Sally noticed the slip she chose to pretend she hadn't. 'My treat,' she said cheerfully, taking my arm again, showing a distinct flair for tact by not asking me if I'd like to stop at home to pick up a jacket first.

Showing a distinct organizational ability too, as she manoeuvred me out of the crowd and along a road I recognized as parallel to ours, and into a quiet neighbourhood pub that must have been our local all the time, though I'd never been there before, never thought about going to a pub either with Sally or on my own or with anybody else. It was unpretentious but comfortable, filled to the capacity of the lounge bar with slightly tatty overstuffed chairs that seemed to invite people to sit down and lean back and not get up again until it was absolutely necessary, to relax and unwind in their capacious depths until the cares of the day were expunged.

I hesitated before sinking into one of them, remembering suddenly that Harry had spoken of a game of rubber bridge he and Andrew were going to play, and that it was getting late; that among other things, he was probably frantic, wondering where I'd got to.

'What would you like to drink, Libby?' Sally said, pulling off one glove and rummaging in her shoulder bag for her purse.

'I, ah, oh dear, I left Charlie in front of *Blue Peter*, eating break – eating,' I amended, flushing. 'I'd better, um, er. . . .'

She looked up, and the gaze of her grey eyes into mine was very level. 'Libby,' she said, 'her father's in the flat with her, isn't he?'

'Well yes, of course, but—'

'Have a drink, Lib. Charlie'll still be there when you go back. And so,' she added gently, her mouth turning up very slightly at the corners, 'will her dad.'

I relaxed and began to laugh and she laughed with me; and all of a sudden, sinking down and down into a chair and saying, 'I'd like a glass of lager, please,' I forgot to be embarrassed.

I remembered how much I'd liked Sally on sight; and how assiduously I'd avoided her over the months of trying to come to terms with the fact that Harry and Charlie and I were not going home as planned.

And the pre-Christmas drink I'd shared with her in my flat, Sally perched on our best chair facing the lighted tree, me opposite on the sofa, trading pleasantries while we downed thimblesful of posh dry sherry.

I'd been aching inside that evening, full of the pain of knowing that all my cherished fantasies of Christmas had come crashing down, encouraging Sally to talk about the

183

holiday she would share with her family as a way of abrading the sore place in my soul, to remind me it was there.

I winced when she spoke of a midnight carol service and champagne on Christmas morning, a Boxing Day chockful of relatives and food. All taped, all hers as of right. I'd been bitterly jealous, and ashamed of being childish.

Sally came back with drinks, set them on the table between us, draped her shoulder bag and coat and scarf over the back of a chair and sat down.

She raised her glass. 'To the new year, and to Friday,' she said.

'And to the rescue.'

She flushed and shifted a little in her chair, as though reluctant to take credit. 'Not really,' she said.

'Yes really. I don't think I have to tell you that sitting here across from a friendly face is a big improvement on wandering around Marble Arch like the village idiot.'

'It wasn't like that, Libby, honestly not. I just thought you seemed a little upset, perhaps that you needed someone to call time-out for a few minutes while you caught your breath.'

'And remembered where I was, and that I'd come out without a coat – oh, and all kinds of things. . . .'

She smiled and reached out to cover my hand with hers, no longer distant and perfect with her smooth brown hair and her neat tartan skirt and neutral jumper.

'It happens to us all at some time or another. I thought you might be – well, perhaps homesick. Forgive me, I—'

'I am,' I said urgently, ashamed of the tears that stood in my eyes threatening to spill, willing them back with an effort, wishing with all my heart I could allow myself the luxury of letting the tears fall with the torrent of words that would share the misery I carried, and halve its burden.

I couldn't afford that. I had lied to my family, my friends, myself, about the nature and extent of Harry's convoluted odyssey in England. And Sally was a virtual stranger, after all; kind, sensitive, certainly concerned enough about me to want to do something to help if she could, but still a stranger.

Oh, she would have listened to my story, I knew that; and I felt she would have tried hard to understand, to put it with her own experiences and make some kind of sense of it, and to accept it. If I could have brought myself to tell anyone what was in my heart, she would have been the obvious choice; she was, after all, available. But it was too late for easy confidences tumbled out casually, too late for crying in my beer.

'I'm homesick for sure,' I said. 'I've been – quarrelling with Harry about it, actually. That's why I came out the way I did. I'm afraid I – well, I threw a bar of soap at him. No way to settle things, I know. . . .'

'A good clean fight, though,' she said, grinning.

I laughed, grateful and relieved; the subject was closed and neatly labelled, and Sally given her due as someone who had seen as much as I could comfortably reveal.

'How was your Christmas, by the way?' I said breezily, free to change the subject. 'It sounded as though it was going to be pretty wonderful, from what you said.'

'I did go on about it, didn't I?' she said. She sipped her drink and reached into her handbag for cigarettes, offered me one and lit it. 'It's the high point of the English family calendar, really, or at least it is in mine. And it is pretty glorious, at least for the first couple of days. But it's always the same in the end. There's the foil-wrapped parcel of food from my mum, to be sure I eat properly while leading a loose life in Sin City, living with a guy without benefit of clergy.'

'You're kidding!'

'Libby, you look so shocked.'

I blushed. 'I'm sorry, Sally, I never thought—'

'That butter would melt in my mouth?' she teased.

'No, not that, but – come on, Sally, you know you don't live with anybody! You don't even have a flatmate.'

'Not any more. However, four years ago in the full flush of being eighteen, I did. Did you really think I came all the way to London from Penzance just to learn how to be a good little secretary and work in an insurance company?'

'I never really thought about it,' I said bleakly honest.

'Well, I didn't. The guy pitched off eventually to marry someone else, and I kept the flat for myself. What with inflation and steady rises, it would have been crazy not to.'

'I'm sorry, Sally,' I said.

'What for?'

'That it didn't work out. I mean, you loved him didn't you?'

'Of course, at the time. Now I'm glad. . . .'

'There's someone else?'

She nodded, misty-eyed. 'Off and on,' she said quietly. 'Would you like the other half?' she asked.

I breathed deeply. 'I think – another time?'

'Right. You're ready to go back?'

'I think I'd better. Harry's probably phoning hospitals or something. I didn't exactly leave an itinerary. . . .'

'It won't have done him any harm to worry for a bit,' she said.

186

11

Sally walked home with me and let us into the house with her key.

Harry caught a glimpse of her as she started up the stairs to her flat; he offered her 'good evening', and she turned to acknowledge and return it before she disappeared from view.

On the way back, I had said to her, eager to consolidate what we'd shared, anxious to be polite, 'Harry'll have to let me in. You can meet him then, you've never met him, he must seem like some kind of phantom—'

'Another time, Libby,' she answered, matter-of-fact. 'You do have things to discuss this evening, after all.'

'I'm not sure I'm in a hurry,' I offered.

'Um,' she said. 'Another time.'

And we had laughed, and I had felt lightened, stronger, for having found another woman to talk to about the difficulties women face.

But as we approached the house I quickened my step. I glanced up to see if there was light coming from the bedroom. The curtains were drawn; I couldn't tell.

I was thinking: what if Harry had lost the knack of fatherhood, what if he was annoyed because I'd made him late for his card game, what if Charlie was difficult and he didn't know what to do with her, didn't want to know.

But when the door to the flat was closed behind me, he said earnestly, 'Honey, I was so worried!' and I relaxed.

He was sorry about the fight too; it had done him good to worry about me. And I was calmer too. I hadn't spilled my guts to Sally. I waited until I was ready to do the only useful thing there was to do about the tangle of our lives: to try to work it out with Harry. I was proud of that.

And I decided I wasn't quite ready to be mollified; I would savour the heady victory of being Harry's centre of attention for the first time in a long while, the one to be humoured and listened to and worried about for a change.

'I was worried, hon,' Harry said again.

'It was your turn. I know you're late for your game, but—'

'I cancelled it, hon. This is more important, don't think I don't know it. Are you all right?'

'You know I came home with Sally,' I said shortly. 'I ran into her on her way home from work. She bought me a beer.'

'She seems nice,' Harry said meekly.

'From what little I've seen of her, I think she is,' I said. For all he'd seen of her she might have been a many-headed monster.

I looked around the sitting room; I noticed that Harry had run the vacuum cleaner the landlord kept on the first floor landing, finishing the tidying I'd had under way when I walked out. It was a peace offering, I decided to accept it. Conditionally, at least.

I offered him a noncommittal smile. 'Where's Charlie?'

'Sound asleep, full of chicken soup *with* rice and toast soldiers.' He chuckled, shaking his head. 'She was still hungry after breakfast. I guess you, ah, talked things over with your friend?'

'She knew we'd had an argument, that's all.'

He put his arms around me and held me close. I wanted to stay where I was for ever, held and rocked, filled with peace and singing exultation.

But we had to talk.

'Harry, let's sit down, okay?'

He nodded. 'Do you want something to eat, hon? A drink?'

'Just a drink, thanks.'

I sat on the lumpy unsprung sofa; when Harry came back from the kitchen he handed me a glass and sat on the armchair opposite.

'I've been thinking,' I said hesitantly.

He nodded, sage and patient, caring and mature. There was a cathedral hush between us in the room.

'Living like this,' I gestured vaguely, 'it's been getting me down, Harry.'

'I know. I know,' he whispered. 'But it's nothing we can't work out, Lib.'

'I'm not sure,' I said. I licked my lips. 'Harry, we can't stay on here, we're not getting anywhere. Charlie's getting older every day, and it's not good for her—'

'Honey, listen. I've been thinking too. Things won't always be like this. I know we need to find a bigger place, for one thing. In fact, I think that's the first thing on our agenda. Now if you were to find a job—'

'I thought of that months ago, Harry. I could find one, sure. But what would we do with Charlie while I worked?'

'Why not the same thing we did in California? There're facilities for working mothers here, surely.'

'After a fashion. But they're hard to find and they offer wildly varying standards of care. This country isn't really geared to the working mother, Harry; not unless she's earning enough to hire a full time live-in nanny.'

'Well, babe, you know you could find a pretty good job. You held one down in California.'

'They don't pay as well over here,' I said patiently. 'I checked. And there's no way I could find a job at anywhere near the level of the one I left at Metcalf Jones, not with one year and three months' work experience—'

'*And* a degree, don't forget.'

I sighed. 'That and my experience will get me a job typing and filing just about anywhere. It's not the same, Harry.'

He shrugged. 'Maybe you don't want to work.'

'I didn't say that. But what about Charlie? What would we do with her all day?'

He ran his hands through his hair. 'Hire a nanny to live in—'

'Where would we put her?'

'I've told you, hon, we'll just have to find a bigger place.'

'Harry, with what? We can just barely afford the place we've got.'

'Okay, okay, so we'd work it out the way we did in San Francisco when I wasn't in school. I'd take care of her. After all, I am home most of the day.'

'But you're asleep then, Harry. You're out most of the night.'

'I'd *be* here, Libby, that's the point!'

I shook my head. 'Not any more. She's growing up, she needs attention, somebody to talk to her and be with her and share things with her. She needs a whole lot more than somebody to slot food into her at lunchtime.'

'Okay, okay—'

'And another thing, Harry. If I did go to work, if we did manage to figure out a way to see to it that Charlie was looked after while I was out all day – when would I sleep?'

'Now look, don't start that—'

'I didn't! But I'm the one who makes sandwiches and chili in the middle of the night, who's up and dressed and expected to dance attendance on a bunch of poker players, and then to get up with Charlie in the morning. I can't take that much longer, Harry.'

'Okay, okay, okay, I said don't start! It isn't getting us anywhere. Now listen, this is the plan I have in mind. Let's just say you can't or don't want to go to work, okay?'

'I didn't—'

'Okay, okay, just hear me out. Now. The alternative is for me to step up my action so we're back in the running here. It won't take long, not if we pull together, I know it won't. But what with one thing and another, I've had to turn the action every which way but loose just to keep my head above water, and I can see I'm going to have to step it up even more, at least for a while. I have a dream here, Libby, and it's more important to me than anything that's ever happened to me in my life, and I'll do anything—'

'More important than Charlie and me?' I whispered, half afraid to ask it, and the answer he might give.

His head came up sharply and he flushed. 'You know you're part of it, you and Charlie Girl! You always have been. And some day we're going to have everything money can buy. A house of our own and a car, more kids. Everything, Libby! All of it!'

I stared at him; I was aware only of his eyes, burning with intensity in his transfixed face, looking through me and beyond me to a vision only he could see.

'Harry,' I said softly, calling to him, praying he would hear me. 'Harry, I know we'll have all that, I know you want it for us. We can make a life like that, sweetheart, we can do it together – once we go home. It's time to do that; you know it is. It's been wonderful, being here, but now it's time for us to leave. . . .'

He bowed his head; I went to him, knelt by the chair and held him, and his voice was deep and resonant against my heart.

'I can't let it go like that, Libby. I can't let it all slip through my fingers – because I failed here. I'd rather walk straight into the Thames until my hat floats, rather than face that.'

'Shh, sweetheart, it isn't like that. You did what you set out to do. You did a lot more, darling, you haven't failed. But now it's time to go back and make our lives and be happy with them. It's time, sweetheart. . . .'

He pulled away from me and his eyes swam into focus.

'You might be right, Lib,' he whispered, anguished. 'But you see, we can't go anywhere. Not now, not any more. We

191

don't have any choice now but to hang on here until I'm back on my feet again. Libby, I've burned the bridges, sold the boats. I owe money, all over town. I don't even have enough to pay our fares back to California.' He looked down at his hands, ashamed. 'Now do you understand?'

I reached out again to cradle him, to touch his hair. 'It's all right, Harry. It'll be all right, really it will. Harry, I have enough money to get us home,' I said.

He straightened in his chair and locked my eyes with a slow smile of pleasure and relief.

'Say that again, sweetpea,' he said.

'I have enough put by to get us home, Harry,' I said softly.

'Oh baby, that's terrific! I kind of thought you might, you know that?' He reached out and tousled my hair. 'Still waters, eh?' He jumped up, totally revitalized, and started towards the kitchen. 'This definitely calls for another drink, wouldn't you agree?'

I followed him, smiling, so relieved and thankful to see him whole again, happy I'd had the foresight to provide for this contingency I'd been so afraid of facing, grateful he had taken it so well.

I leaned against the doorway with my arms folded, watching him as he prised ice out of the tray and into our glasses, loving him, warm and secure now he'd come back to me, back to reality, and we were going home at last.

'Now the very first thing we need in this establishment,' he said lightly, 'is a decent ice tray. Harrods'll have one if anybody does.' He chuckled.

I shrugged. 'Why bother? When we get back we can go out and buy a decent refrigerator.'

'Back?' He blinked at me, uncomprehending. 'Back? Oh baby, who said anything about going back? We're here, sweetpea! We're saved in the eleventh hour!'

'Harry, I just explained—'

'That you've got some dough stashed away,' he said,

nodding sagely, dousing ice with scotch. 'Sure, I heard you. Best news I've had in a long lonesome while. Why, it set me right up! Hey, that's a pun, "set me right up", get it? If we've got enough to pay for two and a half air fares to San Fran, we've got more than enough to pay our way back into the grandstand right where we are!'

'Harry, we've already said we'll use it to pay for our tickets—'

'Wrong, babe, *you* decided. Now that I know it's there – *voilà!* The captain of our little ship is back in business!'

'It isn't there for—'

'I just wish you'd told me sooner, hon. Would've saved me a lot of unnecessary worry,' he mused. 'But I thought it might be, and I was right. Oh baby, just think! Back on course, right in the thick of things again. Say, what do you say we ring Andrew and invite him to step out on the town with us tomorrow night? We haven't done that for a long—'

'Harry?'

'Hmm?'

'We can't use that money for prolonging this nightmare. I can't let you do that.'

He said nothing; we stood there in absolute silence, facing one another. I began to feel cold, and then a little frightened as the silence stretched.

'You can't, can you?' he said softly, finally.

'No.' I took a deep breath and closed my eyes, summoning all the courage I owned. 'I want to go home, Harry. It's time for us to go home.'

'You know, babe, I might have been mad at you for this. You know, for holding out on me the way you did. Instead I decided to let it pass, even suggested we go out on the town to celebrate. I thought that was a pretty generous gesture on my part, didn't you?'

'Harry, stop it! You know damned well what I think! Not five minutes ago you were telling me that the only

193

reason we're still here is because you didn't have enough money left to take us home again!'

'Ah! That was five minutes ago, baby doll! Times have changed.'

'Nothing's changed, Harry. I'm not about to sink every last dime we've got into a pipe dream. It won't work – it hasn't worked. And we were happy once in California, we can be happy there again.'

'We can slot right into the nine to five number, right? Isn't that the way you've got things worked out? I take every penny I've been able to scrape together for years and bring us to London, and then when I run into a temporary slump you come up with all the nickels and dimes you put away in the secret cookie jar and tell me you're calling the shots, right? Well babe, let me tell you something. You've got another think coming!'

'Harry, I—'

'Yeah I know, you want to go home. Well, if you don't like the kind of life I can provide, *where* I can provide it, then you can just get the hell out and go anywhere you like. But let me tell you something else, toots. If you do that, you can forget all about taking Charlie with you. She's mine, got that? Mine!'

'Harry, please—'

'Aw, stow it! Now I'm going out, got that? And while I'm out I suggest you write a nice legible letter to your bank, or wherever you've squirrelled away your butter and egg money, and see to it that it's on its way by the time I get back. You know when you've got it good, don't you, Lib?'

He threw the ice tray into the sink. It knocked into the full tumblers on the drainboard; they broke, and ice and whisky and shards of glass flew everywhere.

He laughed. 'And you can clean that up too, while you're at it.'

He brushed past me impatiently. I could hear him stalking across the sitting room, opening the bedroom door, going in for his coat, slamming the door behind him as he came out again, careless of whether or not he woke Charlie.

He came back into the sitting room and I was still rooted to the spot, unable to move, staring at the mess in the sink and on the kitchen floor. Unable to absorb what had happened.

At last I forced myself to turn, to watch Harry as he shrugged into his coat and walked to the front door.

I ran to him then, to plead with him to stay, to talk things through, to make sense of the slivers of ice and glass that seemed somehow to have lodged where my heart should have been.

I touched his arm; he threw off my hand without a word.

And he was gone.

Short of following him, pleading with him in the public street, there was nothing I could do to stop him. There was nothing I could do but go to bed, and try to sleep, and when I couldn't sleep to try to read.

But the words swam before my eyes and made no sense, and I was forced back down into my teeming reeling turmoil.

Until at last, though dimly, I began to see the central problem: Harry had married me expecting unreserved and unconditional love, and I had promised to give it. By my irresolution, my spineless yielding to him on every issue, my self-effacing need to keep him happy so he would go on loving me.

I had systematically and willingly painted myself into an emotional corner for a man who threw tantrums to get his own way in much the same way Charlie threw tantrums when she was tired and wanted ice cream. I didn't give into her; I shouldn't have given in to her father.

All that insight had come far too late. My dilemma was so central and so huge I hadn't seen it coming; I was powerless to make it go away, to backtrack over the years and make it right and start afresh and honestly with Harry. Loving him didn't change that; if anything, it made it worse.

But it wasn't until Charlie woke up, whimpering, and I

195

took her into bed with me and held her, rocked her in my arms until she slept again, that I could find the strength to face knowing what I would have to do to save her, to save us both.

I fixed a reassuring smile on my face while I heated Charlie's dinner; when she had eaten, I dressed her warmly for the wintry April night. I hummed to her while I took down the biggest suitcase, and filled it anyhow with her things and my own. I tried to be methodical and remember everything: my most recent statement from the bank in California, the cash I'd drawn earlier that week for buying groceries, the name of the hotel in Bayswater I'd passed one day when I was shopping.

Harry hadn't come home in all the slow sad night and day since our terrible quarrel; he hadn't rung.

I wrote a note for him. In it I said I was sorry for what had happened, and for what I felt I had to do, but that I had not been able to think of any less drastic solution to our differences. I told him I loved him, that I would always love him and wish him well.

I signed it with a scrawled 'L' and three scribbled x's.

I put it with my keys on the telephone table, and as I did so, as if on cue, the phone rang.

I jumped – caught, discovered, trapped – as though the telephone was a living thing that could reach out and grab me, stop me. I was certain Harry was at the other end of it.

My eyes went wildly around the room, taking terrified inventory: Charlie, the suitcase, my handbag.

I grabbed. I fled.

12

'Where the *hell* are you?'

'I told you, Harry, we're in a hotel. I just rang to tell you we're okay—'

'Oh yeah, sure! Who the hell do you think you are, taking off like that with Charlie? Listen, if you're not back here in half an hour, *with* my daughter, I'm coming out to find you. You won't much like it when I do!'

'I don't have to listen to this, Harry.'

I couldn't, not much longer anyway. Not with the rapid pips about to start up again and me with no coins left, nor with Charlie grizzling and bewildered and sucking her thumb in the pushchair, which I was moving back and forth with my free hand to try to soothe her. Nor with a longish queue outside the open kiosk in the hotel lobby and none too patient with the wait, and one or two beginning to look faintly alarmed at the passion I was pouring down the phone.

Not unless I told Harry where we were.

'I'll – ah – call you when we're settled,' I said, trying to sound reasonable.

'Jeee*sus*! What kind of cockamamie bullshit *is* this?'

'Harry, I'm serious.'

'Libby, for the last time: Where the hell *are* you?'

The pips began. 'I'll ring tomorrow, Harry.'

I hung up.

It took every ounce of the strength I had left after a sleepless night tossing in the double bed with Charlie, and the greasy fry-up in the hotel dining room at six, and the faintly suspicious noises the hotel management had made at

197

my sudden appearance with a baby the previous evening, not to hurl myself and Charlie into the nearest passing taxi and do as Harry said – go back.

I had to put the panic aside, and hang on like grim death to every ounce of resolution I'd mustered to walk out on him. I had more important things to do. I even had a plan, of sorts.

I would send to California for the money I had saved; I would then fly to Montana, to mother and father. That was the plan; I'd thought no further.

My mother would tell me she loved me, that everything would be all right, that she was there for me, for Charlie; she would cook stuffed peppers and French toast and bring me coffee in bed until I was on my feet again and could get a job. And after that I could make a new life for Charlie and myself.

It was simple, clean and easy.

Except that already, after one restless night, I bitterly regretted what I'd done.

I missed Harry, I ached for him. My mind and heart kept veering away from the firm intentions I had for my brave new Harryless life.

How could I have thought that way, when I loved him so much? How could I have walked out on him just because he wanted to stay in England to pursue his dream, and I wanted something different for us? I had to keep reminding myself I'd had other, better, reasons; that I had to make a decent life for Charlie, for myself.

For most of the rest of that day I practised being strong and adult. I made lists, businesslike, in my neat square block-printing in bold black ink on a lined pad I bought in a news-agents: money, airline reservations, call mother, buy dispos-able nappies. Get coins for telephone.

Ring Harry, try to explain. Try to find a way back to the golden circle of love, to Sunday mornings with crumbs in bed and us not caring, to the moment of exultation that was the day of Charlie's birth. Try to jolt him out of a nightmare . . .

When I called him again, Harry said: 'Honey, come back.

Please. Look, I'm sorry I yelled at you. I was upset, I'm sorry. Come back, Libby baby, please. Oh, life'll be so sweet for us, you'll see. Honey, nothing in the world means a damned thing to me except Charlie and you. Honest to God. Libby, you still there . . . ?'

'You've said all that before, Harry.'

'Don't I know it? Oh, don't you think I've been doing a little soul-searching over here? Oh hon, I can't even find the coffee!' He laughed; I could almost see him grinning; my heart turned over.

I bit my lip. 'It's – it's on the shelf over the stove.'

He laughed again. 'That's my girl! Look, sweetie, check out of there and grab a taxi, okay? I'll be here. I'll be here on my knees, babe, promise. . . .'

Oh Harry, how many promises have you made, and how many times have you broken every one of them? How many more before I'd be bleached, sucked dry, too old to try to start over?

'I want to go home, Harry. I have to go—'

'Sure! Oh sure, honey, *home*! Come on, I'll be right here. Hell, I'll even make the coffee!'

He was desperate, stunned I'd actually left him and was gone, out of reach. I could hear it.

I looked down at Charlie sitting at my feet and tried hard not to cry, seeing in her a perfect miniature of all of Harry's beauty; seeing in her the way he looked the day I met him – and the evening he asked me if he could kiss me, outside my college dormitory. When I was very young. . . .

'Harry, I can't—'

'Hey babe, come on! What'dya mean *can't*? It's easy, one two three! You just march up to the man and pay your bill, then pick up your stuff and go outside and find a *taxi*!'

He lost control on *taxi*. He'd forgotten all about the water under the bridge, and was concentrating hard on the big black shiny cab that would glide up and disgorge us.

'I don't mean that, Harry. I meant home to Montana.'

There was silence, then. 'Do you really? Home to mama,

eh? Just leave all your responsibilities, hop a jet, and that's it?'

'I'm taking my responsibilities with me, Harry. Charlie's right here with me.'

'Uh huh. And where's her passport, toots?'

'Her . . .'

My head spun. I had her passport with me, hers and mine. Didn't I?

I cradled the receiver between ear and shoulder while I rummaged frantically through my handbag, cursing its many compartments stuffed to capacity with essentials as well as the usual non-essential junk. I was sure I'd—

No, I hadn't.

I'd taken them out of the writing desk drawer where we kept them and put them. . . .

I remembered, with the beginnings of wild panic, where I'd put them – and forgotten in my frenzied flight when the telephone rang.

They were on the telephone table; Harry was probably looking right at them.

'I'll come and get them now, I'll be—'

'Your own, maybe. But Charlie's? Oh no. No, you won't. She's not going anywhere.'

'Harry, you can't—'

'Oh can't I?'

'I can go to the Embassy—'

'Go right ahead. It's slap bang in the middle of Grosvenor Square; you can't miss it.'

'Harry, they'll help me! They won't let you do this to me!'

'They won't let you do it to me, either. Try them. Better still, come on back where you belong. Why d'ya think they insist on separate passports for children, honey? They're not so dumb,' he finished, almost crooning, switching his tone so fast it made my pulses race. And chilled me at the same time. 'Come on back, sugar. You know you want to.'

I steeled myself. I closed my eyes very tightly, and my lids were gossamer dams against hot searing tears.

'Don't hold your breath,' I said.

I got to the Embassy just before they closed for the day. Harry had already rung them.

The young-middle-aged American who held the slim file folder marked 'Charlotte Louise Franklin' told me that, when I identified myself. He ushered me into a small private office and invited me to sit down.

Charlie squirmed in my lap and pointed at him, looking up at me; he smiled at her and said 'Hi, honey?' He offered me a cup of coffee.

He wore American clothes and a sympathetic smile displaying beautiful teeth. He understood my plight, he said; he was sorry, there was nothing the Embassy could do to help. Cases in which there was a dispute over the possession of a minor's passport between American parents living in Britain were subject to British jurisdiction, and had to be adjudicated through the British courts, he said. Unless my husband and I could work out a reconciliation . . .

When I said, dry-mouth and stunned, that I doubted we could – trying to finish the coffee while Charlie tried to grab the cup – he advised me to consult a solicitor.

It was. dark when we emerged into the square again, bleak and foreign and indifferent unknown territory in which I was a prisoner of war.

My mother said: 'Honey, say that again. This line is awful bad.'

And then: 'Honey, we'll send your tickets. Don't worry, it'll be okay. Is the baby all right? She's with you, isn't she? Oh honey, don't let her out of your sight!'

'Mom, I have to stay here,' I said. 'They won't let me bring her home. Harry has her passport, and he won't—'

'Aw, that's bull!' she shouted from Montana. 'He can't stop you! Hell, she's an American citizen, ain't she?'

'Sure, but—'

'Now just you listen to me a minute, Libby! You have every right to bring her home. Just go straight to the American Embassy—'

'I just came from there, Mom. There's nothing they can do to help. I have to stay here and work things out with Harry, maybe hire an English lawyer.'

'You're *American*, Libby! Don't you forget it! That still means something, you know, even over there.'

'Mom, so is Harry, and he's got Charlie's—'

'Honey, just go to the airport and tell them you've lost her papers. You know, act real flustered and helpless. They'll let you through!'

'No, they *won't*! They have a file on her now; they've got her name down on all their lists in all the airports and seaports. Harry called them up and told them I was trying to kidnap her—'

'That don't make good sense, Libby. After all, you're her mother.'

I clutched the receiver very tightly; it was slippery in my hand.

'I know,' I said. 'But that's the way things are.'

Charlie and I holed up in that hotel for a couple of expensive weeks, posing as out-of-season tourists while I waited for cash from my bank in California and wrote an urgent letter to my mother. *What shall I do now? I can't leave the country. I don't know what to do. I'm scared.*

She must have written back to me the day she got my letter, but she didn't write to the point.

202

I can't help wondering if you and Harry can't work things out after all, honey. If you didn't want to stay with him pretty bad, you'd have got on a plane home when I told you to. And maybe you should stay with him. You know, I remember the day you were married, and how happy you were, and how much fun we had. Oh, you were so radiant, the most beautiful bride! You know, honey, divorce is a terrible thing. You know that, I don't have to remind you. And what about the baby? You know you don't want to give her a broken home. You don't want that for Charlie, honey, believe you me. So if you can work it out, I sure hope you will, if only for her sake. Remember, honey, marriage is for ever, and Harry is still the same wonderful guy you promised to love, honour and cherish till death do you part.

Over the page, as though it were a different letter entirely, or a letter to someone else:

This may be for the best after all, you and Harry coming to a parting of the ways, though only you two can decide that. I never said anything against him, you know that, but I never really trusted him. Think of all that time he lounged around in college while you worked. Even when you were pregnant he was in Vegas playing cards, remember? He *played* while you worked your goddamned fingers to the bone! Your dad and I have never really understood why he dragged you all the way over to England like he did. So think about it carefully, honey. We'll send the tickets for you and the baby just as soon as we hear from you. I love you.

My father wrote a succinct postscript, expressing his ambivalence.

I always said he was a no-good bum. On the other hand, nobody in our family has ever been divorced.

203

Not even his sister, my Aunt Julie, whose husband drank.

And then, in heavily underscored capitals: 'WHEN ARE YOU COMING HOME? TICKETS READY WHEN YOU ARE! LOVE.'

I cried when I read all that: it felt as though my last exit had been closed and locked. And all because my patiently detailed explanation in writing of why it was impossible to leave England had been dismissed as an irrelevance, something my parents understood as a rationalization of my lingering hankering for Harry, a little hiccup I could get around if I really wanted to. I couldn't have found my way out of a paper bag at that stage, I was so distraught. And I knew I had to be strong for Charlie, and that made it worse.

And living in a hotel with Charlie was horrible; much worse than it had been nine months earlier. She was that much older, less portable and more demanding. She was active and inquisitive and bright; she was fretful and restless when we couldn't go out.

But it was a blustery April, raining half the time, and even when it wasn't, I was so preoccupied with my quandary, so tired, that we seemed to be wandering in endless and ever-tightening circles.

I wasn't sleeping well; half the time I wasn't eating either. And I was worried about money. I had no idea how long it would take to find a job – if I could find one, if I could find somebody to take care of Charlie while I worked – and therefore no idea how long I'd have to support us on what I'd saved.

All I could think of was how cosy life might have been with Harry in the flat.

Day by day the reasons why I'd walked out grew hazier and less valid in my mind until I sometimes had the clear unshakeable idea that I'd been in the wrong, that what I'd done in leaving – bag, baggage and baby – had been the childish self-indulgence of a spoiled brat.

And oh I missed him so terribly. Just hearing his voice on the telephone – even when he'd shouted at me, because I didn't really think he meant it, or that he really meant the threats about keeping Charlie's passport if I really, seriously meant to use it – made my knees turn to jelly.

I kept thinking he was like Billy Goat Gruff, hollering at me to bluff me into going back to him. And following that further, I would see myself as a frightened and bleating and very childish billy goat; and then I had to admit that I was trying to cross a very rickety bridge. Wandering dull-eyed and listless around Bayswater, pushing a striped pushchair full of precious cargo wherever it would take me, day after endless day.

It was not the road to freedom, that was for damned sure. It was a circular road, leading nowhere at all. And even if I found the road to freedom, what was I so busily trying to be free of? I no longer knew.

And then there were the nights.

I saw Harry in every dream, close enough to touch. And every crazy thing he'd ever done was wiped out and cancelled in the sheer glory of his tangential physical presence.

I began to wake up in the night, jerked out of a restless doze, needing to bury my head in my pillow to stop myself howling. And I wasn't able to remember why he wasn't beside me in bed, why he didn't reach out and take me in his arms and tell me everything was going to be just fine. I wanted him there, needed him. In the morning, the full horror of the situation would wash over me. The pale light of another April dawn was the beginning of another day of limbo verging on hell.

Finally one morning I'd had enough. I rang him.

'I want to see you,' I said. 'I think it's time we talked, don't you?'

'Oh Lib, oh sweetpea, I've been frantic to hear you! Is Charlie Girl okay? Where are you?'

205

He'd been asleep, I could tell. I felt terribly guilty; he'd been gambling – *working* – all night long, working for us. I'd been so thoughtless.

'I'm sorry, Harry, I should have rung later—'

'Libby, don't hang up!'

'No. No, I won't.'

'Where are you?'

'It doesn't matter. I thought – I thought perhaps I could come to the flat so we could – talk.'

I could hear him fumbling for a cigarette, striking a match, exhaling, mumbling something. He came back.

'Sure, hon, you can come right now. I'll make some coffee. Has Charlie Girl had breakfast?'

'Ah yes, yes. But Harry, I want to come on my own, just so the two of us can talk – alone . . .'

'Okay, sure. But what about Charlie?'

'I'll get a sitter. I'll come about 1.00. Okay?'

By the time the sitter arrived at 12.30 I was in a fever of excitement and hope, certain that no matter what Harry and I said to one another – or how long it took – we could somehow work things out. If I made sure to give more than my sixty per cent to the effort.

I found a taxi at once. Harry opened the door as I was about to ring the bell.

Looking into Harry's face was like looking into the sun; it was dazzling and dangerous. It was all I could do to look away before it was too late.

He reached out to take my arm, to draw me in. I yearned towards him, magnetized; I could yield so easily to the languor that threatened to drain all my resolution.

'There's coffee, sweetpea,' he said. 'I even bought fresh flowers, your favourites.'

'I love you, Harry,' I whispered. 'Really and truly I do. Remember that. . . .'

I turned and ran, and he called after me.

'Libby, Libby, come back! Please come back. . . .'

I didn't turn. I was sure that if I did, if I weakened once, I would be transformed like Lot's wife into a pillar of salt, and that I would never be able to leave him, ever again.

'He doesn't know where we are,' I said to Sally, speaking as quietly as I could into the coinbox phone when I got back to the hotel. 'Could you come over, maybe later on? I hate to ask you like this, but I'm not sure what to do. I need someone to talk to, someone who can help me to calm down while I think things through. You're the only person I know here who isn't Harry's friend. . . .'

She came that evening after work – with take-away pizza, cigarettes and wine – soon after I'd got Charlie off to sleep. I draped the bedside lamp with a handkerchief so as not to waken her, and ran to answer Sally's soft tap at the door.

'Thank you,' I whispered, seeing her there. 'Thank you for coming. It all happened so fast, I never dreamed – that it would – go this way. . . .'

'You're sure, Libby? About leaving?'

I hesitated, shuddering at the force of sudden pain that shot through me. Then I nodded slowly, and strangely it felt marvellous, an act of affirmation, as though a heavy weight had at last been lifted from my shoulders.

It was a release to sit in a semi-darkened room, aware of the sweet easy breathing of my baby, while Sally poured wine into tooth mugs and listened while I told her the whole story, including what had happened earlier that day.

And she in turn told me everything she knew about the mundane practicalities I'd have to deal with: finding a place to live, and a job, and someone to look after Charlie while I worked – all in a country that was not remotely geared to the needs of working mothers or, more specifically, to single parent families.

'Though God knows there's need for change,' she said. 'It's happening all around us here, though we try hard to be stoical and British and pretend it's not. It happened to my own sister.' She looked thoughtful.

'What did she do?'

Sally sighed. 'Fortunately my mum and dad were there for her, not that it hasn't been hard enough even so. She's got two smashing kids, but she works hard to keep them and it's difficult for her, even with the help our folks can give.'

And then she said, shyly, 'Have you got enough money to be getting on with until you're organized? I mean, I don't mean to embarrass you or pry, but I'd like to help. . . .'

She gestured with open hands and I was touched. I nodded.

'Squirrelled away,' I said, really smiling for the first time for weeks. 'For the monsoon season.'

'You're sure now?' she said.

It was late when she left. When she'd gone I felt very much alone, truly on my own for the first time in my life. There was no one to protect me, no one I could run to who could fix my world and my life for me, no gauzy pink naive illusions that Harry and I could work things out.

I slept deeply all the same, soothed by Charlie's fragrant warmth, comforted by Sally's friendship.

But I dreamed about Harry.

At first glance Glamorgan Crescent seemed at odds with the neighbourhood surrounding it, an area in which boutiques and Roaring-Twenties hamburger cafés were not far to seek, where just around the corner in the Gloucester Road a young flirtatious Cypriot sold ice-cream cornets from a stall in front of a shop that never seemed to shut.

By contrast the Crescent was lined with tall terraced houses in a gracious arc, overlooking trees. Each house boasted an elegant Edwardian façade, regularly maintained by applications of twentieth-century paint. The total effect from the street was quiet elegance.

Inside, however, the reality was seven narrow twisting flights of stairs to an attic bedsitting room with groceries and Charlie in tow.

Once there I set about devising ways to cook nourishing meals on one gas ring; I suspended cartons of milk from the dormer windowsill in carrier bags to keep it from going off; I tried hard to be philosophical about living like that. And I tried to keep Charlie as happy (and as quiet and invisible) as possible.

I didn't mention Charlie when I took the place. That sounds dishonest and it was, deliberately so.

I knew from my experiences trying to find a larger flat for the three of us how many landlords refused to rent to children; I knew, from the kind of building it was, how very unlikely the landlord of 81 Glamorgan Crescent was to let an attic bedsitter to a mother and her small daughter. At that stage, however, I was in no position to be scrupulous about landlords' rules.

Of all my priorities, shelter was the most basic. And 81 Glamorgan Crescent was central (and the irony of that struck me forcibly, after all my entreaties to Harry to let me look for a place that was not so); it was within easy walking distance of a tube stop, and by some miracle it turned out there was a registered childminder in the near vicinity who had a vacancy for which I pleaded on bended knee and was granted; and the attic bedsitter was (relatively) cheap, particularly when compared to the astronomical tarriff even of the modest hotel we moved out of.

The money I'd put aside in my secret bank account had seemed so protective and plentiful in dollars on my statement; but it had shrunk alarmingly when it was converted into pounds sterling and applied to all the priorities among which I had to juggle it, especially as I was jobless. Until I was working, my nest egg was going to have to stretch until the eagles on the dollars screeched for mercy.

Harry still didn't know where we were, but I rang him

once after moving out of the hotel, just checking in, letting him know that Charlie was all right, maybe even to find out for myself if what I thought I saw that day on his doorstep – that if I once walked back to him I'd never again find the courage to walk away again – was really true.

It appeared, after I talked to him, that walking back to him was one more of my closed options.

He told me that he had gone out and hired an A-1 top-flight legal team who were going to wipe the floor with me; who were going to chew me up in little pieces and spit me out; who were going to see to it that he was granted the custody care and control of Charlotte Louise Franklin. Come hell or high water. I wondered where he'd found the money.

'You'll have to find me first,' I pointed out through gritted teeth.

'Yeah well, you can't hide out for ever, can you?'

'I can hire lawyers too, you know,' I said.

'Sure, but I'm going to fight you all the way, and I'm going to win!' That sounded so good to him he hollered it again, before I hung up.

Sally saved my sanity. She dragged me out to dinner as often as I would go, and paid the bill with quiet tactful insistence whenever I would let her; it was Sally who showed up in Glamorgan Crescent with bunches of daffodils she just happened to have seen in a stall on her way to me from the tube, pieces of harmless gossip about the girls she worked with, a bag of sweets for Charlie.

And she gave me the best advice she could.

'Libby,' she said, shortly after I'd rung Harry, 'since it looks like you can't leave the country and go home, I think there has to be a point where you do something to get the whole thing sorted out. You're not afraid of him, are you? I mean, that isn't why you haven't, well, tried to find out where you stand?'

210

I thought about that. I wasn't sure if I was afraid of Harry or not, if that was the true reason I hadn't told him where we were.

'Not really,' I said. 'But he sounds so fierce on the subject of getting hold of Charlie, I. . . .'

'Oh I shouldn't think there's any real danger of his being able to do that,' she said confidently. And then, wavering a little, 'Not within the law, at least.'

'You don't know Harry.'

'No. But Libby, maybe you should go to a solicitor. Surely he'd know what can be done.'

And I did want it cleared up – if such a thing was possible. The loose ends tied, the drama played to its conclusion; above all, I wanted to be free to take Charlie and go home.

Surely it would be simple enough to do that, even if it meant going so far as to a court of law; I knew that if I didn't do something, I could never go home again at all.

So when Sally offered to ask her boss to recommend a good solicitor he did, and I made an appointment to see him.

'First things first, Mrs Franklin,' the solicitor said, when I tried to pour out my whole story in a garbled rush. 'Your husband's full name is. . . .'

I started over, and we worked through the whole mess, fact by recordable fact, while his pen scratched on his pad of lined yellow paper. Then he cleared his throat, and made a little tent of his folded fingers on top of what he'd written down.

'I think the best thing you can do in the circumstances,' he said, fixing me with sharp blue eyes, easing his podgy bulk further back into his swivel chair, 'is to book the first available flight back to' – he glanced through his notes – 'Montana, is it? Where your parents live?'

I clenched my hands in my lap, and tried to keep my voice level, polite, reasonable. 'Yes, that's right. But I think

I already mentioned that my husband has both our passports. Mine and my daughter's. And that he's refused to
give them back to me.'

'Oh, ah, yes, yes indeed you did. I beg your pardon,' he
said, consulting his notes. 'In that case, I see no alternative
to your suing him for their return. Which will probably
involve, ah, suing him for divorce.'

'Divorce?'

I hadn't thought it through that far, hadn't articulated the
word 'divorce' as a two-syllable symbol of our final parting,
hadn't faced the implications of that irrecoverable step away
from Harry.

'You did say that your marriage had broken down, ah,
irretrievably? Mrs Franklin, I am so sorry, perhaps I
misunderstood the matter. If you feel there's the slightest
hope of reconciliation, then by all means—'

'No, no, you didn't misunderstand.'

'Then it only remains to determine what grounds you
have for such an action. Perhaps adultery?'

'No. There was no other woman,' I said stiffly.

'That can be settled later, I'm sure,' he said affably. 'Now
then, you did say your husband has retained a
solicitor. . . .'

He had. A team, as he had claimed. A prestigious firm of
West End solicitors, and a well-known and formidable
barrister to speak in court on his behalf. He must have had a
good run at poker.

'He has no intention of contesting your petition in
divorce,' my solicitor said blandly. 'In fact, to facilitate the
matter he has indicated that in principle he's willing to
admit committing – ah – adultery on – er – at least one
occasion. . . .'

'There was no other woman, I'm sure of that,' I said.

The lawyer studied me from under beetled brows, patient, pitying; I controlled a violent tremor with an act of will.

I felt stripped naked, exposed and naive and gullible, my certainty doubted by a stranger in a pinstripe suit who could no more know of my investment in my life with Harry and what had triggered its abrupt and painful end than he could know my shoe size or the colour of my bra.

It was too soon to be forced to see Harry as a cold-eyed calculating schemer who had figured out the quickest way to be rid of me as coolly as he assessed a poker hand, to whom I meant so little he'd give me grounds for a quick divorce, who would do anything to best me and defeat me in a court of law.

'Adultery,' the solicitor continued, hammering the lie into my heart, 'with a lady whose name he is willing, if necessary, to supply.'

'There isn't one.'

He shrugged. 'Then he is willing to invent one.'

'I see.'

I eyed the papers on his desk, and fingered the smooth blue passport in my hand. I opened it. 'This is mine,' I said, 'but where is Charlie's?'

'Mrs Franklin, your husband intends to sue you in the Family Division of the High Courts of Justice for the custody, care and control of your infant daughter. While that suit is pending, her passport has been placed in safekeeping with our bankers.'

'I don't understand,' I said faintly. 'I thought. . . .'

'Alas, as he intends to take this line, it won't be as simple as we'd hoped. He appears to be determined to pursue the matter just as far as it will go.'

I closed my eyes briefly and breathed deeply, the way I'd been taught to do in the final stages of labour.

'On what grounds?' I said.

He cleared his throat, arched his brows, and continued to read from the papers on his desk.

'Mr Franklin alleges that you kidnapped your daughter

213

from the – um, um – marital home – on or about the – 2nd of April last.'

'I took her with me when I left him. Charlie's only two years old—'

'Quite,' he said briskly, 'I quite see that,' making a note on his lined pad as though he did. 'He further alleges that you intended to remove her from the jurisdiction of the British courts without his knowledge or consent.'

'I couldn't! He saw to that! Mr Franklin had Charlie's passport, *and* my own. He refused to give them back to me, he called the Embassy, he—'

'But that *was* your intention, Mrs Franklin?'

'You're damned right it was! What else could I do? Where else could I – go?'

He handed me a tissue. 'Tea, Mrs Franklin?' he offered.

Harry had a job, a fixed address, means on which he could reasonably be expected to support Charlie; he had already, he alleged, hired a full-time housekeeper to that end.

He went on to allege that in addition to having none of the above, I was of a nervous disposition and highly strung temperament, and that in evidence of that he would show that I had consistently refused to undertake my rightful duties as his hostess when he was entertaining clients in his London home.

'At 3 in the morning, for God's sake?'

'Calm yourself, Mrs Franklin. The courts are reasonable, but they are not at all likely to be favourably impressed by hysteria—'

'Hysteria! Do you realize, sir, that my husband is a gambler? A hustler? A poker player who decided that London was full of suckers and rich fools?'

The man sighed deeply and shook his head. 'Mrs Franklin, *please*. In evidence in support of his affidavit your husband has produced an apparently perfectly legitimate statement from his employer—'

'I've already *told* you—'

214

He held up his hand like a traffic cop.

'Yes, Mrs Franklin,' he said, faintly pityingly, 'but can we *prove* it?'

'What happens if we can't?'

'Early days yet, Mrs Franklin. Early days indeed; we mustn't allow ourselves to get discouraged. The first hearing is set for – let me see here – oh yes, here it is, in three weeks' time, to determine interim custody. Most important. You do have a place to live now, don't you?'

'Yes. You have the address.'

He consulted his notes again. 'So I do, yes. A bedsit, didn't you say?'

I nodded.

'A single room,' he mused, tapping his pen against his teeth.

'Yes. I share the bath with the three other tenants on the landing,' I said; and I felt my face burning with shame for my inadequacy.

'Can't be very comfortable for you and your little girl.'

'It's all I could find; all I can afford until I find a job.'

'And a work permit and visa to go with it, of course.'

'Well, but I'm already listed on Harry's visa—'

His hand came up again.

'As a housewife, Mrs Franklin. I've taken the step of making enquiries about that. Once you and your husband are divorced, you'll not be on his visa any longer. You'll have to find a job for which you'll be granted a full working visa in your own right.'

Was there no end to it?

'Oh well, I'm sure I can.'

'Quite. Meanwhile, you're living from your savings.'

'Yes.'

'Unfortunately, it would appear, an amount just a bit too large to allow you to qualify for legal aid.' He sighed.

'I don't understand,' I said.

He waved his pen vaguely. 'It doesn't matter. This

215

litigation *may* be quite expensive before we're finished, and you *do* have prospects of being able to find suitable employment in the near future?'

'Oh yes! Yes, I have a college degree and work experience. I've already—'

'Quite.'

He folded his hands on his desk and looked up, frowning slightly.

'I must warn you that this may not be an easy case, Mrs Franklin. However, as they say, possession is nine points of the law. So our first priority is to make certain your daughter remains in your custody while the Court Welfare Officer is in the process of preparing his report on the circumstances.'

'Court Welfare Officer?'

He heaved a long, patient sigh. 'Court Welfare Officers are highly trained social workers assigned to difficult custody cases. They visit each parent in his or her home, and they usually – though probably not in your case because your daughter is so young – arrange private interviews with each of the children involved in order to determine which parent can provide the most suitable environment for the child. He or she will want to be quite sure that your daughter is being properly cared for. That you can provide adequate accommodation for her, and on things like proper childminders—'

'I've already found a childminder, near the place where I live.'

'Not always the most salubrious arrangement for the care of young children, so I'm given to understand,' he murmured.

'This one is! I've been there, naturally, talked to the lady. 'She's properly registered, and—'

'I'm sure she's perfectly fine, Mrs Franklin. Now please, you must try very hard to be calmer. The point is that the Court must be satisfied that your daughter is receiving the best possible standard of—'

'Why the hell shouldn't she be? I'm her mother! I wouldn't do anything—'

'Quite. Mrs Franklin, I know how very upset you must be about all of this. But we really must try to work through it reasonably and sensibly, with the object of leaving the Court in no reasonable doubt that you are a perfectly adequate mother. Otherwise the Court may decide she would be better off with her father, after all?'

'Oh God, you mean there's a real possibility of that happening?'

'There are recent precedents in which custody has been awarded to the father. In a case of this kind, where there's considerable dispute between the parties to the matter, the Court is most careful to protect the best interests of the children involved. Sometimes,' he added gently, 'the best place for a child *is* with its father.'

'Not in *this* case!'

He grunted noncommittally. 'You must not only look after your daughter, Mrs Franklin; you must be *seen* to be looking after her.'

I rang Sally at her office from the first telephone kiosk I came to after leaving the solicitor's office.

'How did you get on, love?' she asked.

'The system,' I said, bursting into helpless tears. 'Oh Sally, the system isn't ready for a mess like this.'

13

I think that Charlie must have been the youngest tenant of Number 81, and I the second youngest; all the others we saw were old, and a few appeared to be octogenarian.

At first, Charlie was assumed, I think, to be a frequent visitor to my room, perhaps Sally's child or my niece. But then one Sunday morning one of the elderly ladies on the floor below ours happened to be on her way out as Charlie and I were toiling up the stairs with a pint of milk and the Sunday papers. Charlie was being quiet and well-behaved, but not so quiet that the lady failed to hear her call me 'mama'.

So our relationship was established, if not the circumstances which had brought us, husbandless and fatherless, to Number 81. If anyone thought this odd or remarkable, no one said so; certainly not to my face.

It was the manageress, steeling herself, who remarked on it on behalf of her employers, the company that owned the property and who employed her to safeguard its interests. She did so when I went downstairs with Charlie one Saturday morning to pay the weekly rent.

'You made out you were alone when you moved in, Miss – er – Mrs Franklin. I took that to mean you'd stay alone.'

I toughed it. 'I haven't, as you see. This is my daughter, Charlotte.'

Well, after all, young as she was Charlie was standing there beside me, peeking out from behind my skirt, so nothing more was said just then.

But later in the day, when I came down the stairs to the lobby alone to use the coinbox telephone, the manageress

218

was coming through the lobby and she hovered as discreetly as she could; when I finished phoning, she came forward resolutely, coughed self-consciously and asked to have a word.

'There's a strict rule here against letting to tenants with children, Mrs Franklin. Quite honestly, this is the first time it's cropped up in all the years I've been here. It never even occurred to me to mention it. But if I'd known about your little girl, I'd never—'

'Now we're here,' I cut in decisively, not quite sure of my ground but very sure I'd have to brazen it out, 'it will take the owners some time to get us out again. I'm afraid I was that desperate, you see, for a place to live.'

Desperate was about right.

And how I wished I could get my family to understand that; how I prayed, opening every letter from my mother, that I had at last convinced her that I needed her more than I ever had in my life. That I needed her comforting presence, or even the presence of one of my brothers – any representative of safety, home and family to bat with me on my side until I was sure I wasn't going to be hit out of the ballpark altogether.

It was touch and go, and getting more precarious all the time. The solicitor's devil's advocate number had been bad enough; the barrister's was worse. He was an imposingly confident presence, thoroughly at ease in his comfortable chambers at Lincoln's Inn, a handsome deep-voiced man with silver at his temples who should have been a Shakespearean actor, and who put the fear of God into me about going to court at all.

'Naturally I'll do my best for you,' he said, offering me a cigarette from a silver case on his spacious polished desk, an expanse of mahogany uncluttered by the grubby pads and pens, loose papers and used teacups of the solicitor's economy model.

'Naturally,' I murmured.

'However,' he added, 'your husband has pushed this matter into the High Court before it's even begun. It's not the least expensive venue one might have chosen.' He shrugged, the epitome of elegant unconcern. 'We'll try to keep the whole thing as brief and painless as possible, of course.'

I nodded, accepting a light, trying not to betray the trembling that started in my fingers.

'It won't alas be very difficult,' he continued, sighing smoke, 'for my learned friend for the opposition to make a mockery of our case almost before I've found my wig and gown.'

'Your gown and wig?'

He smiled, deprecating my ignorance but not forgiving. 'Some of those films you may have seen aren't too inaccurate, Mrs Franklin. The British High Courts of Justice may be the last bastion of formality and true respect for equity under the law. And although it isn't tax deductible' – he shrugged, smiling at his cigarette and his little joke; I smiled back as though I knew what the devil he was talking about – 'we do robe up for court, and we wear black within its walls at all times.'

I glanced – not too pointedly, I hoped – at my watch. He noticed; he smiled to himself. 'Yes,' he said, 'as I was saying, Mrs Franklin, on the *prima facie* evidence of the thing, I'm afraid you really don't have much of a case.'

Terrific.

Two could play. I smiled at him. 'I think I do,' I said evenly.

'Ah, a fighter, and potentially a good witness. Good, I like that. Now tell me if you will, what exactly happened?'

'You've been briefed by my solicitor, surely,' I said, glancing at the poor man squirming in the chair beside me, clearly unnerved by the magnificence of superlawyer.

'Of course, and very competently too,' he said generously, beaming at my solicitor, who relaxed visibly and glowed with gratitude. 'But I want to hear it again from *you*, Mrs Franklin. If you would be so good.'

'Sure. My husband is a gambler, and he earns his living playing poker under cover of a job he holds with a computer firm, ostensibly designing video games—'

'Space invaders, that sort of thing?'

I nodded. He snorted. 'Go on,' he said.

'He works by night, and sleeps by day. He brings people home after midnight to play cards and eat and drink. I had taken as much of that as I could without going under. Our daughter will be two in July, I think she deserves a better life.'

'And, Mrs Franklin, there was another woman?'

I glanced towards my solicitor; I swallowed. 'Yes,' and qualified the necessary lie. 'So I have been told, yes.'

That was about it in a nutshell; I felt sick and shaken.

I drew a deep breath. 'So I packed our things and left, leaving my husband a note. Stupidly, I forgot to pick up our passports at the last minute. I – I'm sorry, it was so stupid. . . .'

'You intended, I take it, to leave the country.'

I nodded.

'But when your husband discovered you had left the travel documents behind, he refused to give them back.'

'Mine was returned, Charlotte's was not.'

He glared at the solicitor, who vibrated. 'Where is the child's passport?' he demanded. 'Why is she not travelling on her mother's document in any case?'

The solicitor told him, stuttering a little.

The barrister looked back to me. 'And when you discovered you couldn't leave the country, presumably to go home to your parents, you withheld your whereabouts from him?'

'Well, yes! He threatened—'

'He threatened?' He leaned forward; his eyes shone.

'To take Charlie away from me.'

He leaned back, disappointed; yesterday's news.

'Which it does seem is his intention. He alleges, as you undoubtedly know, that while he can provide a comfortable house and a full-time housekeeper for her, you have no job and no adequate accommodation. And also that your highly-strung and nervous disposition have contributed to the breakdown of the marriage, and make you unfit to be a mother, and so on and so on as usual in these cases.'

'Sir, Harry would never say such things. . . .' I swallowed hard.

He threw back his head and gave a full-throated laugh; the solicitor withdrew a hanky from his breast pocket and wiped his forehead, and tittered.

'I'm sorry,' I said, 'but all this—'

'No need to apologize, my dear, I do understand. You're having to handle a good deal of pressure in a strange country while trying to deal with a man you undoubtedly cared for very much. But I must warn you that under no circumstances must you break down in tears when we're in court—'

'You *are* going to take my case.'

'Oh, I should think so. And by relying heavily on your strong character and will to succeed in caring for your daughter – as against your husband's somewhat rackety lifestyle and the issue of his admitted adultery – we may just squeak by.'

'Squeak – but why must we go through all this palaver at all?'

'You may well ask, Mrs Franklin. But once the cat is set, so to speak, among the pigeons. . . .' He shrugged. 'Then the court is bound in law to satisfy itself that the child involved is receiving the best possible care. You understand.'

I nodded. I was beginning to.

'Good. Oh, and just one more thing. A small point really but important. I don't know exactly how to phrase it – delicately. . . .'

He toyed with a crystal paperweight.

'You're a young and, if I may say so, a very attractive woman, Mrs Franklin.'

I straightened in spite of myself, conscious of the coral linen dress and how good it looked.

'Thank you,' I murmured.

'While the case is in progress, Mrs Franklin, both the divorce *and* the custody matter. . . .'

'Yes?'

He smiled; my God he was charming.

'As I believe it's phrased in popular slang . . .'

'Yes?'

He grinned. 'No live-in lovers.'

In one room with Charlie in a cot in a corner? And who with? The building maintenance man?

'I wouldn't dream of it,' I said.

So there was him to keep me hoping for the best. Charm was his stock in trade, and I could see that charm was what was required to put a case like the one I'd somehow wandered into against all reason – sued and pursued and hounded by the guy I'd followed halfway around the world because I'd fallen in love with him when I was too young to know my arse from my elbow.

God only knew what had been in his mind all that time, or in his heart at any given time. If he'd ever had any real feeling for me – but that line was pointless.

Anyway, charm was bound to be the stock in trade of whoever Harry had hired to be my guy's opposite number. And I figured, from what I knew of Harry's intense determination to win every contest – and it seemed, especially this one – that Harry would come up with a barrister who was every bit my man's match.

Meanwhile I went running after every job I could, dressed in my Sunday best and primed with my most convincing sales pitch about why I was the one and only candidate worth considering.

I didn't believe my own pr, of course, but I hid self-doubt beneath silky hair and careful makeup and good clothes; when it came right down to little brass tacks, I had nothing much to offer any firm except a college degree and comparatively brief work experience in another country. I was hardly in the must-not-miss class as the potential chairman of anybody's board. And no matter how desirable a potential employer might find me, there were still bureaucratic hoops to jump through to satisfy the Home Office that my services were essential to British industry.

For that to happen it had to be demonstrated that I was not usurping a job that might be filled by one of those gingerbread-men shaped figures that marched in depressing graphs through the financial pages in the daily papers, depicting the millions of British unemployed.

But if I couldn't find a job – and this one caused me many nights of gut-gripping terror – I supposed I'd have to abandon ship and go back to the USA and home to mother, leaving Charlie behind.

All of it was fair, I guess. Most of it was my own fault. That didn't make it any easier to bear.

It made it real hard to open letter after letter from Montana in which my parents, while assuring me of their love and deep concern, made it perfectly clear that until and unless I abandoned my foolish determination to remain in a foreign country, they couldn't offer me any help at all. Not even money.

It was not the ideal time to be evicted from my bed-sitting room.

The manageress studied me for a moment. 'You're American, aren't you Mrs Franklin?'

I smiled and nodded. 'But I'm here now,' I said, 'and I – er – plan to stay for awhile. In England, I mean,' I rushed on, 'not here in the building. Not any longer than I can help.'

'Well, I've not told the company about your daughter;

but it's only a matter of time before they find out from somebody. You are looking for another flat?' She looked hopeful.

I held up the folded newspaper I was carrying so she could see all the circled small ads. 'I think of very little else these days,' I said. I smiled again.

She sighed softly. 'Ah well, the company wouldn't like it but as you say, it'll take them some time to force you out. As and when they get on to me about it, I'll just make out I didn't know, which is true. I think I can fob them off long enough for you to get yourself properly settled.'

I could have sworn she snorted delicately, her complicity clearly aligned with me against the property company.

'They'd look awkward, wouldn't they,' she said, 'pitching you out into the streets with a little one?'

No more awkward, I thought tiredly, than anybody else who's making my life as difficult as they possibly could.

The Law Courts in the Strand are awe-inspiring, their lofty ceilings suggesting majestic goings-on. The footsteps of strolling barristers and scurrying solicitors and clerks and litigants ring along the marble-floored corridors, echoing with portentous intentions and far-reaching decisions that dwarf the parties to them, rendering human frailties insignificant beneath the panoply of justice being seen to be done.

The corridor outside the room in which the Interim Custody hearing over Charlie was held was filled with people.

Barristers stood and chatted and joked with one another, unconcerned, or were in earnest confab with the business-suited solicitors they were working for; solicitors rattled papers and patted the hands of weeping women, sitting beside them on polished wooden benches; one man, distraught at the far end of the hall, cried out in rage or pain as a shrieking woman – presumably his wife, or former wife –

225

began to belt him with her handbag, and a guard was forced to separate them.

I sat on one of the wooden benches between my solicitor and my barrister, numb and shaking, and asked if I could smoke.

My barrister, looking splendid in his regalia, said, 'Better not, my dear.' And then, smiling, 'Oh well, let's both chance it. But be prepared to put it out quickly when the judge walks through.'

I turned to him to accept a light; I smiled at him and started to say something. But then Harry walked in, tall, broad-shouldered, handsome, his hair freshly washed and falling soft and touchable in the expensive lines of its cut, and I could hardly breathe, seeing him.

The man beside me sighed, as though he witnessed similar reactions every working day. 'Steady on, my dear,' he murmured, inhaling, looking bored.

'Yes, of course,' I said, contrite. But I was far from being steady. I trembled as the full force of what I was about to do washed over me for the thousandth time, and I realized yet again there was nothing on earth I could do to stop it.

I had rung Harry, tearful and despairing, a few days before the hearing date.

'Harry,' I had whispered, 'say you don't really intend to put us through all this.'

'Oh hi, toots. Hey Lib, you're crazy, you know that? I mean it. Hell, you've really gone right off your kook. They tell me you're living in a slum at the moment. And that can't be right for you, not to mention Charlie Girl.'

'Harry, I don't want to be here! I told you, I just want to go home!'

'Go right ahead, toots. I'm not stopping you.'

'I can't go anywhere without Charlie!'

'Yeah well, that's a problem, isn't it?'

'Harry, what else can I do? I've got to make some kind of life for us—'

226

'You go right ahead and make a new life, Lib. God speed, I mean it. Just so long as Charlie Girl doesn't have to share it with you. See you in court, doll.'

Then Harry had hung up.

I tried to shut down my emotions then, to put all the pretty fading fantasies away as quickly as I'd made my decision to leave him, because I had to.

But I still loved him, that would never change; it ran too deep.

And then the clerk could be heard coming towards us, stepping smartly down the corridor crying 'All stand! All stand!' and the judge came sailing through the respectful, awed crowd, his robes swishing, looking neither right nor left.

And then it was our turn.

We were ushered into a room, not the informal room with the big table and the atmosphere of genial discussion I had been lead to expect from the big book I'd taken out of the local library, but a full-fledged courtroom. With a dais for the judge, and a witness box flanking it, rows of wooden pews below it and a boxed-in row of pews for a jury at the side.

I felt panic rising; it was as though for some reason I'd been shown to the wrong place. I wasn't Dick Turpin or the Boston Strangler, about to be tried for murder.

No, it was the right place; my lawyers were there with me, Harry was there with his; the judge was there, and a stenographer to take down what was said.

But it wouldn't be a trial, after all; there wasn't any jury, no bulb-flashing photographers, no voyeuristic spectators. The whole thing would be conducted *in camera*, they'd already told me that, because of the delicate nature of the matter under consideration.

It was Harry's turn first; his man in flowing black posing and pausing for effect and rustling the papers in his hand while he paced before the bench and put Harry in the

227

witness box and paused respectfully while Harry was sworn in.

And begged the bench, while Harry stood up there looking obediently virtuous, to understand that 'this young husband and father worked hard to support his young family, and had been confronted by a monstrous *fait accompli* from his unbalanced—'

'Objection!' My barrister jumped up and stood poised, rattling his papers, ready to defend me and my sanity to the death.

'Sustained.' From the judge, who looked up and out at the tableau before him with tired eyes beneath his wig. 'Now please get on with it. What precisely is at issue here?'

'She kidnapped my child,' Harry said quietly, almost under his breath but loud enough to be heard by the court.

The judge regarded him balefully. 'Mr Franklin, such outbursts are unseemly here. Now you sit down while we try to get to the bottom of this unfortunate – '

'I tell you, sir, she took my daughter and left me! Without warning, without reason, and without having a suitable place to go.'

' – matter,' said the judge, 'or I shall hold you in contempt.'

Harry stepped down, mumbling under his breath; his barrister wound himself up to start talking again; the judge waved vaguely. 'Please keep it simple; and try to keep to the essential facts of the case, if you please.'

'As your lordship pleases. My client fears for his small child's safety while she remains in the care of a young woman who would do what Mrs Franklin has done—'

'What exactly has Mrs Franklin done, Counsel?'

'She removed the child, Charlotte Louise Franklin, from the marital home, and for several weeks kept her where-abouts hidden from my client. He had no idea where the child was, or in what appalling conditions she was forced to live—'

228

'Objection!' My man got up again.

The judge banged his gavel as though silencing a bunch of fractious children, and glared at Harry's man.

And then said to me, 'Mrs Franklin, perhaps *you* should try to tell us in your own words what has happened.'

My man jumped up again but the judge closed his eyes and shook his head; my barrister sat down with alacrity.

The judge leaned back and smiled kindly at me, avuncular and reassuring; I rose and started towards the witness box.

'No, that won't be necessary, I think. Just stay where you are and tell us what this is all about. Now, first of all, is your daughter safe?'

I gripped the edge of the pew in front of me so tightly my knuckles went white. 'Certainly! I love her, and—'

'I have no doubt you do. But this is a serious matter, Mrs Franklin. Your husband has made certain allegations which give rise to the court's grave concern—'

'It's very *simple*!' Harry cried, to an urgent 'Shhhhh!' from his solicitor, who grabbed his arm. Harry yanked himself free. 'She's a kidnapper!'

The judge rubbed his eyes as though he had a severe headache.

'Mr Franklin,' he said patiently, 'I have already warned you once, and I shall not warn you again. This is a court of law, and it is up to the court to decide where your child will be safest until we have seen reports on the conditions prevalent both in your home and your wife's. Surely you must realize that your wife must have thought she had sufficient cause to leave you as she did—'

'*Insofar* as she can think at all!' Harry said.

'Oh Harry!' I said, my eyes brimming. 'Harry. . . .'

Everybody glared at me, and the respective solicitors passed hasty notes back and forth to one another in a flurry of paper, and the judge banged his gavel again. It was, or would have been, like a three ring circus. God knows there were enough clowns on board. Except no one was laughing.

'I'm sorry, sir,' I said, looking up at the judge. He nodded.

'Now, Mrs Franklin. Why *did* you leave your husband?'

I clenched my fists at my sides. 'I couldn't stay there. He – he came home in the middle of the night with people to be entertained—'

'Clients,' Harry's man slipped in smoothly, jumping up. 'Business associates whose good will was necessary to furthering Mr Franklin's career—'

'Sit down and be quiet!' the judge said, banging the gavel sharply. 'Now, Mrs Franklin, if you will please continue.'

'He came home at three or four in the morning with people who played cards with him, and he woke me up and told me to cook for them, and he – he woke the baby up as well. . . .'

My chin was quivering; I couldn't speak. I stopped and gulped back tears.

The judge looked towards Harry's team. 'Have you anything to say to this?'

Harry's man popped up. 'Occasionally, sir, my client entertained his business associates at his club. He brought them back afterwards to—'

'He's a member of every gambling club in town, sir,' I said quickly, licking dry lips, 'and he spends most of his life in them gambling, which is his *only* career, to the best of my knowledge.' I glanced nervously at my barrister, who was frowning.

The judge said gently, 'The only thing that really need concern us is that your daughter is being properly cared for. That is why we are here today. Your husband has alleged that in his opinion you are not in a fit state to be looking after your daughter, and he has therefore applied to the court to adjudicate the matter.'

'Yes,' I whispered, bowing my head. 'Yes. . . .'

I had seen Harry's affidavit, read it carefully through tears of disbelief and shock. That, and affidavits from

230

people I'd never met, never even heard of – people who'd been willing to say that I was an unfit mother, that in their opinion Charlie should be returned to her father's home forthwith, where she would be adequately cared for in his necessary absences by the housekeeper he had employed for that purpose.

And I had thought, through the fury of my mounting disillusionment – sure, a housekeeper. When I'd had to squeeze the rent out of the food budget more often than not? When Harry had a tailor to pay?

Andrew hadn't played, hadn't made an affidavit for Harry. I never heard from him or saw him again, but I remembered him fondly for that, and with respect.

'Yes,' I said again, looking up. 'I have seen the affidavits, sir. None of them are true.'

He grunted and shifted papers. 'Mrs Franklin, please tell me the nature of the accommodation you have provided for your daughter.'

'We live in a bedsitting room at present, sir.'

Harry muttered audibly and there was a commotion in his little group as he tried to struggle to his feet; the judge stared him down, and he subsided.

The judge turned his attention back to me. 'And what facilities have you for cooking and bathing and so on?'

I told him. 'I am looking for something larger, and for a job,' I added.

'Jobs and flats are not always so easy to come by.'

'I'll find both, sir, I'm sure of it.'

'Um. And what arrangements have you made concerning your daughter's care while you look for a job and accommodation?'

'I take my daughter to a registered childminder, sir.'

'Thank you, Mrs Franklin,' he said gravely. 'You may sit down.'

He swivelled his gaze and addressed us all.

'So we have got somewhere after all, I am pleased to say.

231

Until we have seen the reports of the Court Welfare Officer, I see no reason to disturb this very young child who is living with her mother in the best conditions her mother can provide.'

He rose abruptly, swept papers together, picked them up, and left the court.

14

That was only the beginning of the struggle.

But if that first hearing hadn't immunized me to the full horror of my situation and the antiquated creaking machinery that existed for dealing with it, it served at least to make me realistically aware of what I would be up against until it was resolved.

There was a lot to get through. There were the investigations of the Court Welfare Officer which might, I was told, take months; there would be at least one further hearing about Charlie's custody, another about the divorce. And my solicitor warned me that it might never really be resolved, not really and truly and finally and for good.

'Your husband will undoubtedly claim access to your daughter,' he explained.

I nodded.

'And naturally if you decide to return to your home in America he will undoubtedly wish to fight it through the courts.'

I nodded again.

'He might be able to prevent your leaving with her, even though you're granted custody. Oh, but that's still by no means certain, Mrs Franklin. The order we have is only for the interim until the final hearing.'

I shuddered. The spectre of golden-haired Charlie being wrested from me screaming 'Mama! Mama!' rising up in my mind's eye.

'If you are granted custody of your daughter, and the court refuses you the right to return to America with her, I am afraid there is endless scope for your husband's applying for variations of access, and the amount of maintenance he may be ordered to pay towards her support, and so on. Oh and always, I must warn you, there is the possibility that he may decide to reapply for custody, care and control.'

'Oh come *on*,' I said. 'Surely the courts don't allow anyone to keep a case like this on the boil *for ever*.'

He shrugged and sighed regretfully.

'Circumstances change, Mrs Franklin. And once the matter has been raised – even in a case where one party is clearly, ah, *litigious*' – he glanced at me to see if I knew what the word meant, and when I seemed to, he went on – 'an allegation that the custodial parent is not discharging his or her obligations in regard to the child – well.'

'But the new divorce laws,' I said crisply, armed with all the information I had gleaned from my extensive reading, 'are supposed to have made the whole thing so much more – civilized.'

'To be sure,' he said sadly, 'that was the intention. But only in the area of the divorce itself. There really isn't any way of legislating against one parent's claim that the other isn't adequate – or preventing his or her case in support of that allegation being heard. It would not be,' he finished, rather primly I thought, 'in the best interests of the children.'

'And constant hassles are?'

'Mrs Franklin, this is, in view of your husband's apparent fury at being bested,' he said, sounding aggrieved, perhaps because I'd married Harry in the first place, 'an exceptionally difficult case.'

'Oh yes, I know that! But. . . .' I gestured helplessly.

He sighed again. 'Shall we cross each bridge as we come to it, Mrs Franklin?'

I sighed back at him. 'Have we any other choice?'

Meanwhile, there was little point and no future in crying over spilt milk. I set about picking up where I'd left off –

organizing the life I was leading, the life I wanted to lead, instead of the life I'd left, or the life that might have been. I congratulated myself that I was getting better at it every day.

That summer was as glorious as the previous one had been. The days were long and hot, the lingering evenings mellow, and all of London was out of doors as much as possible, revelling in it.

I realized one day, unwrapping the sandwiches I'd brought to the park for a picnic with Charlie, laughing with her as we wiggled bare toes in cool grass, that in spite of all the difficulties I had to get through I was enjoying her as I'd never had the time or energy to enjoy her when my life had been wrapped so totally around Harry's. When I'd been bowed by exhaustion most of the time.

I began, cautiously at first and then with increasing confidence, to count my blessings.

I still had youth, and some claim to beauty if you liked tall gangling blondes. Regular meals and regular hours had even begun to put the sparkle back into my eyes, I thought.

I had a beautiful daughter who was blooming too, who was beginning to discover the world and the words to express it, who was reaching out to each new day with exuberance and joy.

So we were living in a bedsitting room and she was being looked after by a childminder five days a week. That hadn't affected her temperate disposition or her health, and there was no reason for anyone half-way rational to think otherwise. We were probably no better and no worse off than thousands of one-parent families living in Britain.

If I had qualms – and I did, serious ones and often – that the outcome of all the fol-de-rol with Harry might not go my way and that I might lose Charlie, I pushed them back. I needed a hiatus from all the pain; I couldn't afford to allow it to dominate me.

I had a good friend in Sally, and she began to introduce

me to other people. She had an astonishingly wide circle of friends and acquaintances of both sexes, some married, some not.

Without exception they were people who led life-sized lives and who seemed willing to accept me at face value, and who were content to accept my brief explanation of my situation: I was divorcing my husband; it was a hassle, but it would be all right. Charlie and I would survive. No one ever pushed for details. And thanks to Sally's absorbent shoulder, I felt less and less need to talk about it.

I began to be invited to parties too, and I went whenever I could. Never had babysitting money seemed better spent. Because they weren't blowouts in appallingly expensive restaurants, or full of card-bores who talked of nothing else, and they didn't go on till four in the morning. They were simple pleasurable get-togethers with people who did things like bake potatoes and fill them with cheese and serve them up with wine; people who talked about everything from the state of the world to the relative merits of the latest films.

But what buoyed me most was that a couple of weeks after the Interim Custody hearing, I found a job.

Wesleysmith and Beckforth was a small firm, and I think they hired me because I could write a credible press release for minor and relatively unimportant clients while I doubled as secretary and general dogsbody. They slung the vital work-permit hook on some tenuous connection they had with an American firm in Akron, Ohio. But essentially I was hired to answer the telephone, to type and take dictation, to do simple bookkeeping, to make the coffee. I was Girl Friday – and Monday, Tuesday, Wednesday and Thursday; I was the only female on the premises.

Once I started working there, the prospects were dangled in front of me almost daily, carrot-before-horse fashion, to keep me hopeful and cooperative. Management made occasional vague references to possible transatlantic accounts they hoped for and which I might one day be entrusted to

236

handle; I made frequent specific references to the fact that I'd been doing that very thing almost since the day I left university to take up my first job in San Francisco. That I'd held the job very nicely, my youth and my early marriage and Charlie's birth notwithstanding.

I would then be tactfully but firmly reminded that I'd not worked since coming to England, that I'd not worked all that long in California, that my degree, though a good one, was in general arts, and that Rome was not built in a day.

The three young (male) account executives in the firm called me 'Women's Libby' when they whistled up tea and sausage rolls from the sandwich bar downstairs, and they indulged in other forms of not-too-subtle reminders that they were on their way up the same slippery slope I was trying to climb, and they were out to kill – in the gentlest possible, very British, way.

Still, I was given a rise in pay when I'd been there a couple of months, and I was hopeful in spite of the running gun battle of office politics.

Having a job was an affirmation. I'd got that far; I could get further; I could rebuild my life, or try to.

Life couldn't wait until the custody issue was finally thrashed out. Nor until I'd be free to go home with Charlie.

Nor when I would win my battle to get over the constant doubts about the legal events I'd set in train, the aching longing I still felt for Harry – when my shell of bravado was nothing more than whistling in the dark. When I soaked my pillow, night after night, with hot and lonely tears.

Life couldn't wait. I had to go forward, take charge of my personal destiny.

I had to grow up.

The Court Welfare Officer was about thirty-five; he looked like a family man; he was soft-spoken, impeccably courteous, and very tactful.

But naturally I had advance warning that he was coming to Glamorgan Crescent to look me over – he had written to request a mutually convenient appointment – and by the time he climbed the seventy-two stairs to our cramped eerie, I had invested him in my imagination with traits that roamed and ranged from nosy interfering insensitivity to fangs and blood-lust.

Who did he think he was, and what did he expect to find when he came snooping and sniffing around what was after all my home? Nits in Charlie's hair? A man under the bed? Gin bottles stacked in the kitchenette?

Christ, a social worker! Paid by the state to save innocent children from their drunken sluttish mothers, just like all social workers everywhere. The papers were always full of it. By God no Olsen in recorded history had ever been subjected to that! We were clean-living, hard-working, self-respecting people for all the generations back to the horse thieves, as my father used to say. And God help anybody who said otherwise. I was defensive.

I got off work early on the day of the evening he was due. I brushed the carpet on my hands and knees and scrubbed the already-spotless kitchenette. I tidied and straightened and fretted about the unavoidable jumbled mess of Charlie's toy box. I bathed Charlie and washed her hair, and when I'd cooked dinner and we'd eaten it, I dressed her in the purity of dimity.

I bathed and dressed too, with great care (dark cotton shirtwaist, buttoned to the top) and arranged my hair in a demure knot at the nape of my neck.

And sat in a chair with Charlie in my lap until the downstairs bell rang, and held her tightly by the hand as we descended to let him in.

'Mrs Franklin?'

'Yes. Good evening. It's a long way up, but it's clean.'

And climbed behind him, Charlie's chubby trusting hand in mine, certain he was counting the stairs.

And watched with resentful, terrified, shamed eyes as he walked into the room.

And answered all his quiet questions through tight and wooden lips, sitting in the chair opposite the one I'd indicated for him (the only chairs we had, apart from two straight ones to sit on while we ate) with Charlie securely in my lap as though he might be about to grab her and run off.

And rose when it was finished and defiantly offered him a sherry – it was my home, and that was hospitality, and damn him if he reported me as a drunkard.

And was so disarmed I nearly wept when he accepted, and when he said, sounding just like an ordinary human being: 'This place is a lot better than the one where my wife and I started married life, I don't mind telling you.'

And when he laughed out loud, when Charlie ran to show him our Italian fridge – our carrier bag slung out the dormer window, containing that day's pint of milk.

Harry felt he was being punished because the court had granted me the right to keep Charlie with me, at least until they'd completed their investigations.

And the hearing awarding final custody, care and control of Charlie would not be heard until late in August, if then; they told me I'd be lucky to be assigned a court date that soon.

'The diaries are always full,' my solicitor said.

'I'll bet they are,' I answered.

Because Harry was hurt, he hit out and tried to hurt me. That wasn't hard; he knew just where to aim. And I was as raw as he was. With guilt, with grief, with doubts, with the huge and looming conviction that I had failed in my sacred duty to create a solid marriage and a happy home.

So I hit out and tried to hurt him too. He had access to Charlie during the interim period. That was standard; I had no objections. No one, least of all me, had said he was a bad father. I hadn't thought through all the implications of his right to access and what would happen to it in the event I took her home; I would cross that bridge, as the fellow said, when I came to it. Meanwhile he'd been granted, as a standard clause in the interim order, the right to 'reasonable access' to his daughter. As she was so very young, and since I had announced clear doubts about the wisdom of raising Charlie in the environment he provided in his home, my solicitors advised me to define 'reasonable access' as two hours every other Sunday afternoon.

Well, that didn't seem too reasonable to me. But I went along with it; and I took a perverse pleasure in knowing that no sooner had he picked her up and bought her a cornet of ice cream or something, it would be time to bring her back again. I was ashamed of myself, but did nothing to help him.

It meant that every other Sunday Harry rang the doorbell and I went downstairs with Charlie to meet him, to hand her over. Every time we went through that exercise it was painful for all of us, knives turning in open wounds.

Harry and I would stand there on the doorstep with Charlie in the middle, very young but by no means insensitive, absorbing the vibrations of shots being fired above her head.

Harry, hunkered down to her level to greet her, would say: 'Hi, sweetie pie! Hey, how about a hamburger and a milkshake? You name it, you got it. You sure look like you could use a square meal, honeychile.'

I would stand there as though turned to stone, my arms folded across my solar plexus, fighting down the pain of guilt and loss.

'Harry, do you think we could keep the throbbing violins down to a dull roar? She isn't Little Orphan Annie, for God's sake. She gets fed.'

'And lives in a fucking slum.' Straightening, standing to face me, toe to toe.

240

'Sure beats hell out of living in a floating crap game!'

'Aw, go to hell! You think you can make me out to be Mack the Knife to your Joan of Arc, you got another think coming, toots. This little contest isn't over yet.'

'It's not a contest, Harry, or a poker hand. It's Charlie, and by the way she's standing right here. Wouldn't you agree we should cool it?'

'Oh we'll cool it, sugar. I'll see to that.'

And then he'd look at me, with that terrible opacity that had finally driven me away for good – that had been driving me away, I realized, almost since the day I'd met him. He'd say, snarling, 'See you around four.'

Sometimes he'd be on time bringing her back; more often he wasn't and I'd worry myself into a frenzy, wondering what the hell to do if he didn't bring her back at all.

We had another audience to scenes like that – ears trained to the closed doors in the rooms along the ground floor corridor. And there were complaints about our raised voices on the doorstep from these quarters – or at least I strongly suspected there would be – from the faded, gently-raised women and solitary gentlemen who occupied them. They had been schooled to restraint and still held proudly aloof because of their real or imagined social standing, long-since accustomed to living in peace among the ghosts of their memories: lost fortunes, fiancés lying dead in youth near the German border in the Second War, the twilight of the Raj, missed opportunities, regrets. There would be whispered, politely-worded, oblique remarks passed about the noise Harry and I made from people who kept themselves to themselves because no one else was left.

But that was the least of my worries; it was Charlie I was worried about, looking from me to Harry and back again, visibly upset and wondering what she had done wrong.

'It can't go on like this,' I said in tears to my solicitor. 'Until this is settled, I think it might be better if. . . .'

'If what, Mrs Franklin?'

'I don't know, I don't know what to do about it.'

Harry did. He went back to court to apply for a variation of access, requesting that Charlie be permitted to stay overnight with him from Friday evening until Sunday evening, two weekends each month.

And it was granted, with a rousing lecture from the judge, more paternal that time than avuncular, about how childishly we'd both behaved – he'd been treated to both versions, blow by blow. He emphasized that we must learn and practise a civilized code of conduct. I couldn't fault his remarks; they were sound and to the point. But on Harry's first weekend with Charlie on the new basis, he didn't bring her back on Sunday evening and I was wild, my worst fears confirmed – convinced by nine o'clock the following morning, when I rang my solicitor after a sleepless night, that Harry had somehow got hold of Charlie's passport and spirited her out of the country.

My solicitors obtained an *ex parte* order demanding Charlie's return. Harry returned her, snarling and hissing and shouting. This time there were definitely complaints to the manageress of the building, and I missed two days' work sorting that one out. Then I received another letter from Montana containing so many of my mother's usual homilies and platitudes and pieces of home-spun wisdom I began to think she might as well have it xeroxed and save herself the writing time and I wrote back and told her so.

When I withdrew Harry's access altogether, he took us back to court. He said 'yes sir, no sir,' and promised never ever to do it again. After another stern lecture from the judge, his limited access was restored, and we were back to square one. Except that he stopped paying the maintenance the court had fixed as his interim contribution to Charlie's keep. I let it slide; after all, it was only money.

I was working hard and worrying. I was weary from climbing all those stairs, fighting the good fight, feeling hard-done-by, deserted and dejected. But I kept myself

242

going by telling myself that it was only a matter of time before the nightmare spun on to the last reel and I would be free to find peace in the land of plenty.

Then the manageress of number 81 approached me again. She said: 'I know you've got a lot on your plate, Mrs Franklin, but – well . . .' She fidgeted with her hands. 'The company's solicitor has been on to me just this morning to ask when you and your daughter are going. It'll not be so easy to put them off now they know, you see. The complaints, and so on – about the disturbances . . .' She trailed off, miserably apologetic.

My solicitor said, 'Mrs Franklin, please calm yourself. You've told them you're looking for more suitable accommodation. These things do take time. . . .'

That was the refrain I lived with: *Mrs Franklin, please calm yourself, these things take time.*

I began to wonder how much more I could take. Then they told me that the final custody hearing would not come to court until October, and I didn't know what the hell to do.

Except, perversely, I wasn't so sure that I wanted to go back to Montana any more. Where was home?

15

I soldiered on. I was stoical when Harry came on his allotted Sundays; I did not react by word or gesture to escalate his smouldering anger. I mollified the manageress of number 81 with token gifts of chocolate, artless bunches of flowers from the stall outside the tube stop, constant assurances that my evenings and weekends were being spent combing London for a flat.

I organized like Superwoman when my childminder suddenly announced a late summer holiday in Majorca, and found a pinch-hitter from among my married friends with children who did not object to Charlie's neatly-timed 'flu.

I even considered making peace with my mother for my harsh remarks about her blithe and hackneyed inappropriate responses to my chronicles of woe. That wasn't necessary, however; apparently she hadn't registered my impatience any more than she had registered my cries for help. She continued to write: 'Gee honey, I sure wish you would either drive it or park it. Get back together with Harry, or come home. We love you. Tickets ready when you are. Mom.'

And I took to writing letters to her which began: 'How are you? I am fine, and so is Charlie . . .' and which ended: 'Love and xxx to all. Libby.'

My virtue was rewarded sooner and more abundantly than I had ever hoped or had any right to expect. One of the bright (male) sparks at Wesleysmith and Beckforth announced his imminent resignation at the end of September, which was coincident with the early planning stages of his proposed campaign for a new and prestigious client –

launching wine from the bottomless European wine lake onto an unsuspecting British public as high quality stuff, although it was to be packaged in indecent quantities, in boxes lined with aluminium bladders.

'Boxed wine is nothing new here, of course,' my boss mused as he paced back and forth before my desk.

'No sir,' I said politely, crossing my fingers, reminded with a pang of the day when I'd done the same thing, made the identical gesture, when Michael O'Neill had asked me to work with him on the Mirrani account. I was reminded how very far I'd come since that day, and the way things were with Harry then, and how proud he'd been of me, and how happy he'd been that I was being given a chance I'd longed for. The pretty dresses he'd bought for me, the care he'd taken not to let me get too tired. I was reminded, God help me, of everything we'd shared when I'd gone back to work after Charlie was born.

This was different. This was, in so many ways, just a job of work, a way of getting ahead financially so I could make a life for myself and Charlie on my own. Without Harry.

'I'd like you to consider working with me on this account,' my boss said.

'I would like that very much,' I said.

'The client is a highly respected and well-established firm of importers.'

I nodded soberly, trying hard to look respectful and responsible.

'I imagine that because of your involvement with similar campaigns when you worked in California, you will have had a good deal of experience along these lines. Your references were, after all, excellent.'

'Thank you,' I said. Big, shy, ingenuous smile.

'Now I wouldn't want you to think we can. . . .' He waved vaguely at the Jackson Pollock print to the left of my desk. 'I wouldn't want you to assume we can assign you total responsibility for the account; but as I've been landed with it myself, I thought you'd be a very suitable lieutenant to work with me on it.'

'I'd be delighted to help, I really would,' I said.

'Splendid. It'll mean an increase in your salary, of course. Oh, it won't be a grand sum, at least not at first.'

'I understand, Mr Beckforth. And thank you very much.'

I was careful to couch my ideas as suggestions, and though not once did he demur or even take very much notice of what I was doing, I was scrupulous about deferring to my boss; and I handled the client with kid gloves. But I managed to accomplish what I set out to do.

The client was persuaded to switch to a package that was the most eye-catching box he could afford to commission, and to rechristen the product from *vin de table ordinaire* to *vin d'aujourd'hui*, and otherwise to French it up as much as possible without actually violating any of the EEC regulations or French codes concerning *appellation controllée*. And to hire a resting actor to dress up more or less like a continental and to tour the provinces from Clapham Junction to Bridlington, playing supermarkets with the stuff in tow.

We shifted more crates of the venerable client's overpriced vinegar in a month than he'd managed to unload in the year before he'd hired our firm. I received the promised rise, and though it was far from grand enough to give me delusions of great expectations in the firm, I appreciated it greatly.

Even so I knew there wasn't going to be any meteoric rise to the top, or even to the middle of the firm. I was still answering the telephone, taking dictation and typing it, running down to the sandwich bar for sausage rolls at lunchtime. And I was still sitting at the same desk, without so much as a broom closet in which to work undisturbed. My reward was that my boss congratulated me warmly on the results of the campaign, and he did it in front of the men, too, at the trattoria lunch he gave to celebrate.

And he said, 'Say, Libby, do you know anything about beer? I've got this brewery account coming up. . . .' And I forgot, for one brief moment at least, to dwell on everything I'd lost by leaving Harry. I'd fallen on my feet; it was enough to be going on with.

I took Charlie out for pizza on the strength of it.

Shortly after that, the friend of a friend rang me at work one Wednesday morning to tell me about a flat in Hampstead that would be available in a couple weeks' time, and was I interested? And although it did occur to me that I might be premature in acting, that the court's decision about my keeping Charlie might go against me, I was on the doorstep in Hampstead that very evening.

The flat wasn't perfect. It was nothing more or less than two big square rooms, with a dining area and kitchen tacked on at the back. That's where the bathtub was; the loo was actually an outside wc, separated from the rest of the flat but only a few steps away. There was a hanky-sized garden at the back, the furniture was not too awful, and the landlord was flexible about letting me get rid of some of it and rearranging the rest to suit myself.

The people who were moving out had a three-year-old boy, and the mother worked, and there was a comfortable body down the road who looked after him. She said she'd be delighted to look after Charlie for me if I took the flat.

So I did. I signed the month-to-month lease and wrote a cheque for the deposit and the first month's rent on the spot, before I could change my mind.

I was touched when several elderly ladies came into the lobby of 81 Glamorgan Crescent the day we moved out, when a couple of them insisted on carrying plastic bags and cardboard boxes to the waiting taxi, as a way of wishing us well; when they pressed sweets into Charlie's hand, the manageress herself a bouquet of flowers into mine.

'For your new home, Mrs Franklin,' she said. 'All the best. Mind how you go now!'

I thanked her and the other ladies courteously, but they didn't seem real to me somehow. I hadn't known any of them except as faces to greet at morning going out, at evening coming in. The entire experience of living there had been a salutary lesson in make do and mend. And grieving. And growing up by painful stages. It was already behind me.

The cold crystal of autumn sunlight threw the bare branches of the street into stark relief against the sky. I was suddenly unbearably happy. I was getting out of there, and on with it. I had a million things to do, and a place of my own in which to do them, a place for Charlie and me.

I was rummaging through my handbag for cigarettes and matches as the driver made a U-turn and drove away. But Charlie scrambled to her knees on the seat beside me, looked out of the back window, and solemnly waved goodbye.

My divorce was granted late in October.

The hearing was a farce. There was a correspondent's name in my petition – a woman Harry named and I alleged had enjoyed the pleasure of Harry's intimate company. But I knew with a certainty that was like the pain in an amputated limb, that Harry wouldn't have touched her with a barge pole; that I was his love, and he was mine. That love had failed us.

The name that appeared clearly and conspicuously in my petition was Mary's, the duchess I'd met so long ago in Andrew's club. She'd allowed Harry to use it because she liked him, and because she had nothing to lose.

The custody, care and control of Charlotte Louise Franklin was confirmed to me in November, by the same judge who had presided throughout.

He said to us: 'Our decision is not based on the fitness or unfitness of either parent, and should not be seen as a punishment for wrongdoing or a reward for virtue.'

And then, 'The Court Welfare Officer's report has confirmed to us that Mrs Franklin is a young woman in full possession of her faculties, and a good mother in all respects, which was our initial impression.'

Harry stood up. His face was white and strained. That time no one shushed him. 'If circumstances change—'

'If circumstances change, Mr Franklin – if they change for the worse – then of course the matter should be reviewed. But there is no reason to believe they will. At the moment, it is clear to the court that Mrs Franklin's circumstances have changed only for the better.'

And Harry said, 'But she's moved all the way out to the middle of *nowhere*!'

'Hampstead,' the judge said calmly, with only the barest hint of a smile, 'is on all the maps of London we have ever seen.'

But after all that, I still couldn't take Charlie and go home.

I became preoccupied with that, with the clause in the custody order that clearly stated that neither parent could remove Charlotte Louise Franklin from the United Kingdom until said child had achieved the age of eighteen years without the written consent of the other parent.

It was worse than being back to square one.

Taking Charlie and going home had been the object of the entire bitter draining exercise. I began to wonder how I could have become so involved in a job that was after all more strain and struggle and jockeying for position than measurable career advancement; with a flat that was marvellous only by comparison to 81 Glamorgan Crescent; with the compromises I had jerrybuilt merely to sustain us until I could abandon them, and take Charlie home.

So I compromised again. I asked for three weeks' leave of absence from work, from 20 December; they said I could take it.

I said to my solicitor: 'I want to go home to Montana for Christmas.'

'*With* your daughter.'

'Yes.'

'Just for Christmas?'

'I'll be honest with you. I'm not really sure. But—'

'Will your former husband agree to that, Mrs Franklin?'

'When hell freezes over.'

'Then,' he said, blowing out his cheeks, 'we'll have to apply for the court's permission over Mr Franklin's objections.'

Of which there were many – some valid, some not – with the same judge listening to all of them with weary patience.

And my application was granted, on the understanding that I would file a written undertaking to bring her back when I'd said I would.

When I told Sally, she said: 'Are you really coming back?'

'I thought I'd cross that bridge . . .'

'When you come to it?'

I hugged her tightly, and we laughed together.

My parents met us at the airport in Helena.

We drove the eighty miles west to Lemonade Springs in their big quiet blissfully comfortable car that ate the broad highway and defied the limitless western sky, and challenged the configuration of mountains majestic against it. I had forgotten there was so much space, anywhere in the world.

My mother sat next to my dad in the front seat, half turned so she could look at me, holding Charlie in her lap and running gentle fingers through her curls, telling me how much she looked like me when I was that age, telling me how thin and tired I looked, telling me how glad she was we'd come home at last, home where we belonged. Telling me that there was nothing at all to worry about, now I'd made the break.

250

'It's all behind you, honey, all the bad times. You can just rest up and get your strength back and then you can think about what to do next. Let us worry about all the rest of it.'

It was undreamed-of bliss, her voice washing over me, soothing me, telling me not to worry; I'd longed for it; I couldn't believe she was really there, close enough to touch.

I'd never really thought I'd make it and yet there I was. And there was Charlie, drowsy in my mother's lap.

I had forgotten how good it felt, all the gloriously luxurious comfort of the land I had left – the land where the telephones worked, and money talked.

I had forgotten the simplest American necessities I had always taken for granted: the feeling of my bare toes sinking into soft deep carpet, getting out of bed in the morning; and the warm needles of water from the perfectly functioning shower in my very own bathroom, coaxing me awake. And my mother's kitchen, a comprehensive high-tech miracle, with its refrigerator that made ice by itself and dispensed it from the door – cubes or crushed, whichever. Wall-to-wall television, operated by remote control; lamps that could be plugged in anywhere, that came with plugs already attached to them.

Disney World would have been wasted on me and Charlie. Fantasyland was right there at our fingertips, in Lemonade Springs. Charlie kept running from one splendid gadget to another, pushing the buttons.

Christmas was a mind-blowing extravaganza. There was a ceiling-tickling ponderosa cut from the wealth of timber on my parents' own land, heavy with the ornaments I remembered from Christmas Past, rich with the scent of pine and nostalgia. There were high piles of presents beneath it for Charlie and me, my brothers and their wives and children – lavish and expensive presents that made the gifts we'd brought from England look small. Soap for the ladies, hankies for the men, sweets for the kids. All chosen as much out of careful, habitual economy as for being lightweight in our luggage. Everyone was reverently careful to make a special fuss over them.

Christmas dinner was a family affair, a gathering of the clan; the table groaned beneath the weight of turkey, ham, roast beef and all the trimmings, and everybody had too much to eat. My mother waited on me hand and foot, as though I was recovering from a long, painful illness. Whenever I tried to do anything, she said, 'You have to concentrate on taking it easy, honey, that's all you have to do.' And I began to feel like a child again, absolved of all responsibility even for the simplest tasks; entitled to the best of everything, as of right.

New Year's Eve was another gathering of the clan, except that after eating the buffet supper mom prepared and drinking a New Year's toast, my brothers and their wives drifted off to parties of their own, and my father fell asleep.

Mother and I were left alone.

'We're sure glad you're here, honey,' she said. 'Glad you finally got sensible and came on home where you belong. Now you can start again, give Charlie a decent life. She's so cute, I can't get over how much like you she is. You can even find another job, as soon as you're—'

'I already have a job, mom.' And suddenly, I felt wonderful. I had my answer.

'Honey, that's in England! That don't count, it's behind you! There's nothing for you over there, honey, and you know it. Now you're rid of that son of a bitch—'

'Charlie's father. The same wonderful—'

'Aw Libby, you know what I'm driving at! Now you're out from under all that, there's no reason on God's green earth to walk back into—'

'I have a job, mom. And a place to live.' The words sounded beautiful.

'Sure! With the tub in the kitchen? Libby, honey, you can't live like that. Think of Charlie!'

252

'I have been. And we've lived in worse places. I've got friends there now—' The joy of that.

'You'll make friends no matter where you go, honey. Now you just keep your mind on resting and relaxing until you're good and—'

'I have to go back so Harry can go on seeing Charlie.'

'That don't make sense! Honey, what's he ever done for you except give you a hard time? He supporting the kid? Huh? Well, is he?'

'No, but—'

'Well then, he don't have no rights over where you go or what you do. If you have to earn your living—'

'I have been, mom. And anyway, I promised to take Charlie back.'

Suddenly she thought she understood.

'I guess you're still in love with him, except you won't admit it,' she said sadly.

It was the only explanation she could accept of why I couldn't go back to being a child again; the only justification she could understand for my going back to Hampstead and our pot plants and our tiny garden and our friends. Back home.

I let her go on thinking that.